THE DOSSIER

By Pierre Salinger

AMERICA HELD HOSTAGE
ON INSTRUCTIONS OF MY GOVERNMENT
AN HONORABLE PROFESSION
WITH KENNEDY

By Leonard Gross

GOD AND FREUD
THE LAST, BEST HOPE
1985
THE GREAT WALL STREET SCANDAL
  (with Raymond L. Dirks)
MIRROR
THE LAST JEWS IN BERLIN
HOW MUCH IS TOO MUCH?

THE DOSSIER

by Pierre Salinger
and Leonard Gross

ANDRE DEUTSCH

First published in Great Britain 1984 by
André Deutsch Limited
105 Great Russell Street, London WC1

British Library Cataloguing in Publication Data

Salinger, Pierre
  The dossier.
  I. Title II. Gross, Leonard
  813'.54[F]   PS3569.A4595

  ISBN 0-233-97716-3

Printed in Great Britain by
Ebenezer Baylis and Son Ltd.
The Trinity Press, Worcester and London

To thirty-two years
of friendship.

THE DOSSIER

1

When it finally materialized, the reality seemed better than the dream. In the dream, André would sit at the piano with nothing around him, no ceiling or walls or even a floor —a reflection, he recognized, not simply of his desire to play again but of his aching private wish to be so isolated that for once no one could get at him, not the news desk in New York or the vice presidents of network news or the correspondents and stringers who worked under him in Paris and elsewhere in Europe, or a contact calling with a tip, an acquaintance looking for a job or a visiting American hoping that a call from André Kohl would get him into Regine's.

The reality filled in all the empty spaces with a texture so rich he could scarcely digest it. The piano rested on a well-polished oak floor underneath a beamed ceiling supported by high, white walls. One of the walls was decorated with paintings collected during his travels, so numerous they had to be arranged in patterns above and below one another. A second wall was covered with books on shelves that ran from the floor to the ceiling. The two outer walls contained four sets of French doors each, through which to the north and west he could see the tidy rows of apple trees, just beginning to flower in the early spring. The brilliant morning sunshine was such a rarity for the Normandy coast that André could be excused for wondering if it might not have been divinely arranged for the occasion. The thick grass glistened with morning dew, a wind had swept the sky, and the tangy air drifting into the study seemed flavored with cider. Except for the soft sound of logs burning in the fireplace, the quiet was absolute. Madame Cartet, his widowed housekeeper and the only other resident of Le Pré Ango, André's country home, had left for the village ten minutes earlier on her bicycle to gather the provisions for his *déjeuner*—too comprehensive to be called merely "lunch"—and the chance of the telephone ringing was infinitesimal. Not even his office in Paris had his unlisted number. Of the three people who did have it, two were his grown children, both of whom lived in the States and neither of whom was in the habit of making transatlantic calls, and the third was Mike Paul, the president of network news, who had been admonished, only half-jokingly, to call only if the world was ending *and* there was a strong European angle.

So this first day of his one-year leave of absence was exactly how he had hoped it would be, and yet he could not bring himself to move into the perfect picture that unfolded before him. Instead, he stood in the doorway of the study— a craggy-faced but surprisingly gentle-looking man of medium height with a soft but not corpulent body and a deferential air—as though waiting for permission to enter. There could be only one reason: as firmly as he had argued for the leave, he hadn't fully convinced even himself that taking a year off to practice the piano at the height of a superlative career in journalism was anything other than what Mike considered it: crazy.

"It's just as crazy as '68," Mike had said in New York

three months earlier when André told him his plan. "You're walking out on the most exotic job in the business . . ."

"I'm not walking out, I'm taking a leave of absence."

". . . and in '68 you walked out on the best job in Washington."

"I didn't want it anymore."

"You realize you'd be the anchor now if you'd stayed in Washington."

"I wouldn't have wanted to be the anchor."

"For a million dollars a year?"

"There's nothing a million dollars could buy me that I don't already have."

"You've got enough to lose a year's salary?"

"Absolutely." It was true. One didn't forfeit a year's pay without serious thought, particularly when the amount of money approached two hundred thousand dollars. But his investments alone covered André's annual outlay. What concerned him far more than the money he'd be forfeiting was the excitement he'd be dropping temporarily from his life: the realization on rising each morning that he might sleep in another city that night; the lunches at Harry's Bar in Venice, the dinners at Annabel's in London; the almost daily encounters with a power elite whose decisions changed the lives of millions; the almost certain likelihood, on his return from a trip, of a message on the answering machine at his apartment from one or more of the notable friends collected over the years who had abruptly turned up in Paris. ("André, darling, it's Betty Bacall. I'm in town for a few days at the San Regis. Love to see you.") Saying: "There are ten thousand people in the world, and they all know one another." The arrogance of the thought made him uncomfortable, and yet he knew he'd rather be one of the ten thousand than not. Life was rich, he was a lucky man, and no one had to remind him.

Which had made his decision all the more inexplicable to

Mike Paul. It was Mike who had brought André into television from print journalism almost twenty years before. It
was Mike who had made media stars out of André and half
a dozen others, creating lives for them in the process beyond
anything journalists had ever experienced or even imagined.
The day of their confrontation, he'd stood behind his glass-
top desk in his ample office on the eighteenth floor of the
United States Broadcasting Corporation (USBC), the top
floor of the network's headquarters on the northern edge of
Columbus Circle. He was a short man, powerfully built,
who rose every morning at a quarter to five so that he could
read for an hour without interruption, run for an hour
around the Central Park reservoir and lift weights in the
gym of his co-op apartment building for half an hour before
beginning his day's work. He radiated good health, which
always made André, who loathed any exercise more strenu-
ous than golf, feel a trifle uneasy. Long hours and nervous
energy expended on the job were his only defenses against a
mild tendency to overweight complicated by a zest for good
food and wines.

"You're how old now?" Mike asked.

"Fifty-six."

"In nine years you'll be able to take off all the time you
want."

"In nine years I'll be nine years older."

"What if I worked it out so that you only got top-priority
stories?"

"You know that wouldn't work," André said. "I'm either
there or I'm not." He watched Mike for a moment, pacing
back and forth beneath a wall literally covered with plaques
and scrolls commemorating awards won by his news staff.
"Why are you making it so difficult?" André said at last.

"What do you want, a testimonial? My job's to beat the
other networks. How do I do that in Europe without you?"

"Europe's a second-rate story to you guys, and you know it."

"But the French elections are coming up."

André laughed. "Come on, Mike. The last election was worth one minute and forty seconds on the evening news. You can use one of the kids in the bureau or send Bill Avery from London."

For some seconds Mike was silent, staring out his window at Lincoln Center. Then he turned to André. "Okay," he said, "I'll tell you what bothers me. In one respect, you guys are like actors. You're as good as your last performance."

"Meaning that if I'm gone for a year I could be forgotten?"

"Let's say your star would have dimmed."

André thought about that for a moment. "I'll take my chances," he said. "In a way, it would be a relief."

He knew how Mike would interpret that remark: as an expression of his weariness, after all these years, of being on call twenty-four hours a day, seven days a week, of chasing journalistic fires—sudden political crises, eruptions of violence, assassinations, calamitous, grand-scale accidents of man or nature—of deadline pressures. There *was* that factor, the counterpoint to excitement, but that alone wouldn't have impelled André to ask for the leave. The real reason was one André couldn't bring himself to confide to anyone. Given all his blessings, how could he explain his growing preoccupation with "the road not taken"?

The question had first crept into his brain in the early seventies, when the various crises that engaged him seemed so similar he began to feel that he was meeting himself coming around the corner. How good might he have become? What kind of life would it have produced? What sort of man would that have made him? His parents and Isaac Stern's parents had been friends, and although they had grown up in different cities, he in Los Angeles and Isaac in

San Francisco, they saw each other several times a year and
played duets together. Their respective talents were favor-
ably compared. *Could* he have had a life like Isaac's? They
had met last in Israel during the Yom Kippur War. André
was there to report on the battles, Isaac to play for the
soldiers. Which of them had affected more people, or felt
more authentic? None of these questions answerable, yet all
of them so tantalizing and ultimately irresistible. André had
no illusions that a year at the keyboard would restore the
strength and agility his fingers had possessed as a young
man or the interpretation of the music his brain had once
conveyed to his fingers. He had no notion of concertizing at
this late date in his life. What he felt, he knew, was a great
need to get in touch with his past—to take, if only for a few
steps, that road not taken—and playing his way back to
some sort of prowess at the piano, he thought, might not
only help him do that, but also clear up the mystery of why
he *wanted* to do it.

Now, at last, the moment was here, and while the textures of the reality might be more satisfying than the dream,
the experience, itself, was not. In the dream, he had never
had any doubts. Here he was, his skin so moist he might
have been in the process of withdrawing from a drug. For
years, his narcotic had been motion; it did for him what
alcohol never could. Could he really attach his seat for a
year to a piano bench in Varengeville-sur-Mer, a village of
less than a thousand souls thirteen kilometers from Dieppe
and three hours from the nearest international airport?

The piano was a Steinway, bought for the occasion. He
uncovered its keyboard with as much nervous anticipation
as he had felt the first time he'd removed a brassiere from a
young girl's body. He let his hands fall to his lap for a
moment and laced his fingers so tightly together he had
difficulty pulling them apart. At last he poised them over
the keyboard, and they fell onto the first notes of Chopin's

Fantasie Impromptu. The Czerny and Hanon exercise books were at hand, scheduled for use, but first the Chopin, the little joke he'd arranged for himself. "I'm always chasing rainbows," he sang aloud in a lusty baritone when he got to that moment in the score. The problem in his playing, he could already tell, wasn't a consequence of stiff fingers; they seemed nimble enough. What had happened was that his responses had slowed. Miraculously, he could hear groups of notes as phrases, almost as clearly as he had when he was practicing four and five hours a day. But the information didn't get to his hands as rapidly as it once had, and he couldn't execute what he saw and heard. That would be the challenge, he thought with satisfaction. What was important was that he'd begun.

He played on, his skin dry, the queasiness gone, feeling almost as though he were floating on a cloud that was rapidly closing on the rainbow, at the end of which was a full symphony orchestra accompanying his performance. It was all so perfect that when the telephone rang he tried to pretend that one of the percussionists had made an awful error.

2

Hello," a man's voice said.

The voice, soft, low, and tinged with an Israeli accent, was unmistakable. André would have recognized it if he hadn't heard it in years. "Shlomo," he said, after a spell, "how nice to hear from you."

Shlomo chuckled. "You'll really mean that after you've heard what I have to tell you."

"I won't even bother to ask how you got this phone number."

"It's better that way," Shlomo said.

André sighed, mixing weariness with resignation. Shlomo's calls were never social. They always meant a tip of major consequence, one that served the Israelis' interests, to be sure, but also resulted in important newsbreaks. At any other time a call from Shlomo would have quickened André's pulse. Now it filled him with foreboding. "Okay," he said without enthusiasm, "what have you got?"

"I'll have to tell you in person."

"I'm not coming to Paris, no matter what it is."

"No problem. I would enjoy a drive in the country."

André thought, for a moment. Whenever he talked to Shlomo, it was better not to be surrounded by walls, even if they were his own. His afternoon had been built around the day's second big event, which could dovetail nicely with the requirements posed by Shlomo's visit. "Meet me at two-thirty this afternoon at the Dieppe country club. It's on the coast road, just west of town."

There was a pause at the other end. "What does one do at a country club?" Shlomo asked.

"One plays golf, Shlomo." When Shlomo didn't respond, André said, "Surely you've heard of golf."

"Of course. We even have it in Israel."

"Okay. Two-thirty." André hesitated, seeking some resource within himself that would enable him to tell Shlomo not to come. It wasn't there. "This better be good, Shlomo," he said at last.

"Have I ever given you a bad one?"

Officially, Shlomo Glaser was a diplomat, and he had served in diplomatic capacities at Israeli embassies in Washington, Paris, Latin America, Africa, and the Middle East. Although he had never outright admitted as much to André, André was certain Shlomo's real work was as an agent—and now probably a deputy director—of the Mossad, Israel's secret service.

André and Shlomo had met in Washington in the midfifties. For a quarter of a century he had been one of André's most valuable sources. When the Mossad warned Anwar Sadat that fundamentalist Moslems were planning to assassinate him, Shlomo told André. Shlomo had also warned André—correctly—that Haile Selassie of Ethiopia would be overthrown. He'd done the same about the Shah of Iran.

Shlomo was short and heavy. But the weight was all muscle. His shoulders and arms were so imposing he seemed capable of uprooting a small tree barehanded. He was eight years older than André, well past sixty, but as he moved easily along the challenging terrain of the golf course, his incongruously cherubic face reddening in the sun and wind, he appeared to be at least eight years younger.

The course, while pleasing to the eye with its rolling contours, lush turf, and clusters of Scotch broom, penalized the golfer in a variety of ways. Many of the greens seemed little more than closely mown fairway. The traps had the consistency of concrete. A ball hit into the Scotch broom, strategically placed alongside a number of fairways, just short of the greens, was almost never seen again. And then there was the wind coming in off the English Channel, so strong at times that a par three hole normally calling for a four iron could barely be reached with a driver. Nonetheless, the course, like the game of golf itself, served André's basic purpose, which was to provide him with a weekly reminder of his imperfections.

"The way you are doing it—is that the way one is supposed to do it?" Shlomo asked as they walked from the fourth green to the fifth tee. They were the first words he had spoken since André had teed off on the first hole and taken up pursuit of his errant ball with swift and silent determination.

André looked carefully at Shlomo to see if he was joking. When he realized that he wasn't, he said, "Since you are obviously unfamiliar with the game, I could say 'yes,' but you might see a good golfer before the day is over and never trust me again. No, Shlomo, this isn't the way one is supposed to do it. What you're seeing is the consequence of a special upbringing. I was a child prodigy. My parents kept me out of school so that I could practice piano. I was educated by a tutor. Until I was ten I never played sports because something might happen to my hands. The result is what you see: massive enthusiasm and poor coordination."

The fifth hole was a par three that descended fifty vertical feet before rising again to the green. André hit a four wood. The ball started out well, but then began to slice sickeningly, winding up almost in a pasture bordering the fourth hole. André watched in silence until the ball had stopped rolling, and then said, "That shot, Shlomo, did not achieve the objective."

They took a path that led below the tee. André, leading the way, stopped and turned to Shlomo, who was looking in surprise at the remains of a German bunker. "There are half a dozen of them on the course," André said. "Rather than tear them down, the club incorporated them into the course."

"Fitting," Shlomo said.

André frowned. "How so?"

"For what I have to tell you."

"Ah."

At the bottom of the hill André's caddy gave him a five iron and a commiserating look and then climbed to the green while André veered to the right. Shlomo caught up to him after a few steps. "So," he said, "what would you say if I told you the probable next President of France was a Gestapo informer during the war?"

André stopped in his tracks and peered intently into Shlomo's mournful eyes. *"Now* you're joking," he said at last.

"I didn't come from Israel to tell you a joke."

"Just a minute," André said. He walked to his ball, took one quick look at the green and swung. The ball shot away on a dead line for the flag, barely visible beyond the crest of the green. A moment later, the incredulous caddy appeared at the crest, holding his hands a foot apart. André scarcely noticed. What Shlomo had just told him had totally preempted his thoughts. He might just as well have said that Charles de Gaulle had been a Gestapo informer. The man he referred to, without question, was a French general who had served with distinction in the colonial wars. Camille Laurent, a conservative, was the odds-on favorite to win the forthcoming French presidential elections. His reputation as well as his career had been founded on his wartime role as one of the leaders of the French Resistance.

"Okay, what have you got?" André asked Shlomo as they walked to the green, just as he had on the telephone.

"An Israeli woman brought it to us. She's German. During the war she got phony papers and wound up working for the Gestapo." Shlomo held up a hand to stifle André's protest. "Hold on. That part checks out. Five thousand Jews went underground in Berlin during the war. They called themselves 'U-boats.' Maybe a thousand survived, and many of those had counterfeit papers. The woman showed us hers. She had a phony identity card and a legitimate Gestapo card. We checked the card. It's real."

"Go ahead."

"She worked as a file clerk. One of the papers she filed was a memorandum from Kurt Hoepner to Gestapo headquarters in Paris, which was then sent on to Himmler. You remember Hoepner?"

"The Executioner of Clermont-Ferrand."

"Exactly. Hoepner reported that he'd managed to infiltrate the Resistance by turning one of its leaders. The man he named in the memorandum was Laurent."

André walked to his ball, stroked it into the hole, then proceeded to the next tee, where he paused scarcely long enough to hit his drive over a ridge 190 yards away. He walked so rapidly to his ball that his caddy had to follow at a dog-trot in order to keep up. The hole was a par four, into the wind, but André's next shot easily reached the green, where he sank his putt for a birdie, as his caddy stared at him in stupefaction. The moment the ball dropped into the hole, André turned to Shlomo. "Tell me," he said, "why does this woman wait until forty years after the fact to come forward with this story?"

"We have no trouble with that one. She knew nothing of Laurent until she read a story about the French elections saying he might win."

"And so, like a good Israeli, she came forward because a former collaborator with the Nazis wouldn't be the Israelis' first choice to be President of France."

"We have enough trouble with the French."

"So what do you want from me?"

"I thought you might want to look into it."

"You guys have the best agents in the world. Why aren't you looking into it yourselves?"

"We'd love to, but we can't take the chance. If we were caught, it would be interpreted as interference by a foreign power in the internal politics of France. That would be a mortal setback. It would put us back a century."

"You could be discreet."

"Supposing we did find something. Who would believe us?"

"On the other hand, if the story checked out and USBC broadcast it, everyone else would pick it up and Camille Laurent would be through. That wouldn't exactly hurt your feelings."

"No, it wouldn't."

André grinned. "You guys aren't trying to run me, are you?"

"Please, André, do you really think I would use you in such a way after all these years?"

He didn't, and not simply because of the enormous regard and affection that had grown between them. André had paid off with major coverage for every tip Shlomo had brought him. The liaison between them was a fact of life with which other journalists and even diplomats had to deal.

"Just a joke, Shlomo," André said. "Incidentally, since you were clever enough to get hold of my unlisted number, you surely discovered in the process that I'm on a leave of absence."

"I'm sorry, André. I really am."

André hit his drive on the seventh hole, a short par four with a hill that crested two-hundred yards out and then descended to the green. The ball snapped into flight, landed on the crest and disappeared from view. "On the other hand," André said, "after thirty years of the most abject frustration, I have finally learned the secret of this game: think about something else."

The first thing André did after returning to his house was to call Mike Paul in New York. "Before I say a word," he began, "I want a promise from you that no matter what I tell you, you won't ask me to come back to work."

"That's a promise."

"I have just been told a story that, if true, is one of the great barn burners of our time. Unfortunately, I can't say a word about it on this telephone. How about getting yourself on a Concorde and paying me a visit?"

"Impossible. Will anyone else do?"

"Not really," André said with a sinking heart, knowing exactly what would come next.

"Then you'd better come in. Or forget the story."

"You'll remember your promise?"

"Absolutely."

André breathed deeply and exhaled slowly. "I'll see you tomorrow," he said.

3

"Longevity in service abroad has major advantages,"
André had once written in a radio piece for the network on
the life of correspondents abroad. "It permits you to develop precious contacts that are invaluable in pursuing major stories. But the journalist must constantly remind himself that he is an American—and that he is talking to
Americans. One of our best fail-safe devices is that we must
speak each day to our New York show producers who never
let us forget that important umbilical cord which must link
us permanently to the United States."

While André's piece had been about American journalists, in general, he was really writing about himself. From
the moment he'd set foot in France, he'd had the feeling
that he was rediscovering a land and a people he'd known in
another life. The French could be, and usually were, courtly
in their professional relationships, but they stiff-armed any
overtures at intimacy. Not with André. To them his name—
which had caused him so much havoc as a child in America
—was proof of a heritage shared, and his French, learned
from his French-born mother, was his passport to the inner

recesses of authentic French life. In a way, it was just compensation for his childhood suffering; not only had he been freighted with an un-American name, when his parents finally sent him to public school, his heavily accented English incited his schoolmates to mirth and special tortures.

André never told his parents of the equality he had gained with his fists lest, fearing for his career, they pull him out of school and back to the solitude that seemed so bleak by comparison to the new world he was discovering. Nor did he explain to them why, when they addressed him in their mother tongues—his father was German and, though traveling on business a great deal, had insisted that André speak that language with him whenever they were alone—he now replied exclusively in English. André's French was not what it might have been had he spoken it consistently throughout his life, but he had quickly regained sufficient fluency to ease his passage into those authentic French recesses.

And how pleasurable they were! The long, ritualized three-course lunches with wine in restaurants that placed as much importance on atmosphere as on food; the dinners in homes furnished in Louis XVI pieces that were hand-me-downs rather than affectations; the exclusive clubs like le Polo; concerts and plays at least twice a week; weekends in châteaus; all of this accompanied by bright conversations laced with literary references by classically educated men and women—politicians, diplomats, lawyers, bankers, academics, writers, actors—most of them with heightened aesthetic sensibilities, who, once you had penetrated their icy fortress, were as warm and gay as any people in the world. What most endeared the French to André was their indestructible sense of proportion, to wit: the objective of enterprise was not enterprise, but pleasure. That understanding gave André a more acute sense of present time than he had ever before felt and made experience itself, more intense.

All the more need to remind himself with great frequency of who and what he was.

There were other reminders in addition to those daily telephone conferences with his producers in New York: the friends, most of them Americans, who kept turning up in Paris; a private telephone number in New York that André could dial from Paris and be plugged in automatically to the network news; tapes of broadcasts shipped overnight from New York to Paris. An invitation to André's apartment to watch a tape of the Super Bowl was much coveted by football-starved expatriates.

There were, finally, trips to the States, more frequent for André than for the others because, as the senior correspondent in Europe, he was often asked to come in to the home office to confer on planning for the coverage of future major stories, or on changes in personnel. Those trips had become even more frequent since the inaugural flight of the Concorde, which had halved the time of a trip between Paris and New York.

Immediately after his call to New York, André had booked a seat on the Concorde for the following morning. There was no question as to whether he would get the seat; he was a member of Air France's Club des 2000, which guaranteed him space on any flight he requested no matter how short the notice, even if it meant bumping another passenger. He left Varengeville at seven the following morning, which would put him at Charles de Gaulle Airport more than an hour before the scheduled 11 A.M. departure. André always tried to arrive at airports at least an hour before flight time; he hated the tension that accompanied tight schedules. There was another reason for the early departure from his country home; it would allow him time to take his favored route.

There are two routes between Paris and Varengeville. The first and by far the fastest is via the autoroute that passes by

Rouen. The second is by way of a mostly two-lane road that passes through small towns and villages separated by rich land used mostly to graze cattle and grow seasonal produce. André vastly preferred the slower route and took it whenever he could. Leaving Paris, he put himself more quickly into the tranquillity of the lush Normandy landscape; returning, he could prolong the time before he was once again caught up in the heavy beat of Paris life. Ten years ago, his choice of routes would have been the reverse. On the other hand, ten years ago, he hadn't even considered the possibility of owning a country home.

It was foggy when he left, a fitting accompaniment to his mood. Now that he had committed himself, he should have felt some exhilaration at the prospect of the trip. It was always a turn-on to go to New York, if only because when you were there everyone you saw professionally wanted to talk about you, the simple reason being that their job was to determine how your activities could enrich their own. But there was no adrenaline this morning, only foreboding.

The truth was that André's radio piece about American journalists had been written out of a deeply felt anxiety that he was losing his own identity. The great danger for foreign correspondents is the insidious osmotic process by which they become like the people they're reporting and lose thereby the ability to comprehend them in terms that their audience can understand. For André, half-French to begin with, the danger was compounded. He had too many quarrels with the French, in spite of his attachments to their way of life, to actually "convert." But France was part of Europe, and Europe was another matter. More and more, André had come to think of himself as a "transnational," his home wherever he was. He had finally had to acknowledge that he no longer thought of America as home and might never return on a permanent basis, and that troubled him a great deal.

Each time André returned to the States he experienced a greater culture shock than he had on his previous visit. He had left America in the sixties believing that he no longer understood his country and hoping that a period away from it might give him some perspective. Not only had that perspective failed to materialize, each trip back in recent years had made the United States suffer by comparison. It was not simply the absence of the balance and sensibility he found so compelling in the French and other Europeans, it was the physical and even social characteristics those qualities translated to. New York was not a feast for the eyes as were Paris and Rome and Stockholm and so many other European cities. Americans did not make careful use of land and other resources as less generously gifted Europeans did. And although the Europeans might not be as wealthy, there were no city landscapes littered with the desperately poor such as those he would be passing through in Queens and Manhattan several hours hence. Surely one of the things that had most shocked André in recent years was the un-American streak of selfishness that was being increasingly exposed in his countrymen. As egocentric as the French might be, no one starved in France and very few people begged.

There were other discomforting comparisons. In America he was gawked at, whereas in France he was left to himself, even though because of his many appearances on French television he was famous in France, as well. Fame had its advantages, particularly in his work. He knew that if he called even the most highly placed person he had an excellent chance of getting through, because famous people will always talk to famous people. But he had never bargained for having a face so public that strangers in the States thought of it as their property and accosted him on the street, in restaurants, or on airplanes and were offended if his reply was less than eager or generous. He always replied, if not generously, at least adequately. He was tired of that; fame was something he'd neither sought nor expected. There was something to be said for a society of people who valued their own privacy so highly that they granted you your own.

Linked to his fame was a public identity that he didn't like at all. To the television audience, he was the quintessential reporter: tough, aggressive, even rough when he had to be, whatever it took to get the story, an image that had been solidified not only by his reportorial successes but by his on-camera presence, as well. His delivery was emphatic and forceful, his manner usually stern. Where his broadcast style had come from he hadn't the faintest idea; his best guess was that it was a cover for the sheer terror he'd felt when he'd first gone in front of the camera. That lack of assurance was a far better clue to his real self than his on-camera image. The man he perceived himself as being was not at all as self-assured as people thought he was, neither aggressive nor opinionated, much more eager to hear others' opinions than to offer his own. But to the network, the on-camera image—an accident of inexperience—was gold and had been nurtured through the years. What could be said of a culture in which aggressiveness was so prized and in which image counted more than verity?

What troubled André most, perhaps, was that he might be as much a party to the deception as the network. The man he thought himself to be loved to wear sports shirts and sweaters and slacks; here he was, all costumed for the role he was about to play.

In the back of his mind, André had known that there might be a summons to New York, and so he had brought a single suit from Paris to Varengeville. He was wearing it now, one of the dozens he bought, four or five at a time, off the rack at Pierre Cardin. His shirt, made for him at Charvet, was monogrammed with his initials. His boots—

never shoes—were from Gucci. His patronage of such shops had nothing to do with snobbery; years before, when money had been a problem, he'd learned that cheap shirts wore out in six months whereas the best lasted for years. But no such clothing would have filled his closets and wardrobes if he hadn't been required to conform to the public expectations of how a chief European correspondent should dress.

Was there any wonder, then, that this trip to New York filled him with such foreboding? It had brought back into focus all the distortions in his life that he had taken a year off to forget.

It had occurred to André after his thirtieth trip on the Concorde that it functioned as something of a club in the air for those ten thousand people who run the world. There had scarcely been a flight in which he hadn't run into someone he knew. He'd crossed four times with Rudolf Nureyev, twice with Andy Warhol, probably half a dozen times with David Rockefeller. Even the people he didn't know by name came to seem like old acquaintances after several trips together.

But today, providentially, while there were a number of familiar faces, there were no old friends aboard, which relieved André immensely because he needed the time in flight to think about the story he was flying in to discuss. To emphasize that point, he scarcely nodded to the stranger in the aisle seat before turning to stare out the tiny porthole as the Concorde left its gate at precisely 11 A.M.

There was, to begin with, the matter of treason, almost unimaginable in nonrepressive societies and even less so in France where love of country was felt with genuine emotion. Yet what the Frenchman felt for France was something akin to what the Spaniard felt about God. The relationship was direct, one-to-one, intensely personal. As God existed to assist the Spaniard in his earthly endeavors and to guar-

antee him a place in Heaven, so the state existed to protect
each Frenchman from the encroachments of all others. Privacy was a birthright, reflected in everything the country
did. It was no accident that telephone bills were never item-
ized; specific numbers might provide a spouse with the clue
to an affair. Unless they were related or associated in business or were of the same class and had been properly introduced, the French had little use for one another. Never
mind that another car was entering an intersection from the
left at the same time theirs was; they would crash if necessary to prove that they had *priorité à droite*. Their soccer
and rugby teams often lacked coherent teamwork principally because of each player's desire to show off his own
prowess. And woe to the corporate hireling who made an
exceptional deal; rather than being applauded for the benefits he had gained the company, he would be despised for
showing up his colleagues.

Was it such preoccupation with self—the essential prereq-
uisite for acts of treason—that also made the French such
ineffective soldiers? It wasn't the worst explanation for the
series of twentieth-century military defeats the French attempted to paper over with stories of individual heroics—
few of which held up under scrutiny.

André knew that service in the Resistance was one of the
great myths of contemporary French politics. Hundreds
upon hundreds of elected officials and aspirants to political
office, who had never resisted anything, were running
around with medals pinned to their coats. The truth was
that millions of Frenchmen had been passive in the face of
the German invasion and bitter at the collapse of the French
Army. Ever since the war, the Communists had boasted
that they had been Resistance fighters from the day the
Germans set foot on French soil, but in actuality they had
collaborated with the Germans so long as the German-So-

viet pact was in force; their resistance dated from the day the Germans invaded Russia.

Worse yet had been the helpfulness of many Frenchmen in regard to the Nazis' war against the Jews. French history books did not record until only very recently that 90 percent of the Jews sent to the death camps were arrested by regular French police; that the Prime Minister of Vichy France asked the Germans to deport Jewish children even before the Germans were prepared to do so; that three thousand Jews died in Vichy France, in concentration camps run by the French, when no Germans were present to kill them.

So there was ample precedent for deceit and treason. But Camille Laurent? The man had been to the Resistance what de Gaulle had been to the Free French, a near-mythic figure, a beacon, transcending, like de Gaulle, the suspicions with which the French generally view their military leaders precisely because of the critical role he had played at a key moment in history. Afterwards, Laurent had served with distinction in the colonial wars, maintaining a careful separation between himself and the rebellious French generals. Physically, he was almost as distinctive as de Gaulle, tall, reedy, with a long, thin nose, unwavering blue eyes, and close-cropped pepper-and-salt hair. Without so much as saying so, he managed to convey to the French what they so desperately wished to believe, that they were still a great world power. De Gaulle had used the same technique to give the French new courage after their humiliation in World War II. In recent years, the French people had become disenchanted, not simply with the devaluation of the franc, but with the discounting of their country that it seemed to represent, and the apparent inability of their government to deal with the economic crisis. Given Laurent's record and image and the current state of the nation, he stood an excellent chance of being the next President of France. Could such a man have once been a traitor?

André heard a muffled boom, felt himself being pushed forward in his seat, and knew without looking at the tachometer in the front of the cabin that they had reached supersonic speed. A few moments later one of the stewardesses put his luncheon appetizer before him, and he turned silently to his food. He noted by the way the man seated next to him handled his knife and fork that he was French and knew his thoughts would not be disturbed.

Due to space limitations, the luncheons served aboard the Concorde weren't as elaborate as those served during normal first-class flights, but they were excellent nonetheless and always included awesome wines. Today's luncheon began with Iranian caviar and salmon with mint, served with a 1977 Meursault, followed by breast of chicken with port wine, accompanied by a 1969 Hospices de Beaune. Normally, André would have drunk a third and even a fourth glass and then dozed for the rest of the flight, but today he held to two glasses, and, once he had finished his coffee, tilted his chair back and feigned sleep.

What complicated the puzzle that Shlomo had given André was that André knew Laurent—or at least thought he did. The two men had even dined together on a few occasions. If they were acquaintances more than friends, it was because of André's caution about forming friendships with important sources, lest he be compromised. Was there something about Laurent that had been hidden all these years, visible neither to the public from a distance nor to an acquaintance close up? Had money been involved? Most military men did not live well; Laurent did. Where had the money come from? Had blackmail been involved? André recalled reading about a Resistance fighter who had informed for the Gestapo in order to save his girlfriend after the Germans had captured her while she was on an underground mission. Or was there some other explanation that at the moment he couldn't even imagine? There *had* to be an explanation—assuming, of course, that the report was real.

Don't get carried away, he told himself. It's someone else's problem. Feeling the wine, he let himself relax and soon he was asleep. When he awakened they were landing in New York. It was 8:45 A.M. A car was waiting for him; as it carried him into Manhattan, he realized that the man with whom he'd be meeting in an hour was on his way to work as well, the only difference being that he was being transported from Fifth Avenue to the West Side, whereas André had come from a tiny village on the French side of the English Channel.

4

Mike Paul was waiting for André when he arrived at the eighteenth floor. With him were the two men directly under him in network news, Charles van Damt and Saul Geffin. Both men were in their forties, both bore the marks of constant deadline pressures: sallow faces, lines around the eyes, quick, deft, nervous movements. Van Damt spoke and dressed like an Ivy Leaguer; Geffin had fought his way out of the South Bronx and lived in fear that someone would somehow conspire to put him back there.

André told them the story from the point of Shlomo's telephone call. He then offered his own assessment very much as he had outlined it in his mind during the flight. When he finished, both van Damt and Geffin turned deferentially to Mike Paul, who was staring out the window, seemingly lost in thought. Finally he said, "So you don't rule it out?"

"Anything's possible in France."

"The Israelis don't like Laurent because he'd be just as anti-Israel as de Gaulle. Is it possible they're trying to use you?" van Damt said.

"I've thought of that. Everything Shlomo's ever given me has checked out."

"And you're useful to him," Geffin said. "He knows he can trust you. If he burns you on this story, you'll never go near him again."

"That's right," André said.

Geffin turned to Mike. "I believe it," he said.

"But how do you do it?" van Damt said.

The three men turned to André. "Don't look at me," André said. "I'm on leave."

"Come on, André," van Damt said. "We wouldn't know where to begin."

André looked at Mike. "You promised," he said.

Mike shrugged. "I haven't said a word."

As the three men waited for his reply, André knew not only that he was trapped: he had trapped himself. He'd known all along exactly what would happen, and yet he'd permitted it to happen by coming to New York. Not to attempt the story was unthinkable, but it was such a difficult story that no one, not even he, might be able to verify it. Yet if he didn't at least attempt it, the story would never get done. This was cold fact, not conceit. He was the network bird dog; few of the other correspondents had anything like his reporting experience. Moreover, France was his headquarters, his beat; either he would know the contacts or they would know of him. He spoke their language; he understood them. Contacts were everything in the acquisition of information. It wasn't enough just to have them; one had to know how to use them: the setting one chose for discussions; the carefully chosen dress, meant to confirm the source's tastes; the unnoticed inflections in one's own voice, and the subtle change in cadence, conforming to the speech patterns the source found most familiar; the timely references to a shared history; the small encouragements as the source begins, at last, to tell you what you have come to hear. Years of on-the-job training went into this rite; without it, no reporter stood a chance. He couldn't perform nearly as well on strange turf as on his own; it was not reasonable to suppose that a correspondent strange to France could come into the country cold and perform as well as he could.

So the rationalization for taking the assignment made perfect sense—except for a man who had determined to walk a road not taken. "Okay," he said, "I'll give it two weeks. If I haven't got anything by then, I'm off the case."

They agreed to refer to the story as "Camellia." No one but the four of them would know of its existence. André would draw a ten-thousand-dollar advance and charge all his airline tickets, if travel was required. He would try to keep them informed, but it was understood that he might be out of touch for days or even the full two weeks.

On every trip to New York, André made a point of dropping in to visit Gregory Harrison, the anchorman of USBC's evening news, and to spend an hour or two in the cavernous fifth-floor newsroom where the news editors and producers put the program together. This time, he decided, neither visit would be wise. Too many questions to duck; too much suspicion aroused. That evening, as he watched the program in the living room of his suite at the Ritz Carlton Hotel, he knew exactly what had been involved in achieving such precision, the hard bargaining that accounted for every second of air time or even a place in the lineup. Yet it was all so seamless, Harrison looking straight at you and speaking so naturally you would never suspect, if you were an outsider, that there was no such thing as ad libbing or spontaneity on the air. The evening news was totally scripted, from beginning to end. Mike Paul had hired Harrison away from another network ten years before because his white hair and rugged looks—he might have been in a savings and loan commercial—gave him an air of credibility, and because he could be counted on to pull off a half hour program every night, five nights a week. He'd been doing exactly that for the last twenty years. He was weary of it, he'd confessed to André, but he didn't know how he could make a million dollars a year doing anything else.

What a good decision he'd made not to stay on the track that would have led to that chair, André told himself. That kind of money made him nervous because it implied an importance vastly greater than the job deserved. Besides, a million dollars a year seemed so unnecessary; he'd never wanted more than enough to live a good life. Harrison was rich, true, but he was so far removed from the excitement of reporting as to be in another business. He experienced reality only by what others reported. If journalism was a spectator sport, André, at least, was out there watching the game; Harrison saw it only on film clips.

Harrison was bridging now, from the Washington report to floods in the western states caused by the melt off of the heavy winter snows. Two and a half minutes for national affairs. A minute for a natural disaster. Minutes and seconds divvied out to another ten to twelve stories. There it was, the inherent, basic defect of daily television journalism, unchanged in thirty years; the need to compress a variety of subjects representing the news of that day throughout the world into twenty-two minutes and fifty-nine seconds—the time left over after commercials. André still carried bad memories of fights with New York over an extra five to ten seconds for a piece. There was simply no way you could deal in real substance with anything, and he was no more comfortable with that fact in this moment than he had been at the outset when he had to learn to convey with two hundred words what he would have said in a three-thousand-word magazine article.

He had known in his heart then, and nothing since had

changed his mind, that the people who might have read his magazine piece, or even a newspaper article, would know more about the subject than those who would listen to his broadcast. And yet the reality was that seventy-five percent of all Americans got most or all of their information from television and almost never read a newspaper or magazine. An even greater impediment to substance was the visual nature of the medium. It wasn't simply that pictures were more valued than words; it was that, given a choice between a plain picture and a spectacular picture, a news editor would choose the spectacular picture, even though that picture might not convey an accurate sense of the story or an indication of its complexities.

For a long time after accepting Mike Paul's offer to join USBC, André had felt that he'd made the mistake of his life. He hadn't needed television and didn't believe in it or even like it. But he'd wanted to see it from the inside; if it was going to be as important as people said it would be, he hoped—naively, perhaps—that he might eventually help make it better. Six weeks into his new job he wouldn't have taken even the most attractive odds that he would last a year. Either the stories he was assigned were completely banal or else he was given a minute and fifteen seconds to talk about matters of such major consequence as Lyndon Johnson's discomfort as President. What had saved André was Mike Paul's recognition that he was gaited to longer pieces, and his decision to assign those pieces to him whenever he could. It was then that André had discovered the real marvel, the true potential of television, when pictures heightened words and words heightened pictures with a synergistic power that no other medium could equal.

From that moment, André had done extremely well on television. He'd done hour-long programs on the future of NATO, on France after de Gaulle, on Israel, Egypt, Iran, and the PLO. He'd even talked the network into letting him

do a show on television's impact on public opinion. A single
picture on television could change the attitudes of people
almost overnight. Nixon perspiring during his debate with
Kennedy. Romney saying he'd been brainwashed. Muskie
crying in New Hampshire. In the early seventies, the French
magazine *L'Express* had done a poll on capital punishment
showing fifty-four percent of the French people against it
and forty-six for it. The magazine had appeared on a Monday. That afternoon French television carried a report of a
prison riot in which hardened criminals took over the
prison, took hostages, and killed several people. The following week *L'Express* reported the results of a second, identical poll made the day following the broadcast. This time
fifty-four percent of the French people *approved* capital punishment.

International terrorism was clearly a media child. Terrorists had learned to strike in those places and ways that
would get the maximum exposure on television. Witness the
1972 Olympic Games when a billion people watched the
work of Palestinian terrorists. André had covered that
story, and it had given him the idea for the longer piece on
television's impact.

The work was all-consuming. He seldom had a moment
to himself. His life wasn't his own. He couldn't make a
dinner date three days in advance because he never knew if
he'd be able to keep it. There were too many empty hotel
rooms, too many airplanes, too much flying to Athens or
Helsinki or Beirut just to be filmed next to a familiar
landmark in a thirty-second stand-up. There was never time
to write anything but scripts. It bothered André terribly
that he wasn't writing books; it bothered him that people
wouldn't be retrieving his broadcasts from library shelves
generations hence. But as heady as it was to hold a book
you'd written in your hands, it was clear to André that he
was reaching a far greater audience as a television corre-

spondent than he ever would with the printed word. And he could not help but believe that if he was persistent he could bring the people who ran the network to look at things in a different way and permit him a little more time to tell even those stories he did for the evening news. Given the incalculable importance of television in shaping public opinion and policy, that seemed like a decent objective—but one he could only achieve from the field. That was why no amount of money could persuade him to change jobs with Gregory Harrison.

On the other hand, Harrison didn't spend half of *his* nights in empty hotel rooms. He spent them at home with his wife.

As soon as the program ended, André called his son, Gene, at his office in Los Angeles, but Gene, a stockbroker, who was at work by seven A.M. in time for the market opening, was already gone, playing tennis, his secretary said. Then André called his daughter, Paula, a cub reporter on the San Francisco *Chronicle,* catching her just after the first deadline.

"What are you doing in New York? You're supposed to be in Varengeville," she said.

"I don't want to lie to you, and I can't tell you the truth because you're a competitor now."

"Oh, Daddy, come on."

"Tell me what you've been up to," André insisted. When Paula had filled him in, André said, "How's Mom?"

"She's fine."

"Give her my love the next time you talk to her."

There was a second's pause. "Why don't you give it to her yourself?"

"No," André said, "just give her my love."

Paris had finished them off. They might have made it had they remained in Washington, but even then they knew the

problem. It was as plain as the freckles and dimples on
Katie's exceedingly Irish face. They had met at UCLA in
the late forties, after André's discharge from the Navy. Katie was an eighteen-year-old freshman. André was twenty-
one and a senior, having completed the equivalent of three
years of college in the Navy's officer training program, in
addition to commanding a minesweeper in the South Pacific
during the last fifteen months of the war. There was the
difference right there. Everything André had done to that
point had been done at a much younger age than anyone
else. He had given concerts when he was six, graduated
from high school at fifteen, assumed the command of his
minesweeper at nineteen. Katie was right on schedule, not
precocious in any way. But that simply didn't matter at the
time. No one would have called her beautiful; she was quite
simply the cutest girl on the campus in the days when the
word "cute" had a valuable meaning, and her freshness and
vivacity were a tonic after three years of the cynicism and
vulgarity that characterized so much of service life. They
were married two years later: the first mistake. André, by
then, was the second-string music critic for the Los Angeles
Times. Katie, with no musical education and no college degree, seemed ill at ease with the young performers and com-
posers André brought around. His mother, a music critic
herself, all but overwhelmed her, and Sunday afternoons,
when Mrs. Kohl held a salon for refugees from Europe such
as Thomas Mann and Lion Feuchtwanger, were terrors. All
that Katie might have survived had they remained in Los
Angeles, where her friends and family in Palos Verdes provided ample support. But the war had politicized André,
and he had quickly tired of writing reviews of lesser musi-
cians. He was also ashamed to be working for a newspaper
that, at the time, was nothing more than a sun-tanned Chi-
cago *Tribune*. He wanted to write about politics, and he
wanted to live in Washington, and he soon had what he

wanted when a job with the Los Angeles bureau of the *Saturday Evening Post* led to an assignment with the magazine's Washington bureau. Katie was dismayed. She had nothing now but André, and later her two little babies. She didn't care for politics, and she couldn't comprehend the values or concerns of the ambitious young men and women she met at Georgetown parties. Katie's discomfort grew in direct proportion to André's success and the stature of his subjects. The day finally came when, to her utter dismay, she found herself in the company of the President and First Lady of the United States. Nor was that the worst of it. The magazine profiles André had written about John Kennedy when he was a candidate for President, and again when he was President, led, finally, to a contract for a book. The manuscript was in galleys in November 1963; after the assassination, André rewrote the book in a month. It was one of the top five nonfiction bestsellers of 1964. That was the year all of the television networks, concerned about the low esteem in which their news divisions were held by the public, began to go after the best print journalists. The networks knew by then that it wasn't enough to have a handsome face read a script rewritten from the New York *Times*. They had to compete with the New York *Times,* and their present staffs didn't know how to do that. All of the networks courted André. Mike Paul of USBC went the others one better: he offered to make André the network's Washington correspondent. Within a year, Katie Kohl was not only living among the ten thousand people, she was the wife of one of them, stared at wherever they went.

All these years André had observed Katie's deepening unhappiness with first confusion, then concern, and finally anger. They were affluent, they lived well, their children were being beautifully schooled. Above all, they were vital —or so it seemed to him. Katie's abhorrence of their life not only made no sense to him, it diminished her in his eyes.

And then Paris, where André, who had spoken French before he spoke English, quickly flourished and Katie was mute. She abandoned her French lessons after six weeks. André was furious. "You won't even try to be happy," he cried one evening after a particularly dismal dinner party.

"How can I be happy when I can't understand two thirds of what they're saying? So I study French and after a year I'll understand half. How much better will that be?"

"Every woman I've ever known would kill to live the life you've led."

"Then you should have married one of them. I hate it."

"Why? For God's sake, tell me why."

"Because it's not me. I'm just a girl from Palos Verdes. I don't know how to deal with arrogant, pretentious, uncooperative people who need a month to do something that should take a week. I like to talk about problems I think I can solve, not whether England should be allowed to enter the Common Market. I like old friends and doing the same things over again every year. I'd like to watch my mother and father playing with their grandchildren. I'd like to watch UCLA play football. I'd like to walk on the beach and watch the waves. I'd like to see something on television that's in English. I'd like . . . oh, shit, what's the use?"

And suddenly André could no longer be angry. How can you be upset with someone for being honest about who she is? He knew then what Katie had known for some time, that they should part as quickly as they could.

It was the one great sadness of André's life.

André sat at the desk in the living room of his suite, looking out the window across Central Park to the apartment buildings along Fifth Avenue. Mike Paul lived in one of those buildings. Gregory Harrison lived a few blocks away, in a brownstone on East Sixty-fifth Street. It was after eight now; both men would be in their homes or if not, out somewhere with their wives. He wondered if the two couples had dinner often together. He figured they probably did.

He continued to stare out the window. He didn't want to turn around. He knew what he would see: a pretty, but empty room. His apartment in Paris was empty, and so was the house in Varengeville, except for Madame Cartet, who didn't count in that way. All of his rooms had been empty since Katie went away.

"Why don't you give it to her yourself?" Paula had suggested when he'd asked her to give Katie his love. He reached for the phone and began to dial the number, which he knew by heart. Halfway through the digits he began to visualize the scene. It would be five-thirty in Palos Verdes, where Katie had lived since returning to the States, first in her own small home and then in the family home, which she had inherited when her parents passed away. It was a beautiful home, he'd grant her that, a Cliff May ranch house all but buried in red bougainvillea, with a large lawn sloping toward the Pacific Ocean a few hundred yards away. The surf would be down now, and the sea a silver sheet. Katie would be fixing dinner for her husband, John Morgan, the man she should have married in the first place. He was a good man; he'd been good for the children. He'd be on the freeway now, coming home from his lawyer's office on one of the top floors of the Atlantic-Richfield Building in downtown Los Angeles. He would arrive at six, and they would have their predinner martini in the living room and watch the setting sun through the picture window. They would do the same thing tomorrow night, and the next, and the next. Katie would be fifty-two now, a beautiful time for a woman, when happy years have placed a light stamp on her face. Thank God she'd had some since their divorce.

Why spoil it? André thought, as the number began to ring. Before it could ring a second time he softly replaced the phone.

5

The Paris bureau of USBC was on the Champs Élysées, just below the George V Métro station in a six-story building with a theater that had been playing *Emmanuelle* for nine years. It was not a location André cherished. As famous as the boulevard was—it ran from the Arc de Triomphe to the Place de la Concorde, two of the city's most notable landmarks—it felt less like Paris than almost any other street in town. Partly this was due to the constant presence of tourists, but other parts of the city, notably St. Germain des Prés, dealt with onslaughts of tourists without losing their Parisian character. Not the Champs Élysées; it proliferated with fast-food shops, automobile showrooms, and other commercial scars. The only virtue to the location, in André's eyes, was that it was virtually across the street from Fouquet's, a glorified brasserie and one of his favorite places for lunch.

But there would be no time for lunch this day, and no inclination for it, either. He sat in his fifth-floor office, feeling exactly what he felt every time he started a story: helpless. More than thirty years at the job and hundreds upon

hundreds of successful assignments should have caused him
to feel otherwise, but it never happened. The only thing he
knew for certain was that every reporting project began
with a telephone call. The object was to find someone who
knew even the slightest bit about what you needed to know
—or who knew someone else who did.

André's first call was to the press attaché at the Ministry
of War Veterans, a man he had known for fifteen years. By
noon of his first day in Paris following his return from New
York, he had a list of all Resistance organizations still active
in France. By four o'clock that afternoon, he knew which
organizations had worked in central France, in the vicinity
of Clermont-Ferrand, Camille Laurent's main sector of operations, and by six o'clock he was aboard a train at the
Gare de Lyon, with three appointments set for the next
morning and a list of promising contacts. By noon the following day, having told each of the men he interviewed that
USBC was preparing a background story on the forthcoming French elections, and that for obvious reasons the network was particularly interested in the role of Camille Laurent as a Resistance hero, he'd heard so many eloquent
testimonials to Laurent's courage that he was beginning to
believe he would be back in Varengeville sooner than he'd
thought.

Late that afternoon, however, he received a call from a
baker in the outskirts of Clermont-Ferrand, a man whose
name had not been on the original list of contacts. One of
the men André had interviewed earlier that day had telephoned to tell him of André's visit, the baker explained. He
had worked in the Resistance with Camille Laurent, he
said, and he would be very happy to talk to André if he
thought it would be useful. André asked if the baker could
join him for dinner that evening. No, the baker said, he
would prefer that André come the following morning to his

boulangerie. André would understand why after they had spoken.

That evening, André took a taxi to Chamalières, a small town four kilometers from Clermont-Ferrand. Chamalières had two distinctions: Valéry Giscard d'Estaing, the former president of France, had once been its mayor. And it contained the only one-star restaurant in the region, the Hôtel Radio. As André ate a broiled *poulet de Bresse* and drank a half bottle of burgundy, he cautioned himself about becoming too optimistic. But he could not help believing that he was working a lucky story.

The baker's name was Olivier Cerbonney. He was well over six feet tall, an unusual height for a Frenchman. He had the ruddy face of a drinker and was, in fact, ready for a drink when André arrived at 10 A.M. That fact might have caused André to discount anything Cerbonney might tell him. But the baker would have been working since three-thirty or four that morning, André knew, which made it well past midday for him. Cerbonney, wearing a white shirt and pants dusted with flour, motioned André to a seat in a little kitchen behind the shop and without asking poured both of them a tumbler full of Côtes du Rhône. *"Santé,"* he said.

"Santé," André said. He raised his glass to his lips, then put it down without drinking.

"You stir many memories, Monsieur."

"I'm sure," André said.

"I was at the side of Camille Laurent from the first moment to the last. Of course, we never called him Camille Laurent in those days. His code name was 'Felix.' I'm sure you have been told of his courage. I, myself, can recall a dozen times when he undertook assignments that I or the others might have done. He did not tell us that they were extremely dangerous. We knew that ourselves. By rights he should not have gone because he was the leader and would

not easily be replaced. But he would not hear us speak of
that."

"So I have heard," André said, wondering, in spite of
himself, why he had been so optimistic, why he had driven
out to see yet another Laurent booster, why the baker had
insisted that they meet in his *boulangerie* rather than in
town.

"Everything that Camille Laurent did, Monsieur, was accomplished against the worst kind of obstacle."

"How so?"

"I cannot prove what I'm about to tell you, but I am
certain that throughout the war there was an informer in
our organization."

André reached for his glass and took a sip of wine. It was
very young and almost totally lacking in body. "I see," he
said. "What made you believe that?"

"A number of our operations were compromised."

"What sorts of operations?"

"Mostly those in which we attempted to help the British
and Americans infiltrate agents into the area around Clermont-Ferrand. They were extremely good operations. There
was no reason for them to fail. And yet each time it seemed
that the Germans knew more about them than we did."

The baker rose and disappeared for a moment down a
flight of stairs. When he returned it was with a freshly
baked *baguette*. Then he removed a terrine and a bottle of
cornichons from a small refrigerator and set them on the
table along with knives and plates. He cut some of the terrine for each of them. "Duck with green peppercorns," he
said. He broke off a piece of bread, covered it with the meat
and took a large bite. André did the same, even though he
wasn't hungry and the baker's story had made him too excited to eat. A refusal might somehow jar the baker; one
tried never to jar a source.

"Being American, you would probably be most interested

in what happened to the American agents, isn't that so?"
the baker said at last. He did not wait for a reply. "By
coincidence, the story I remember best concerns an American operation, code name 'Screaming Eagle,' in the fall of
1943, six months before the invasion. Six Americans parachuted in with some new equipment they were to teach us
to use. We never got near them. Twenty minutes before the
drop, we got to the target area on foot. The Germans were
already there. There was nothing we could do. We couldn't
attack the Germans because we didn't have enough men or
guns. So we just had to stay there and watch from the edge
of a woods. Some minutes later, we heard the plane, and
then we could see the Germans flashing a code. The same
code we had arranged with the Americans."

"How did you know it was the same?"

"I was the communications man, Monsieur. I was to send
the very signal that I could see the Germans flashing."

"Couldn't you have sent a signal yourself? Wasn't there a
signal arranged to abort the mission?"

"I tried, but they didn't see it. I was too far away. In any
case, before I knew it, the parachutes were in the air. There
was a great wind that night. The result was that the agents
landed a quarter mile from the target area. The Germans
went after them. They were between us and the Americans,
so there was nothing we could do. For the next hour we
heard shots. Can you understand how we felt, Monsieur?"

"Of course," André said. "All of the Americans were
killed?"

"No, Monsieur. I was just coming to that. Three days
later, one of them was brought to our headquarters. The
man was badly wounded. He had been shot in the lower
back and could not move his legs. Somehow, in the night,
he was overlooked and managed to drag himself into the
woods. A farmer found him and hid him and then got in
touch with a member of our group."

Cerbonney cut another hunk of terrine and put it on his plate. André forced himself to wait until the baker had taken another big bite. "What did Camille Laurent have to do with this?" he asked then.

"He was the leader of our group, Monsieur. It was his decision to hide the American and get him medical help."

"Did the American survive?"

"Oh, yes. He remained with us until the end of the war. We got on very well. He was extremely intelligent, with many good ideas."

André tried to make his next question sound as offhanded as he could. "I know it's forty years ago, but you wouldn't by any chance remember the American's name, would you?"

For an answer, Cerbonney smiled, reached behind him and took hold of a photo album that had been laying on the table. "I can do better than that, Monsieur," he said. He opened the album to a premarked page and pointed to a photograph. "This was our Resistance group. The photograph was taken at the end of the war. That's him," he said, indicating a tall young man, unmistakably American, who was standing with the aid of two canes in the midst of a dozen Frenchmen. "His name was Charles Houghton."

André's hands were trembling as he took the album and drew it closer. Lucky story, he said to himself, lucky story. Standing next to a young Camille Laurent, he was absolutely certain, was the current deputy director of the CIA.

Olivier Cerbonney waited until André's car had disappeared from view. Then he returned to the *boulangerie,* entered a tiny office next to the kitchen, closed the door and dialed a telephone number in Paris. A woman answered. "I wish to speak to Boris," Cerbonney said.

"I take messages for Boris," the woman said. "Boris is not here."

For the next several minutes Cerbonney described his visit with André in full detail. As he spoke, the woman took notes. When they had finished, she made a call of her own, to a private number at the Soviet Embassy, and repeated verbatim the story told her by the baker.

Five minutes after her report was finished, a telex message was en route from the embassy to KGB headquarters in Moscow. It said: "Phase One is complete."

6

For the third time in six days, André was flying the Concorde. He perceived it as an excellent omen. Lucky stories had a kind of irresistible velocity, one lead leading to another and then another in such rapid succession that you were simply picked up and carried along by the momentum.

But the faster he went, he knew, the farther he distanced himself from Varengeville, the piano, and whatever it was that he had hoped to find by playing his way back to his past, to that moment when he had taken one road and not the other. The momentum was totally beguiling. It gave you a sense that you were going somewhere. As long as you went fast and kept moving, it didn't seem to matter where you were heading. But every time you got there you knew that what you'd discovered, as valuable as it might be, wasn't what you'd been looking for. So you moved on again, at the first moment you could. But you never found what you were looking for. Was it because you didn't know what you were looking for? How else could he explain his restlessness with what he had, which almost any journalist in the world would trade him for hands down?

Was Olivier Cerbonney restless with his station? André doubted it. Like his father before him, and *his* father before him, Cerbonney had known that he would live the life of a baker. He wasn't restless with that fate because he knew there wasn't much chance of changing it. In a sense, that was unfortunate. His counterpart in America would be wondering how he could get another bakery, and then a chain or a franchise, and then incorporate and sell shares until he had become the chairman of the board. That hunger to succeed, to grow, to change was what fueled America and caused its miracles. But which was the happier baker? The man who knows there are limits to what he can become learns to appreciate what he has and is. That kind of contentment scarcely existed in the States. Maybe it was a matter of history, André thought. You couldn't go anywhere in Europe without being reminded that history did not begin two hundred years ago. Understanding that you dwell in a place that has been centuries in the making relates you to time in a manner that Americans don't experience. Without that sense of their place in time, no wonder Americans feel so restless and are so susceptible to suggestions that the world will end tomorrow.

Was that what he was trying to work back to—that European sensibility with which he'd been raised? Was that why he'd come to Europe, bewildering all of his colleagues in the process, to find that sense of proportion that he perceived as European? If so, he had totally failed, because for fifteen years he'd been leading exactly the kind of life he had led in the States. That was why the year off was so important, a year of developing a sense of his own place in time, a year in which to slow down each day to its hours and minutes and seconds, each of them experienced in the here and now. How many good years did he have left? Ten? Fifteen? Twenty? If he was ever to experience the contentment he was seeking, he had to kick the narcotic of motion.

And yet how could he drop this story now that it had taken this turn? Charles Houghton in the company of Camille Laurent during the last eighteen months of the war! It could be no other Charles Houghton than the CIA deputy director. Yes, the photograph was forty years old, but the resemblance was there in all ways, face and physique and height, and there was, above all, the matter of the canes. The deputy director of the CIA still used them to assist his all but useless legs.

André had never had dealings with Houghton, but they had met several times in Washington, and he knew a great deal about the Houghton legend because Houghton was one of a kind, a war hero and victim who had overcome his handicap to forge a career for himself in the agency. He'd been recruited for the OSS out of Yale, where he'd played end with distinction, and also varsity basketball, on an athletic scholarship. He'd waited tables, as well, a poor boy from an Iowa farm family come to the Ivy League, a "Jack Armstrong, the All-American Boy," ruggedly handsome and a straight A student. Since the war he'd been confined to desk jobs, of course, but with all of his energies focused, by necessity, on his mind, he had developed into an awesome analyst. His powers of concentration were legend. Not only did he have a prodigious memory—once he read something he never forgot it—he could learn a language in a few months. He spoke twelve and read twenty. For years he had been in charge of that unit of the CIA assigned to the interrogation of foreign defectors; it was to interrogate these defectors personally that he had learned a number of tongues.

Over the weekend, André had asked Saul Geffin at USBC in New York to contact Houghton. He would need the help of the network's Washington bureau, André told Geffin, but he should talk to Houghton himself, telling the deputy director only as much as necessary to secure an interview, and to give André the green light if all was well. The green light had flashed late Sunday night. "I told him it was a matter that concerned him personally," Geffin said. "So he suggested you come to his apartment as soon as you got in."

Houghton's apartment was in the Watergate, that complex of high-rise buildings—hotels, offices, shops, and apartments—adjoining the Kennedy Center and next to the Potomac River. He answered the door himself, supported by his two canes, the metal kind with a brace for the forearms and handles for the hands. André was stunned by his size, not his height so much as the breadth of his chest and shoulders and arms, unmistakable under his blue buttondown shirt. There wasn't even a hint of gray in his full head of wavy brown hair. He had to be in his midsixties, André knew, but he had the look of a man not quite fifty. Those rugged and handsome features had been lightly marked by the years, considering the fate with which he'd had to come to terms. His smile seemed to ignite his face. "Well, you've certainly aroused my curiosity," he said to André once they'd been seated in his living room in facing chairs next to a window with a view of the river.

"Then I'll dispense with the preliminaries," André said. "I've come to talk to you about a man you knew as 'Felix.' "

It took him twenty minutes to tell Houghton everything he knew. He held back nothing, having decided that the only way he could enlist Houghton's help was to "throw in" with him. As he spoke, Houghton's brown eyes never wavered from his and scarcely blinked. There was a minute's silence after André finished, so complete that he could hear the traffic nine floors below.

"You're asking me to believe that the man who saved my life was actually my enemy at the time," Houghton said at last.

"I'm not asking you to believe anything," André said. "I'm simply telling you what I know."

"But you believe it."

"That's not true. At this point I can't afford to believe it or disbelieve it. I was hoping you could help me."

"I'd be happy to help you if I could, but I don't see what I could do."

"The first thing you could do is tell me your opinion. Do you think it's conceivable that Camille Laurent was a Gestapo informer?"

"The word you want is 'preposterous.' "

"What about the baker's theory that there was an informer in their organization?"

"You said yourself that the French tend to enlarge their roles as Resistance heroes."

"But you remember him?"

"Oh, very well. He was extremely entertaining."

"What about those other drops?"

"There were no other drops in that area."

André hesitated. "You're sure?"

"Positive."

"What about that Gestapo memo?"

"I have a feeling your friend Shlomo might have been playing games."

"Never," André said. "He's never done that."

"Perhaps he was ordered to do it. The Israelis haven't many friends these days. They need all the help they can get."

It was true, and André knew it. Perhaps the time had come for the Israelis to play their trump cards. André didn't want to believe it. But why would Houghton believe it? He, of all people? "Look," André said, "you flew in on a mission that was compromised. There *had* to be an informer."

"Perhaps. But not Camille Laurent."

"What makes you so sure?"

"I watched him work. I helped him run missions. I've seen him dozens of times since the war. I feel about him like any man would feel about another man who had saved his life."

André studied Houghton for a moment. "You're telling me I'm spinning my wheels," he said at last.

For an answer, Houghton shrugged and smiled enigmatically.

André could almost feel himself slowing down and coming to a halt. In a way, it would be a blessing. He'd be back in Varengeville in two days. It wouldn't be the first story that hadn't checked out. Yet he couldn't help feeling disappointed. In theory it was an incredible story, not simply because of the sensation it represented, but because of its international implications. He couldn't quite bring himself to give up. But to continue, he would need some kind of lead, and he was down to one possibility. "I don't suppose you'd be willing to help me find that Gestapo memo, would you?"

Houghton laughed. "We're good, but we're not that good. I'm afraid we couldn't help you even if we tried. Most of the Gestapo's files were captured by the Russians at the end of the war. As far as we know, the files were taken to Moscow and stored in the archives of the KGB." He laughed again. "As much as we'd love to, we haven't got a prayer of getting into the KGB archives."

André rose, and Houghton with him, heaving himself from his chair and catching himself with his canes in a single, uninterrupted movement. "Thanks for seeing me," André said.

"Not at all," Houghton said. "You returning to Paris right away?"

"Tomorrow."

"You wouldn't know anything about the contemporary art scene in Paris by any chance?"

"What contemporary art scene? All the good artists from Paris are living in New York."

"Then that's the problem," Houghton said.

"What problem?"

"My daughter's an art dealer, as of two months ago. She opened a gallery in SoHo in New York. She got this great idea—at least I thought it was a great idea—to go to Paris and try to find some artists at the source, before they get discovered and their prices go through the roof."

"It's a great idea, except that she's looking in the wrong place. She should be buying art in places like Rumania and Czechoslovakia."

"There are good artists in those countries?"

"I have a house full of art from Eastern Europe that I could never have afforded to buy in the States."

Houghton frowned for a moment. "Would you mind terribly if I suggested she call you when you get back to Paris?"

"I wouldn't mind at all," André said. "Have her call me on Wednesday." He gave Houghton his private number in Paris and put the matter from his thoughts. He needed to concentrate on how he was going to get a certain dossier out of the KGB archives in Moscow.

7

The headquarters of the Central Intelligence Agency is set in a vast expanse of undulating Virginia woodland a few miles beyond the western edge of Washington, D.C. There is nothing secret about the location; a brown sign with the white letters CIA tells you when to turn onto an access road off of the George Washington Memorial Parkway. But from the moment you approach the large, white modern building security is of the essence. A twelve-foot fence, crowned with barbed wire, encircles the building. Teams of armed guards patrol the compound, accompanied at times by attack dogs. The heart of the security system is an elaborate identification process that exempts no one. To gain admittance to the building proper, each employee must produce, each day, a laminated card bearing his or her photograph, and wear that card visibly at all times. To gain entry to any of a multitude of special enclaves within the building, the employee must have a special authorization, signified by a red letter in a small box bordering the identification card. This authorization must be shown to a guard caged behind impregnable glass just outside the enclave. Only then will the guard activate a turnstile through which the employee must pass. To gain access to the innermost reaches of the CIA, there is one further phase to the security gauntlet: doors that open only for the right combination of coded symbols.

The more important the CIA employee, the more red letters on his card, and the more knowledge he has of the coded symbols. Charles Houghton's badge was rimmed with red letters, and he knew all the secret combinations. His office was in one of the more secure areas, but there was nothing otherwise to distinguish it from any one of hundreds of offices of important bureaucrats in the service of the government.

Houghton was seated at his desk, thirty minutes after saying goodbye to André. In front of the desk stood his assistant, a trim man with a crew haircut who looked as though he had been recently discharged from the Marine Corps after several tours of duty. His shoulders were back and his fingers were curled, as though he was standing at attention.

"I want the files on all of the clandestine parachute jumps that we did in France during World War II," Houghton told him. "I want them all. Get hold of our liaison man in the Army. He'll be able to help you. And then I want you to do a computer check on all interrogations of Gestapo personnel that relate in any way to the French Resistance. Your cross-check is the Office of Strategic Services, the predecessor to the CIA. Their personnel did the interrogations at the lower levels. Check names like John Kenneth Galbraith and George Ball, too. They were part of a team sent to Europe to interrogate top Nazi officials. I'm pretty sure what I'm looking for will be in the OSS interrogations, but let's not overlook anything."

"May I know what it is you're looking for, sir?"

"Not now, Billy. In due time."

"Yes, sir," Billy said. He did an about-face and walked

quickly from the room. When the door was closed, Charles Houghton slammed his right fist into his left palm and ground his teeth together.

It had seemed exactly right when the recruiter came around a month after Pearl Harbor, during Houghton's last year at Yale. He'd had his eye on him for some time, the recruiter said. They were organizing a special service for exceptional young men. He couldn't say much about it now, and Houghton was to say absolutely nothing, but if he was agreeable, he'd proceed as though he was taking paratrooper training, and then simply disappear for a spell to a farmhouse in Connecticut where they'd open a new world to him, a world of small and secret weapons and detonating devices, of secret codes and Dick Tracy radio wristwatches, of techniques that could give one man the effect of thousands and tens of thousands.

What better role for Jack Armstrong, the All-American Boy? That joking reference to the hero of the afternoon radio serial they'd all listened to as kids was his friends' way of handling the awe with which they viewed Charlie Houghton's exploits. The straight A student, the triple letterman, star and captain in football, basketball, and track, the class president, the boy of every prom queen's dreams. He took the kidding well but he knew that he was blessed and he was determined once the war started to serve with distinction. He wouldn't wait to be drafted. He wouldn't be a dogface. This was a just war, and he would give it everything he had.

Houghton graduated from Yale in June of 1942. Fifteen months later he was a first lieutenant in the OSS, seated in the office of his commanding officer at a base fifty miles from London, being briefed on his first assignment: to capture Kurt Hoepner, the Gestapo's chief in Clermont-Ferrand and smuggle him back to England. Five OSS agents

would jump into France with him under the impression that
the purpose of their mission was to bring in sophisticated
communications equipment and teach the Resistance fighters how to use it. Only Houghton was to know the real
purpose of Operation Screaming Eagle.

"Sorry, pal," his commanding officer, Victor Bernstein, a
small, wiry man with a dark complexion and almond eyes
and jet black hair had said when Houghton objected to the
secrecy. "That's the way it is."

"That may be the way it is but I don't think it's very
enlightened," Houghton said. He'd known Bernstein only
three months, since shipping to England, but he knew that
in spite of the difference in their ranks and ages and back-
grounds—Bernstein was a colonel, nearing forty and a successful Washington, D.C., investment banker in civilian life
—the CO liked as well as admired him, a principal reason
being that Houghton wasn't afraid to speak up. "I happen
to believe my men would perform a hell of a lot better if
they knew how important this mission was," the lieutenant
said.

Bernstein smiled. "That's exactly why I'm going to explain it to *you,* but *you're* not going to say a word until you
decide the second half is go. I'm authorized to tell you only,
Charlie. Got it?"

Houghton had been slow to reply. "Yes, sir," he'd said
finally.

"Good," Bernstein said, his manner suddenly all business. "How much do you know about the role of the French
since the Germans moved in?"

"Why don't we assume that I don't know anything."

"Okay. In brief, it's nothing they're going to be very
proud of in years to come. The invasion itself went very
easily for the Germans. Whether it was the superiority of
the German equipment and fighting force we'll have to
leave to the historians, but given what's happened since, you

can't discount the possibility that the French Army didn't have its heart in the job. After the armistice in June of 1940, France was divided into an occupied zone, with the Germans headquartered in Paris, and an unoccupied zone, with the French government in Vichy, a health resort built on the supposed curative powers of its natural mineral waters. You can draw any inferences from that choice that you like. In any case, the Vichy government has been headed since then by Marshal Pétain, France's big World War I hero, who calls himself the 'French chief of state' and looks upon himself as a French Franco, protecting the country's Roman Catholic values against the insidious left. We get the impression that Pétain wouldn't at all mind seeing the Germans kick the shit out of the British, turn England and France into protectorates, and summon Pétain to Paris. What Pétain has going for him is that the Germans can't run the country without him and the French bureaucracy he represents, and he's playing that card for all it's worth.

"You can explain the Pétains of this world as cynics or pragmatists or opportunists, or combinations of all three. They pop up in every occupation. What's inexplicable, and heartbreaking, is the attitude of the French themselves. There were a lot of tears when the Germans marched down the Champs Élysées, but since then there's been almost nothing except docility and acceptance. In a country of forty million, there probably aren't more than a hundred thousand in the Resistance—and a big hunk of that hundred thousand probably came over since the Russians stopped the Germans at Stalingrad and the Allies landed in North Africa. What complicates the hell out of your mission is that some of the people in the Resistance may have been collaborators before they joined up. They're hedging their bets, and they're just as capable of swinging back the other way again if the Germans get lucky. So you can't take anybody for granted. Okay so far?"

"Okay."

"Of the genuine articles, there are two varieties, those who organized spontaneously after the invasion—they called themselves *'le mouvement'*—and those who were organized at a later date by Allied agents, mostly British, dropped into France once the occupation was a fait accompli. That group called itself *'le réseau.'* The *mouvement* wasn't so much interested in military resistance as it was in printing newspapers and otherwise getting the word out to the people not to give up hope. The *réseaux,* as a rule, don't go in as much for propaganda as they do for sabotage. They know how to put a few sugar cubes into the gas tank of a panzer, or how to short out a communications cable with a thumbtack, or how to turn road signs around to confuse the German convoys. That sort of thing.

"For the first couple of years of the occupation, what was possible varied greatly from zone to zone. The *réseaux* in the occupied zones were much more restricted than those in Vichy, where most of the problems were from the Gestapo rather than the troops. To a great extent, the Allied invasion of North Africa changed the ball game. Before the invasion, the Germans had no need to station troops in the south. But with the Allied forces just across the Mediterranean, the southern flank had to be protected.

"Even though the greatest concentration of Germans is in Normandy and Brittany, where they figure the invasion will come, all areas of France are important to us, the objective being to slow the movement of troops and supplies to the critical areas both now and once the invasion begins. Since May, the RAF has been dropping containers of weapons to selected *réseaux.* Each container has half a dozen light machine guns, three dozen rifles, and two dozen Stens, grenades, pistols, ammunition for all the weapons, and a good supply of field dressings. Not much, but enough to cause some trouble when the fun begins. Unfortunately, we haven't been able to call the shots as to which *réseaux* get what. That privilege has been reserved for the Free French in London, and especially de Gaulle, to try to keep him under control. So there's no large single force we'll be able to count on. It's all terribly fragmented and politicized, Communists at one end and Gaullists at the other, with Socialists and middle-of-the roaders in between. You sometimes get the feeling that they've already discounted the war and are fighting for the future control of France."

"Shades of China."

"Exactly."

"What's Hoepner's role in all this?"

"You're one step ahead of me. We've got to talk first about de Gaulle. He's a big problem for us. An arrogant man with a preposterously inflated image of himself. The truth is that he's poorly educated and ill mannered, and totally unreliable. Tell him a military secret and you might as well broadcast it on the BBC. He places the British in the same category with the Germans as France's natural enemy. He'd love nothing more than to see the Russians beat the Germans all by themselves, thus keeping us and the British out. Despises us as well. Anything you read in *La Marseillaise,* the Free French newspaper, or hear on Radio Brazzaville has been cleared by de Gaulle. Maybe 'invented' is a better word. What they're suggesting is that the Americans want to negotiate with Pétain—totally untrue—that American help came too late and that the United States shouldn't involve itself in European affairs. Where the problem comes in for us is that the overwhelming majority of French people, probably 90 percent, look upon de Gaulle as the symbol of French Resistance and, although they don't have much use for him beyond that, they tend to accept what he has to say. So here we are, preparing to liberate France and having to worry about how much help the French will give us. Not just us, but the British, as well."

"You're not suggesting that they're against liberation?" Houghton asked incredulously.

"Nothing of the kind. What they're against is a liberation in which they don't play the leading role. That's obviously impossible, but tell that to de Gaulle. So as long as he keeps putting out this crap about the divine destiny of the French and what bad guys the Allies are we've got ourselves a problem. The solution, as we see it, is to pull off some kind of caper that proves to the Resistance not only that we're their friends and can be trusted but that we've got the ability to help them."

"And that's where Hoepner comes in?"

"Exactly. Of all the Nazis in France, he's the one the members of the Resistance most fear and hate. He's chief of the Gestapo in Clermont-Ferrand. His principal responsibility is to track and crush the Resistance. In the process, he's murdered thousands. *Thousands*. Women. Children. Jews. You name it. But the one that sticks in all their minds was the murder of Jacques Ferrer, the president of the *Comité National de la Resistance*. Ferrer was arrested by the Nazis in 1940 and tortured pretty badly. At one point, he broke a window and slashed his throat, hoping to kill himself before they could break him. After they finally released him he got to London somehow, saw de Gaulle and won his approval for a plan to unite the Resistance. In December of '41 he parachuted back into France and successfully executed his plan. Last June, he was arrested at a Resistance meeting in Lyon. No one knows who betrayed them. Hoepner himself led the raiding party and then personally tortured Ferrer until he was near death. Only then did he find out who he'd been dealing with and what a monumental piece of stupidity he'd accomplished. Here he'd almost killed the man with more information about the Resistance than anyone else in the country. He immediately put him on a train for Berlin, but Ferrer died en route."

"Hoepner's still in Clermont-Ferrand?"

"Right."

"How do I kidnap him?"

"That, Charlie, is something you're going to have to figure out on the ground, along with the Resistance people
we're sending you in to see."

"And if I'm successful?"

"There are several small airfields in the vicinity. They're
all lightly guarded. Pick the best of the lot, knock out the
guards at the appointed hour, and we'll be there to collect
you."

Houghton stared at Bernstein for a moment. "Sounds
swell," he said then.

"We know it's tough, Charlie. That's why you got the job.
That's not a platitude."

"Thank you, sir." Houghton hesitated. "I'd still like to
tell my men. They're entitled to know what they're risking
their lives for."

"When the time comes, Charlie. What they don't know
they can't talk about if they get captured. It's really in their
interest."

"Yes, sir," Houghton said.

Billy returned in less than an hour with files on all the
clandestine jumps into France. Six of them had been
wipeouts in addition to Screaming Eagle. All six had been
attempted after Screaming Eagle. All six attempts had been
made within one hundred kilometers of Clermont-Ferrand.

By the time Houghton finished reading the last of the
files, Billy was back with several volumes of transcripts of
interrogations, as well as summaries and analyses by the
interrogating officers. It was tough going, filled with ram-
bling statements, detailed explanations and descriptions,
and an overwhelming sense of horror even forty years after
the fact. Most horrifying of all was the sociopathic portrait

of Kurt Hoepner, the Executioner of Clermont-Ferrand, the man Houghton was to have kidnapped.

He was a small and chubby man, scarcely a master-race prototype, but he made up for his physical shortcomings with his devotion to the Nazis, and his sadistic zeal and inventiveness. As a lesson to the region under his domain, he locked several hundred children into their school one day, then blew up the building. He was particularly zealous in his quest for Jews, many of whom had fled to Vichy from the north in an attempt to escape the persecutions. At one point, Hoepner ordered several hundred Jews loaded onto cattle cars and sent them off to the death camps without food or water. Before the two-week journey had ended, most of them were dead.

According to figures compiled by the French after the war, Hoepner had been involved in 5,123 murders and was directly responsible for 9,571 deportations to Dachau and Auschwitz. "Repentant?" he answered one interrogator. "Why should I repent? I was and am a believing Nazi. I believed in what I did."

For three hours, Houghton read through the transcripts, reawakening to the rages and frustrations he had felt during that time in France when he had heard stories of the atrocities and deportations and had been helpless to do anything about them. Could he have diminished them even to some degree had he been able to kidnap Hoepner? Perhaps if he had succeeded, the boost to morale might have made the French a little less cooperative and acquiescent. But the mission had ended almost before it began, in a farm field twenty miles southeast of Clermont-Ferrand.

Suddenly, Houghton's thoughts were frozen by a paragraph in one of the interrogator's reports. He read it over and over again until he had it memorized: "Hoepner was a master at recruiting the French. By the end of 1943, more than two hundred of them were working for him. They formed a network of informers, the members of which constituted a cross-section of the city's society, including many from the very top. His network of intelligence agents was led by his French mistress, Simone Theron. Perhaps his greatest coup was in penetrating the Resistance itself, a feat that enabled him to frustrate several Allied efforts to make contact with the *réseaux* in and around Lyon. Hoepner's contact inside the Resistance was ███████████."

The document had been sanitized. The name had been blacked out.

8

After his conversation with Charles Houghton, André had returned directly to his hotel, the Sheraton-Carlton on Sixteenth Street, two blocks from the White House, looked up a telephone number in the small but thick black book he had carried with him, even on vacations, throughout his career, and then placed a person-to-person call to Moscow. That done, he stretched out on his bed and instantly fell asleep. The telephone awakened him. As he reached for the receiver he noted the time on the traveling alarm clock he had placed by the telephone. Two P.M. That would make it ten P.M. in Moscow.

"I have your call to Mr. Gondrachov. On the line."

"Thank you, operator," André said, and then he was yelling, "Gennady, my boy, how are you?"

"You don't have to shout, André," a soft voice speaking British English replied. "Our telephones work quite nicely."

"Oh, you've invented them, have you? Excellent. How are you, my boy?"

"I was fine until you called. The next time I see you I will explain to you in detail precisely what you interrupted."

"I take it you're not at home."

"How well you know me. As a matter of fact, I'm not even in Moscow."

"Where are you?"

"On the Black Sea."

"In April?"

"The only time to come, old man. Before the proletariat get here."

André laughed. He knew Gennady Gondrachov for the cynic that he was. He would never trust him for a moment, but he cared for him just the same. What André most liked about Gondrachov was how readily understandable he was. Events did not register with him in terms of right or wrong or good or bad. They were either effective or not effective in realizing an objective. The Western world would call him a sociopath. The Russians probably didn't have a name for it. His mind was dead to such considerations. He was a soldier in the ranks, prepared to follow orders no matter what they were. He had learned long ago that in his society privileges existed only for the very few, and that one earned such privileges only by demonstrating faith, doing what is asked of you and never rocking the boat. The man who is prepared to plod his way up the ladder of Communist society will reap many of the benefits of the wealthy class in the Western world. It did not concern him that such benefits were available only to the very few; he had achieved his objectives without ever registering the failure of his own society to produce the life he esteemed for more than a handful of people. Gondrachov's belief in the system extended only to what it could do for him; he had no fundamental commitment to the system at all. "Admit it, Gennady," André had said to him one night in Paris many years before when they were celebrating their special triumph. "Your system's no good. Your agriculture stinks. Your production stinks. Your distribution stinks. Your *system* stinks, now doesn't it, my boy?" And Gondrachov, his guard, too, lowered by a great deal of champagne, said, "You don't understand, old man. The system is what we've got. My problem's to survive within it, and I've learned how to do that quite well."

They had just made history together, Gondrachov, at André's suggestion, arranging an interview for USBC with Nikita Khrushchev after the Soviet leader's forced retirement—persuading the new regime it would serve the national interest to show the world that he was alive and well and hadn't been eliminated. If you wanted to do a story in the Soviet Union, independent enterprise would get you nowhere—unless it was directed at finding a fixer in the system. There was no fixer better than Gondrachov, who paraded as a free-lance journalist for hire by Western media and was in reality a colonel in the KGB.

"What can I do for you, old man?" Gondrachov said.

"Do? What makes you think I want you to do something? I was just calling to see how you were."

"I'm just fine. Well, then, call me again when you'd like to chat."

"There *is* one thing . . ."

Now Gondrachov laughed. His laughter was as surprising as his voice, soft and restrained, yet mellow.

"It's my understanding that the KGB has a piece of information which I'd very much like to have," André said.

There was a moment's pause. "I have always insisted that your sense of humor was underrated," Gondrachov said.

"It's nothing like that," André said quickly. "It's ancient history. You guys captured the Gestapo files when you took Berlin . . ."

"Or what would have been left of them, if in truth we did."

"What I'd like you to do is find out whether there's anything in those files on the Gestapo's operations with the French Resistance."

"That's a lot of work, old man."

"You've got computers."

"That's right. We *did* invent them. I'd forgotten."

"That's all I want to know—that, and whether I can look at the files."

Gondrachov was silent again. "I suppose what you're asking isn't impossible, but I do think, old man, that your chances would be better if you could be a little more specific."

Now André hesitated. He really didn't want Gondrachov or the KGB to know anything more about what he was doing than they had to. The last name he dared mention was that of Camille Laurent. He knew that anything he asked for would be scrutinized by the KGB in an effort to discover what he was up to. But he would have to take that chance. "Okay, I'd like to look at memos written by Kurt Hoepner . . ."

"The Executioner of Clermont-Ferrand."

"You know him."

"Know *of* him."

"Memos by Hoepner to the home office."

"You realize the chances are one in a hundred that such a dossier exists?"

"Give it a try. I'll owe you one, Gennady."

"You'll owe me nothing, old man. For me it's just a phone call. But supposing I do get something, are you prepared to come to Moscow to look it over?"

"Of course."

"When did you have in mind?"

"As soon as possible."

"Tomorrow? Next week?"

"Thursday, maybe. I'm in Washington. I'll get back to

Paris tomorrow. Give me a day to rest up. Can you do it that fast?"

"If the right people say yes, no problem. But how should I let you know? Shall I call you in Paris?"

A small alarm went off in André's mind. No point in making Gondrachov any more curious than he undoubtedly was already. "I don't know why not," he said. "On the other hand, just as a matter of policy, I don't like the locals to know too much about what I'm up to."

"You're not suggesting that they tap your phone, old man?"

"You never know, my boy."

"Shocking," the Russian said, and chuckled himself after hearing André do the same. "Tell you what," he went on, "let's leave it this way: if I find something, I'll have a visa sent around to your apartment and assume you'll come on Thursday unless I hear otherwise."

"Perfect."

"Will you fly Air France?"

"Would you fly Aeroflot if you had an alternative?"

"Then if it works out, I'll meet the Air France flight from Paris on Thursday."

"Great, Gennady." André chuckled again. "Sorry to interrupt your work."

"No problem," Gondrachov said. "It's right where I left it. I'll be back on the job in moments."

The actress Gondrachov had brought with him from Moscow stretched out her arms from the bed as he put down the telephone. "Two minutes, I promise," he said, smiling at her. Then he dialed a number in Moscow and waited for an answer. "Gondrachov," he said to the voice on the other end. "Phase Two is completed."

"Excellent," the voice said. "Then you'll return to Moscow tomorrow."

"I see no need for that, Comrade Chairman. The arrangements are all in order."

"You're taking too much time." The voice was suddenly impatient and heavy with authority.

"It takes the time it takes," Gondrachov said, his own voice calm and soft.

"We don't have that much time, Comrade. It was your recommendation to take this roundabout route. I accepted it because of your experience and record and in spite of the protests of several men who outrank you. Neither one of us will be served if your program doesn't work."

Gondrachov reached behind him and moved his hand until he found the actress's breast. "It will work. I know this man. We work extremely well together, but he does not understand our system and he is totally unsympathetic to our progressive objectives. If he even begins to suspect that this project was undertaken at our initiative, he will abandon it at once. That was the reason for the roundabout route. But now the most delicate part is over, and we are only a few days behind schedule. I promise you that he will be in Moscow the day after tomorrow."

"It will be good for you if he is."

And bad for me if he isn't, Gondrachov thought as the actress moved under his arm and put her head in his naked lap. "I have a suggestion for you, Comrade Chairman," he said. "When it's over, you should come to the Black Sea for a rest."

9

Virginia had never looked more beautiful as Charles Houghton's car, driven by a CIA chauffeur, carried him along a back road forty miles from Washington. In the late afternoon sun, the gardens of the immaculate homes were ablaze with red and pink azaleas, framed with white dogwoods and accented with purple, pink, and white rhododendrons. The beauty, however, did not enhance his mood; if anything, it served to darken it. Since 1947, he'd seen the same blossoms each spring. For him, spring was not a renewal so much as a reminder that in his case options didn't exist. He would always be bound to a desk.

The only gratifying aspect of yesterday's devastating series of events, beginning with André Kohl's revelations, was that they had provided him with a problem that required him to leave his office. He wasn't assigning this problem to anyone but himself.

In the twenty-four hours since he'd finished reading the transcripts of the interrogation of Kurt Hoepner, he'd not only learned everything he wanted to know about Hoepner's interrogator, he'd also discovered that the man was

still alive and living in the Virginia countryside. His name
was Virgil Craig. A graduate of Amherst, he'd been teach-
ing German history at Rutgers when the war began, had
enlisted at once even though he was past thirty, had gone to
Officer Candidate School after basic training, been commis-
sioned and then recruited by the OSS. After the war, he'd
remained in Europe, transferring to the CIA when the OSS
was disbanded. Because of his knowledge of Germany and
fluency in the language, Craig was stationed in that country
throughout his tour in Europe, which ended in 1959, when
he moved to Latin America, ostensibly to become an executive in a joint development with Latin American companies.
He remained in Latin America until his retirement in 1978.
He had never married and had no family.

Although they had worked in the same branch of the
agency for a quarter of a century, the two men had never
met. That was not surprising. As an operations officer,
Houghton dealt with numbers of agents who were known to
him only by their histories and capacities. In Washington
between assignments, Craig would have maintained his
cover by pretending to work either for Defense or State. He
wasn't expected to drop in to say hello.

If the two men had ever worked together, Houghton
didn't remember it, and Craig, for his part, had given no
indication of it when Houghton telephoned him to say he
wished to see him that afternoon. There had simply been a
very long pause followed, at last, by directions to his house.

It turned out to be an old colonial house, a quarter mile
from the road, not at all in good condition. The white paint
had yellowed, the porch sagged, the columns were chipped,
and the hinges on the shutters were rusted. There were no
azaleas or dogwoods or rhododendrons here, just a lawn
that did what it could by itself. What kind of a man would
spy for thirty years and then squirrel himself away? Houghton asked himself as he sounded the tarnished knocker.

For a full minute, there was no acknowledgment from inside, neither a shout nor the sound of footsteps. When the door finally opened, Houghton could only wonder whether Craig had been there all along or had crept up on tiptoes. One look at him gave Houghton at least a partial answer to the kind of man he was. He obviously hadn't exercised in years. His slack face looked almost windburned but his hands were as gray as ashes, suggesting that his color came from something other than the sun. A net of tiny red lines encircled watery blue eyes. When he took Houghton's hand his own was moist and limp. Obviously, the man did not live alone. He had his bottle with him.

Craig led him into the study, which was laden with Scotch vapors and cigarette smoke and desperately needed an airing. He offered him tea, which Houghton declined. "A drink?" he asked. Houghton declined that too. "I'll just freshen up," he said, pouring some Scotch into a teacup. Then he settled into a paisley-covered wing chair and attempted to look Houghton in the eye. "I haven't the vaguest idea what this is about," he said uneasily.

"Would it help if I identified myself?" Houghton said.

"No, no. I'm well aware of who you are. Tell me how I can help you."

"You interrogated Kurt Hoepner in 1945."

Houghton noticed the almost imperceptible change in Craig's aspect: the eyes suddenly focused, the features frozen, the back pressing into the chair. "Good Lord, is this about Hoepner? I hope you're not going to ask me to remember something that happened forty years ago."

"I'm afraid I am." Houghton drew a piece of paper from his jacket pocket and handed it to Craig. "That's a copy of the last page of your interrogation report. As you see, a name's been blacked out. I'd like you to supply it."

Craig studied the report long past the amount of time it would have taken him to read it. Twice he raised his teacup to his lips and sipped without looking from the page. His hands were trembling but that, Houghton knew, could be from age or the alcohol rather than from surprise. At last Craig looked up. "I can't remember," he said. "For the life of me, I can't remember."

"Would you remember the name if I told you?"

"Try it."

"Camille Laurent."

Craig frowned deeply, loosening flakes of dried skin. "The general? Whatever would make you think that he could have been a collaborator?"

"I won't answer that for the moment. Do you know why this document was sanitized?"

"No."

"Did you sanitize it?"

"No."

"Do you know who did?"

"I haven't the vaguest idea."

Until this moment, Houghton had taken some satisfaction from his ability to remain under control of himself and his circumstances in spite of the devastating news André Kohl had brought him. He would treat it like any other of the bizarre twists of fortune he dealt with almost daily. Almost forty years of practice had inured him to surprise and its consequences. Losses occurred all the time; one accepted them so long as the gains were greater. The important thing was to remain analytical. He knew this better than anyone. His cool persistence had enabled him to break down the toughest defectors, find and tweak their nerves, expose their lies, learn what he had to know. But to his utter bewilderment, Houghton suddenly felt himself unable to deal with Virgil Craig and, worse, about to lose control. "Why are you lying to me?" he demanded.

It was the worst thing he could have said.

"I beg your pardon," Craig said.

"Come off it, Craig," Houghton said, unable to stop himself, "who else would know what's in that report but you? I want the name of Hoepner's man in the Resistance."

Craig sipped from the teacup. His hand no longer shook. His watery eyes held steadily on Houghton's and before he spoke—in a voice that was suddenly and glacially calm—he smiled lightly, revealing stained and misaligned teeth. "I believe you're out of order, Mr. Houghton. I'm not in the agency any longer."

Had he somehow contrived to cause Houghton to stand, take his canes from him and then push him, Craig could not have produced a more devastating effect. Houghton felt that he *had,* somehow, been toppled. He was the nation's top intelligence professional, with an array of forces at his disposal beyond the imagination of an Orwell, yet in this one crucial instance he had suddenly been rendered powerless. He could *not* compel Craig to tell him what he wanted to know, could not order him or pressure him or force him. The man was simply beyond his reach, as was the information Houghton was now certain he possessed. The frustration broke the last vestiges of rational restraint and, to his horror, he heard himself begging. "Please!" he implored. "This is a matter of great importance to me. You see the way I am. I got it during a clandestine jump in France during the fall of '43. Someone betrayed the mission, probably the man Hoepner named. I'd like to know who it was."

"Why now?" Craig said.

"I can't tell you."

"And I couldn't tell you who the man was, even supposing I knew."

"Why not?"

"Because it's not in the national interest. That period opened up some terrible wounds, and many of them haven't healed yet."

Houghton's eyes searched Craig's face for some clue to

what he meant. He saw a man who looked at least as old as his years, six to seven years past retirement, who would have spent the majority of his waking hours during those six to seven years seeking to validate his existence from the perspective of enforced obsolescence, angry that he no longer mattered, critical of any policy that did not extend the line of history he had helped to draw. What was that line? Craig was a Cold Warrior. It had to be the Cold War. The national interest, by his terms, meant not simply containment of but dominance over the Soviet Union. What could a minor league betrayal involving the French Resistance and the Gestapo during World War II have to do with the Cold War? Seeing the set of Craig's jaw and the tiny ripples in his cheeks caused by his grinding teeth, Houghton knew that the answer to that question wouldn't come from him.

The two men stared at one another in silence. Then Houghton rose and swung rapidly on his canes to the door.

10

André walked into his Paris apartment at one o'clock Wednesday morning, following his return from New York on the Concorde, his fourth supersonic trip in ten days. His body was hopelessly confused by the series of back-and-forth time changes, and his mind scarcely registered where he was. In spite of his fatigue, sleep was out of the question. It was scarcely dinnertime in Washington, where he'd awakened that morning. And he was too excited, all but drunk with excitement, the only kind of excitement that transported him like this. There could no longer be any concern for Varengeville, not until the momentum stopped.

He rewound his answering machine and began to play back two weeks' worth of calls. He'd missed some good friends: Art Buchwald, William Styron, Yves Montand, his agent, Sterling Lord. There were calls from French students writing theses about American politics, asking him for help; a call from an expatriate Polish screenwriter to say he was broke again and would like to borrow some money; a call from Bernie Frizell, the former NBC correspondent, who had retired and stayed on in Paris and now ran the Sunday night poker game that had once been a tradition at the apartment of the late novelist James Jones, André's former neighbor on the Île St. Louis.

The last message was from Meredith Houghton. "I'm calling at the insistence of my father, whom I have always obeyed. As I'm sure you get several hundred such calls each year, you are free to ignore this if you wish. If on the other hand you have a few moments to straighten out a somewhat mystified fledgling art dealer, I'd be very much obliged. I'm staying at the Hôtel de l'Avenir."

If there was anything for him in Moscow, he would have one night between planes. No one in Paris knew he was back in town, which was just as well because it saved a great deal of explaining. He would take Miss Houghton to dinner. He might learn something about her father.

He called her at 9 A.M. He asked if she was free that evening and when she said she was, he said, "Why don't you come to my place at eight o'clock?" There was a brief pause, and then she said, "Don't I get dinner first?" and he was so surprised he said, "What?" and then she began to laugh and said, "Forgive me. I couldn't resist. I'll be happy to meet you at your place." He spent the day reading and listening to music, starting with Bach, Vivaldi, and Telemann, moving onto Brahms and Beethoven and then Wagner, whose music he loved but always listened to with a tinge of remorse because the man had been such a profound anti-Semite. About half an hour before Miss Houghton was supposed to arrive he began to play Rachmaninoff, an event that, by contrast with Wagner, always produced an extremely pleasant association of the man and his music. He'd been very young when his parents had taken him to a concert by Rachmaninoff, who had a shaved head and looked like a Cossack soldier and then sat down and played music with such sweep and beauty and romanticism that it didn't seem possible it could have been composed by him. And it was only as he was listening to the Rachmaninoff as he illuminated the paintings Miss Houghton would want to see that he realized how unsettled he had been all day about this engagement, and why.

It had been years since a woman had surprised him. He could remember exactly when. It was in 1970, a few months after Katie had returned to California with the children. French friends had suggested that he and a certain Madame Durand, a divorced woman in her late thirties, might enjoy one another's company, so he had telephoned her and arranged to pick her up at her apartment and then take her to dinner. But when he arrived she had some champagne waiting and as they finished their first glass and poured a second, she said to him, "How would you like to make love before we go to dinner instead of waiting until afterward? That way you can relax at dinner instead of worrying about the outcome." He'd accepted, of course, and when he'd recovered from his astonishment, her suggestion struck him not only as totally civilized but as an exquisite example of the difference between European and American women. Not that all European women would have made the same suggestion, but André was convinced that they did tend to approach sex with more integrity, as something extremely interesting to them, rather than using sex manipulatively, as so many American women seemed to do—or, at least, as memory persuaded him they did. Miss Houghton's remark had verged on an invitation, even if she was joking. Maybe he was out of touch, he acknowledged to himself, but it had seemed to him like an extremely un-American remark.

His first moments with her did nothing to settle him or solve the puzzle. She certainly looked American, tall, almost as tall as he was, and clean-looking with almost no makeup that he could discern, her hair straight and long and held back at her neck by a bow. In his first brief glimpse of her, her face seemed classic, like Grace Kelly's, but he had almost no time to register details because she looked at him so directly and openly and with such serenity that he was completely flustered. Then she walked past him into the living room, a European presence in an American body, her carriage regal, walked to the French doors that looked across the Seine to the rear of Notre Dame, turned, smiled and said, "It's perfect, isn't it." It was not a question.

"I was very fortunate to find it. It makes a lot of my French friends jade green with envy . . ."

"And drives your American friends wild, I'll bet."

"Why do you say that?"

"I can see them walking in here and realizing with utter dismay that you were right and they were wrong. They stayed put to climb the ladder, and here you are, removed from the corporate battles they fight every day, and you've got everything they want."

"I would not be good at corporate battles," André said.

She turned to the paintings then and looked at them silently, and as he watched her he had the feeling that even when she wasn't speaking she had completely taken over the room. No matter that it was just the two of them; it would have been the same had there been a party. What was it? Self-possession. Meredith Houghton was pleased to be who she was.

She turned to him suddenly, smiling again, and said, "Your collection tells me something nice about you."

"What's that?"

"That you believe in your own judgment."

"How so?"

"Most people who collect buy for value, which means they stick to painters with established reputations. These paintings have no market value because the painters are all unknowns, and because they live where they do, there's little prospect that they'll ever be known. So you bought the paintings for only one reason: because you liked them."

"And because they were inexpensive. There's not a painting in this room that cost me more than three hundred dollars. The average price is probably a hundred dollars."

"How did you find these people?"

"Whenever I go to a new country, I check out two things: films and paintings. They give me a pretty good idea of what's on people's minds."

"What a sensible idea."

"There are more in here," André said when she had finished touring the living room, indicating the door to the bedroom. As she went through the door and saw where she was, she turned back to look at him and laughed appreciatively. He suddenly felt his face grow hot and he said quickly, "No, no, I promise we're going to dinner," and she laughed at his embarrassment and squeezed his arm and he laughed with her but could not get over the charge that her touch had shot through him.

She looked at the paintings and then at the bed and said, "How long have you been divorced?" and he was so stunned by the question that he said at once, "Twelve years." There was a pause and then he said, "How did you know I was divorced?"

"I saw the pictures of your children on the piano. Since there doesn't seem to be a Mrs. Kohl on the premises, I took an educated guess."

"And why did you ask?"

"Because you still sleep on your side of the bed," she said, and he looked at the bed and saw that, sure enough, there was a shallow indentation on the left side. He turned to watch her as she walked past him to the living room. After a moment he followed and poured some champagne, and as he handed her a glass he said, "Do you always get so quickly to the point?"

"Don't you prefer it that way?" she said in a tone that indicated his answer had to be yes. "Men and women think nothing of screwing on their first night together, the most intimate act imaginable, and yet they wouldn't dream of opening their minds to one another, which is just as much fun and a lot more rewarding."

"Cheers," André said, for lack of an alternative.

"I like your paintings a lot," she said. "They're all so expressive."

"Exactly. They're by people with a lot on their minds."

"I find nothing like them in Paris."

"You won't. France isn't the great cultural center it used to be. The French don't understand that yet, but it's true. French artists of any consequence all go to the States because they find the creative climate there more invigorating."

"But why?"

"It's a function of power. Culture is geared to power, just as language is. French used to be the diplomatic language because France was a major power. Today English is the diplomatic language because America is the major power. French culture flooded the world when France was an important power. And now the world power is America and attached to that power is the spread of American culture. When you aren't a world power you become a cultural victim of the world power. You lose your artists . . ."

"And you're invaded by blue jeans and Big Macs."

"Which the French deeply resent. But it's not an invasion, really, it's bits and pieces being sucked into a vacuum. What the French don't realize is that there's been a recession in their own culture. If their culture were still flourishing, the inroads made by foreign cultures wouldn't be so important."

"But the myth of French culture prevails. Look at me, coming to Paris to find artists."

"That's because the history is so impressive, and all that history's still here. France is still living on its past reputation." He raised his glass to toast her. "And, fortunately for us, it still does a few things extremely well. Let me take you to dinner."

He took her to Chiberta, an expensive restaurant just north of the Champs Élysées on the Rue Arsène-Houssaye. He had chosen Chiberta not simply because the food was so adventurous, a happy marriage of classic cooking and nouvelle cuisine, but because—principally because—the decor was so unusual, art deco reconsidered, its original stamp unmistakable but refined with deep textures and subtle lights. The linens were pink, the crystal glistened, and plants embellished the room. "Oh, thank you," Meredith said a moment after they had entered, turning and putting a hand on his arm once again. It was the perfect tribute to a choice made so obviously with her interests in mind. Once again her touch sent a shock through him. He couldn't remember the last time such a simple and—he was quite sure —uncomplicated gesture had done that to him.

"I have to confess I've never before heard of the Hôtel de l'Avenir," he said when they were seated, "and I thought I knew every hotel in Paris."

"Of a certain class, perhaps. The Hôtel de l'Avenir is not in that class."

"Is it decent?"

"Of course."

"How did you find it?"

"I run, and one day I ran right past it, on my way to the Luxembourg Gardens. It's just a block from the gardens, which makes it very handy for me."

"You run, you say?"

"I do."

"I think we should come to an immediate understanding.

I have nothing against running, per se, or against your running. But I want it understood that you will never try to convert me."

"You're anti running?"

"I'm anti exercise in almost all forms. Only golf."

"How can you stay in shape, living in France, if you don't exercise?"

"I did not come to France to stay in shape. Furthermore, haven't you ever noticed that the French are thinner than the Americans? The one thing that impresses French people when they go to the States is how fat Americans are. Americans are fat because they live on junk food. The French didn't even know about junk food until the last few years. Their diet is rich, but it's also well balanced, and it's not very copious. Also, the French don't drink a lot before dinner, like Americans do."

He ordered *Kir royale,* made with cassis and champagne instead of white wine. They clinked glasses and sipped. "Well, shall we trade life stories?" Meredith said.

"I thought we already had," he said with a laugh, and when she had finished laughing with him, he said, "You're quite a contrast to your father."

"I take it you mean that I'm very open and he's anything but."

"That's what I mean."

"He has his reasons. Not just the obvious ones."

"I'd love to know about your father."

"Then I'll tell you," she said at once.

She began with the part he already knew, but he let her tell it because he wanted to perceive Houghton through her eyes, and there was always the possibility that she would include some detail he hadn't known. There was such a detail, it developed, and it turned out to be critical to an understanding not just of Houghton but his daughter. During his preservice years at Yale, there had been a romance with a girl from Smith. Her name was Amy Meredith. The family was old Virginia, tobacco growers dating back to the 1600s. Just as Charles had seemed destined to play a larger-than-life role, so did Amy seem destined to match up with a leader. When he left for the service, there was an understanding, but no engagement, at his insistence not hers, in case something happened to him. To Amy's credit, she refused to give up hope after he was reported missing in action, and to her further credit, she insisted on marriage when her beloved returned a paralytic. It was Charles who put the marriage off, hoping that intensive therapy might restore his legs and then, when that had failed, hoping to discourage Amy. They were married in 1946. Meredith was born the following year. Nine years later, Amy finally lost her battle, acknowledging that she really didn't want to spend the rest of her life with a physically diminished man.

"I lived with Mom during the school year," Meredith went on. "She remarried almost immediately, a very nice man from Greenwich, big Wall Street stockbroker. He was the other man in her life when she met Daddy. All Mom had to do was wiggle her finger and he came running even though he was married and had kids. He was very good to me, and Mom did her best, but I never got over her walking out on Daddy. I spent all my summers with him, trying to make it up."

"Is that why you've never married?"

Meredith tilted her head and looked quizzically at him. "What makes you so sure I've never married?"

"Your name's still Houghton, for one thing."

"I could have assumed my maiden name after a divorce."

"True. But there are no indentations on your ring finger." He took her left hand and turned it over and felt the pad just below the ring finger. "And no calluses."

She smiled. "You took a chance, didn't you?"

"A small one," he said. "You didn't answer my question."

"Is your question, 'Am I unwilling to put myself in a position where I can be devastated by another human being?' Is that the idea?"

"Something like that."

"If I thought I really knew the answer I'd tell you. What I do know is that being single has worked extremely well for me. I enjoy being independent. In theory I'd like to have a child, but if I pass through life without producing one I figure I've done the world a favor. I'm just not that happy with what's going on in the world to be sure I want to subject a child of mine to it, and I've yet to meet the man with whom I've wanted to make the child. Does any of that make sense?"

"It seems perfectly clear. One more question?"

"Sure."

"How did you happen to open an art gallery?"

"Art's my life. I majored in art history at Wellesley. I worked at the National Gallery in Washington and then at the Museum of Modern Art in New York. Every summer I take Daddy on an art tour." She paused. "It never occurred to me to do Eastern Europe, though. You've opened up a whole new world."

She withdrew her hand only when the waiter brought their plates. At her request André had ordered for both of them. She marveled her way through marinated salmon, duck with pink peppercorns and pears, a 1977 Château Margaux, and an Île Flottante. "You don't know what you're missing," she kept insisting to André, who never ate desserts and refused to even taste hers.

When she had finished and they were drinking coffee he said, "I'd like to hear the rest of that life story."

"Not until I've heard some of yours," she said.

"I'm usually the one who asks the questions. I'm not sure I'd know how to begin."

"Then let me ask you some questions."

"Shoot."

"Your name is both French and German. Explain."

"Mother French. Father German."

"Both immigrants?"

"Exactly."

"That explains your French. Do you also speak German?"

"As a matter of fact, it was almost a contest between my mother and father, each of them trying to make me more proficient in their own mother tongue than in the other's."

"Wasn't that traumatic?"

"Only when I discovered that wasn't the way every other boy was being raised." He explained about being tutored then, so that he would have time for the piano. "It wasn't until I was ten and started going to public school that I spoke English with any regularity." André laughed. "Can you imagine what a freak I seemed to my peers—an American kid who couldn't speak English except with a French-German accent."

"Why did your parents finally decide to send you to public school?"

"They were very worried. I'd become extremely introverted. I didn't want to go out or play with other kids. By this point I didn't know how, and the prospect scared me to death. So rather than try, I practiced. One day my parents told me they were declaring a one-year hiatus. No piano. No tutor. I'd go to school just like other kids. I had to learn to make friends, to deal with girls, to play sports, to get over the fear of hurting my hands. At first it was terrifying but then it was wonderful. By the time the year was up I couldn't bring myself to give it up in order to practice four hours a day again."

"Have you ever regretted giving music up?"

He frowned and looked closely at her.

"Something wrong?" she asked.

"You've asked this year's question," he said after a moment. It had taken him only that long to decide that he would tell her what he hadn't told anyone. He couldn't imagine why he would do that. He was by nature a guarded person, particularly about his private life, a nature that had been reinforced time and again by the need for professional discretion. But there was a need now to tell this virtual stranger his innermost secret—exactly why he didn't know. He explained then about his leave of absence and his desire to get in touch with his past, in the hope that it might tell him how he wanted to spend the rest of his allotment. He felt uncomfortable talking to her like that, because it made him conscious of the difference in their ages, but he didn't know any other way to answer her question honestly. Gradually, as he spoke, he thought he could hear himself getting a little closer to the truth that he was looking for. "Maybe the big imponderable is the notion of success," he said. "If success is measured by acknowledgment, that means you have to go public, and to the extent that you go public you distance yourself from the intimate aspect of your own life. One day you wake up and you realize that this whole aspect of life has been lost, and you finally understand the cost of what you've done. This may not be entirely fair, but in the last few years I've come to view the public aspect of my experience as the American side, and the private aspect, the one I've lost, as the European side."

"It's not exactly your conventional midlife crisis, is it?" she said.

"As I understand it, midlife crisis happens to people who haven't achieved what they set out to do. That's not the case with me at all. I'm successful beyond my wildest imagin-

ings. I'll go you one better. I never imagined being successful in this way."

"But you must have imagined something."

He thought for a moment. "I guess all I ever really
thought I would want would be the esteem of my peers."

She leaned toward him. "But don't you see? That's why
you had to go public. There's the trap right there."

"How so?"

"What makes your peers esteem you? Success and recognition."

André nodded. "I never thought of that," he said.
"Maybe what I need are different peers."

He paid the bill, and they walked the fifty feet from the
restaurant to the Champs Élysées and put their backs to the
Arc de Triomphe and began to walk toward the Place de la
Concorde. "May I?" Meredith said, and without waiting for
an answer put her arm through his.

Within two minutes they were adjacent to the theater
playing *Emmanuelle*. "That's my office up there," he said,
pointing to the fifth floor.

"Is that where you do your broadcasts?"

"It's not quite as simple as that, but basically, the answer
is yes."

"What do you mean?"

"Most of our stuff is taped, goes to London by land line
and then to New York by satellite. But we're in the throes
right now of setting up the facilities to broadcast direct."

They walked a few steps further, and then she said,
"You're not at all the person you seem to be on television."

"What kind of person is that?"

"Assertive. Aggressive, even." She smiled at him. "I
don't think I would have liked that person."

He couldn't have been more pleased. She'd seen through
the image to the man he believed himself to be. Had she also
divined the uncertainty he felt in situations just like this

one? She was telling him that she liked him, and he didn't know how to reply. "We haven't talked at all about where you should look for young painters," he said to cover his confusion.

"It didn't seem appropriate. We can do it tomorrow, if you can spare a few minutes." She looked at him as she said it, and he could see that she hoped it would be more than a few minutes. All evening he'd had the feeling that he'd been skirting posted land. Since his divorce he'd dated many women younger than himself, but Meredith was too young, as well as too bright and beautiful. He had tried to persuade himself that she was off-limits, someone to befriend, perhaps, but not a woman with whom he could become involved. But her face was very soft now, her eyes steady on his, and he was certain she was telling him that she wasn't off-limits at all.

A few minutes later he put her in a taxi. Before she got in she kissed him goodnight, half on the cheek and half on the mouth, leaving him to wonder what such a kiss implied. He thought of her all the way back to his apartment, and he was still thinking of her when he settled into the indentation on the left side of his bed. He moved to the center of the bed, but it wasn't comfortable and he was soon back where he always slept.

But he couldn't sleep, and he knew why. Ever since his divorce, André had existed on the assumption that he would never get deeply involved again. He loved the company of women, but it was a woman who had hurt him as no one ever had before. He was perfectly content to make it through the rest of his life with successive pleasant attachments that provided him with companionship and sufficient sexual release.

In one evening, Meredith had upset the balance so carefully and painfully constructed in the years since his divorce. He wasn't at all sure that that was a good idea, but he felt helpless to do anything about it.

When his doorbell rang at 6 A.M. it seemed to him that he hadn't slept at all. It was the concierge, angered to the point of injury at having been disturbed at such an early hour. He shoved an envelope into André's hands and stalked off without a word. André opened the envelope. Inside was his visa to Moscow.

The Air France flight to Moscow departed Charles de Gaulle Airport at 8:55 A.M. As soon as he had checked in, he telephoned Meredith. "I won't be able to see you today," he said. "I've got to go to Moscow."

"Oh!"

"You sound shocked."

"Do I? I can't understand why. All the nice men I meet go off to Moscow the morning after I meet them."

"I'll be back in a few days," he said. "Will you still be here?"

There was a moment's pause. "I'll make a point of being here," she said then.

Before boarding the plane, André called his florist and ordered a dozen roses sent to the Hôtel de l'Avenir.

11

Although André had been to Moscow a dozen times since the sixties, he still found the prospect unnerving. He knew it was as much a consequence of what he brought to the experience as it was of what the Russians made of it, and he wasn't proud of that fact. He, of all people, should have been able to resist the exaggerations and clichés with which the American image of the Soviets had been invested. Yet the first moments of every trip he had made seemed to validate the caricature. The intensive scrutiny of the young soldier who took his passport would make him wonder if he would ever get it back. The young man would look at the picture in the passport, and then at him, and then back at the picture, and then once again at him, repeating the process any number of times, and always with an expression that said, "I know it's not you, and I'm going to get you." When, at last, André was past passport control, he had the customs gauntlet to run. Once again, the silent stares would make him feel that he must have done something wrong, even though he had scarcely entered the country. What the customs inspectors wanted to know, most of all, was what

kind of literature you were bringing into Russia. By his fifth
or sixth trip, André knew better than to fly in with a book
he wanted to keep, because the chances were that it would
never leave the airport—not, at least, with him.

There had been some changes for the better, however,
since his initial trips. A new international airport had been
constructed near the old one and opened in 1980, in time for
the Olympics. Modern, handsome, and roomy, it was as
impressive as the best airports in Europe and, wonder of
wonders, even boasted a first-class lounge. The catch was
that it was run with the same inefficiency as the old one. If
eight passageways had been provided for passengers by the
architects, only one or two would be open.

This time, however, all such details were lost on André.

Gondrachov awaited André just outside the door of the
plane, an unspoken statement of his status. None but the
highest officials were permitted to greet passengers until
they had passed through customs.

"Do you have any baggage?" the Russian asked.

"Just what I'm carrying," André said.

"Good." Gondrachov grabbed André's overnight case
and began to guide him briskly through the corridor. "I
hope you can read German," he said.

"No problem."

"There's a thick dossier on Hoepner awaiting your pe-
rusal."

"Fantastic," André said. Lucky story, he told himself,
lucky story.

"What's all the fascination with ancient history?"

"Can't you guess?"

"I haven't the foggiest."

"Come on," André said, playing it just as he had decided
he would on the flight from Paris. "You guys aren't exactly
stupid."

"Well, we don't have much interest in Hoepner."

"That's because he worked in France and not on the Eastern front."

"But that was forty years ago. What's that got to do with you and your network today?"

"Hoepner's alive and well and living in Bolivia."

"Ah ha! And someone's going to pluck him!"

"Who knows?" André said. His cover had been spread and he hadn't had to lie. Why it would bother him to lie outright to Gondrachov he couldn't understand, since he went on the assumption that Gondrachov lied to him when it suited his cause to do so. Perhaps it had to do with the nature of their causes, ends justifying means for Gondrachov, André, ingenuously perhaps, still unable to accept that.

They were outside the terminal. "Hey," André said, "what happened to customs?"

Gondrachov smiled and guided André smoothly past half a dozen tired-looking taxicabs to his car, a black Mercedes 450 SEL, which André duly noted had been parked in a no parking zone, even though there weren't a half-dozen cars in the parking lot. The interior of the car smelled and looked new. He checked the odometer. Less than five hundred kilometers.

Gondrachov settled his big frame into the driver's seat, looked at André through his thick eyeglasses and said, "Nice, eh? I bought it from a West German diplomat."

"Gennady, someday I should do a story about you."

"God forbid. I'd be ruined."

"You could defect."

"Never. There's nothing in the West that could touch my life here."

"Oh, come on."

"You'll see," Gondrachov said. He drove swiftly out of the airport and onto an almost deserted highway, where he promptly floored the accelerator. In moments they were fly-

ing past birch forests on either side of the highway. André
leaned to his left, just far enough to read the speedometer.
The needle flickered at 160, a hundred miles an hour.

"Too fast for you?"

"Not as long as you think you know what you're doing.
Where are we going, anyway? This isn't the way to town."

"You're a clever fellow, old man. If you really put your
mind to it, I'm sure you can guess."

André grinned. "At last! The famous dacha!"

As long as he had known Gondrachov, and as close as
they'd been, André had never been to the Russian's country
home. Others had told him about it, and he had read about
it as well, in a file the U.S. ambassador to Moscow had
shown him after Gondrachov had offered to help USBC get
its interview with Khrushchev. The idea for the interview
had originated as one of those why-not-try-it-we've-got-
nothing-to-lose propositions during a conversation between
Mike Paul and André. André had drawn the assignment
because, although he was still based in Washington, the
project required high-level staffing and he was then the most
visible correspondent in the network. He'd gone to Moscow
in the summer of 1966 on the pretext of negotiating with the
Soviets for major coverage of the fiftieth anniversary of the
Russian Revolution, which was to be celebrated the following year. Those negotiations were carried out with the
Novosti Press Agency, a KGB front whose personnel as-
sisted foreign journalists in the Soviet Union. But neither
they nor Leonid Zamyatin, the chief of press relations at the
foreign office, would even discuss the possibility of an interview with the deposed premier. One day Gennady Gondrachov had materialized at André's hotel, unannounced
and unbidden, introduced himself, shown André a scrap-
book of his byline articles clipped from newspapers in the
West, and said, "I understand you want to interview Khrushchev. I'm a friend of his and I can do it for you. He'll talk

to me." His price had been a stiff one for those days, fifty thousand dollars, the money to be deposited in a numbered Swiss account. A good bit of sophisticated and expensive electronic equipment was to change hands as well.

With that much at stake, André felt he should know a little more about the recipient. What he discovered was as puzzling as it was reassuring. Gondrachov had been a student radical, agitating for democratic reforms at Moscow University, when he was arrested, tried, and sent to a work camp in Siberia. There, for reasons no one understood, he had turned informer, cooperating with authorities to identify troublemakers in the camp. His cooperation won him privileges within the camp—special food, a hut of his own, an occasional pass to the nearest town—and an early release. He was immediately recruited by the KGB and, after training, assigned to Novosti.

That arrangement apparently proved too confining for Gondrachov's talents because he was soon traveling abroad, offering his services to news agencies in England and France. A London paper picked him up and ran his reports from time to time. They were extraordinarily accurate and always at least a day ahead of official releases. In Moscow, where he maintained an excellent apartment by Russian standards—one filled with canvases of artist friends whose work was not sanctioned by the state—Gondrachov played host to Western correspondents, who jumped at the opportunity to talk to the highly placed government and party officials as well as the film stars who always showed up at his gatherings. The puzzling part was that no one really understood what his role was supposed to be and how he lived as he did. The reassuring part was that he continued to live that way and to produce valid information, which meant that he could be trusted to do what he said he would. On André's recommendation, USBC had paid twenty-five thousand dollars down for the Khrushchev interview. An-

dré had written out a series of questions and given them to
Gondrachov. The Russian had disappeared, only to reap-
pear a week later with what turned out to be a perfectly
professional tape of an interview with the deposed Russian
leader. Only Khrushchev was seen on the tape, but all of
André's questions could be heard as they were asked by a
voice that was unmistakably Gondrachov's. A week later
the remainder of his money was in Switzerland, and the
electronic gear was in his Moscow apartment.

But Gondrachov didn't stop there. Whether or not he
saw that in the tapes he'd just completed—five hours' worth
—he had something very valuable and should press on or
whether he had always had the intention of going forward,
the fact was that he then interviewed Khrushchev for another twenty-one hours, and those twenty-six hours of tapes
became *Khrushchev Remembers,* the memoir that Gondrachov sold to *Time* magazine for $300,000. The deal was
consummated in a room at the Hotel d'Angleterre in Co-
penhagen between Gondrachov and *Time,* although both
Gondrachov and *Time* always denied that the Russian had
anything to do with it.

André cast a sideways look at his enigmatic friend, whose
face seemed so fittingly inscrutable: almond-shaped, faintly
Mongolian eyes protected behind the thick lenses of his
wire-rimmed spectacles, high cheekbones, a thick but or-
derly mustache. There was a light smile on his face, as there
almost always was, as though he was in possession of some
extremely funny information to which no one else was
privy. Mysteries, mysteries, the indigenous Russian style,
the product of a people for whom conspiracies were as vital
as breathing, the most xenophobic people in all the world,
mauled through the centuries by foreigners, a people ad-
dicted by centuries of rule and religious habit to authoritar-
ian structures, of which the present system was simply the
latest variant. It's a terrible system, André would tell each

of the successive USBC correspondents assigned to Moscow as they passed through Paris en route to their new post, but you will make a terrible mistake if you try to interpret what's going on in terms of your own expectations and values. The Russians are different from you and me. They want a lot, but not an awful lot. Group instincts prevail over self. They worship science and belittle religion but they're nothing if not believers. Independent thought makes them uncomfortable. They may scream their disagreement on local matters but when it's Russia against the world, they all play follow the leader.

How many times André had tried to persuade the Moscow correspondents to turn the volume down on the stories of the dissidents, not because the stories weren't true and pitiable, but because when you run so many strident stories of the plight of the dissidents your American audience understandably concludes that the Soviet Union is populated solely by dissidents, when the reality was that they were a minuscule component of an accepting civilization that scarcely cared about their fate. But he couldn't blame the correspondents for being attracted to the dissidents. They were not only good copy, they expressed the very rage against the system that the correspondents felt themselves. Tony Cook, a bachelor then, had spent his first New Year's Eve in Moscow alone in the apartment that also served as the network's bureau. At 11:30 P.M. he'd opened a bottle of Russian champagne and at one minute past midnight, he'd raised his third glass to the ceiling and shouted to the bugs he was sure were planted there, "Happy New Year, you poor bastards. I'm up here drinking champagne, at least, while you're down in the cold cellar listening to me. What a cold fucking way to celebrate the new year. Happy New Year, you poor bastards." Five minutes later the phone had rung. "Hello?" Cook had said. For an answer, he heard a champagne cork popping.

They'd been driving for thirty minutes when Gondrachov slowed at last and turned off the highway onto a secondary road. Two miles farther on they turned again, this time onto a dirt road, at the end of which was the dacha. It was almost dark when they arrived, but there was enough light for André to make out the Porsche Gondrachov had been driving the last time they'd been together in Moscow. Next to the Porsche was a Land Rover, both of them parked in a gravel driveway. The house reminded André more of a hunting lodge in Canada or northern Minnesota than it did a dacha, but in any case it was the kind of second home anyone anywhere would be pleased to have. It was huge by Russian standards, a two-story log structure. Gondrachov reached above the sun visor of the Mercedes and pushed what appeared to be a garage door opener. The house and grounds were suddenly and completely illuminated.

"Come on," the Russian said. He led the way down a path that wove through a sloping garden, its flower beds still covered with the remnants of winter. They passed a gazebo and then an empty swimming pool and came at last to a tennis court. Gondrachov looked expectantly at André.

"I didn't know you played," André said, and then could not repress his laughter. "Okay," he said, "I'm impressed. I'd be even more impressed if you'd tell me how you got this."

"As my friend André Kohl would say, 'My lips are sealed.' "

They retraced their steps. As the top of the path, Gondrachov said, "Bring your suitcase. You're spending the night."

The interior of the house was not at all elegant, but it was old-fashioned and roomy. The living room was organized around a stone fireplace. There was a fire in it, indicating someone else's presence, although no one had come to greet them.

Gondrachov took André upstairs to a large guest bedroom and disappeared. André found a bathroom, then returned to the bedroom and took a sweater from his suitcase
to slip on under his coat. He checked his appearance in an
antique mirror above an equally ancient chest of drawers
and was about to turn away when he saw, reflected in the
mirror, a folder on a table against the opposite wall. Wheel-
ing, André reached the folder in three strides. It was
crammed with papers. He turned back the top leaf of the
folder and saw a document written in German. It was
signed with Kurt Hoepner's name. Quickly, he looked
through the other papers. There were memoranda and letters and telegrams, all written by Hoepner. There was no
doubt about it: he was holding the dossier kept by the Gestapo on the Executioner of Clermont-Ferrand.

"Dinner!" Gondrachov shouted from the bottom of the
steps.

"You bastard," André said when he joined his host in the
living room.

Gondrachov laughed. "Come," he said. "You'll have
plenty of time tomorrow."

"If you think I'm going to wait until tomorrow . . ." He
cut himself off, knowing he'd made a mistake, and followed
the Russian into the dining room.

It was a small room adjoining the living room, with a
table for eight. The table was laden with food—herring,
tomatoes, cucumbers sprinkled with dill, green onions
mixed with sour cream, radishes, a fruit and vegetable
salad, cold tongue, pickled mushrooms, and many others.
"Good God, all this for us?"

"There's a family in the kitchen that will eat what we
don't."

"Not your family?"

"No, old man. My wife is in Moscow and my children are

no longer children and no longer live with us. The family I speak of takes care of the dacha."

"Servants," André teased.

"Caretakers, old man."

"Gennady, do you know the difference between capitalism and communism?"

"Tell me."

"In capitalism, 50 percent of the people oppress the other 50 percent, and in communism it's just the reverse."

Gondrachov smiled lightly. Then he poured brandy for each of them. "To the oppressed peoples everywhere," he said, raising his glass. They clinked glasses and drank. "Two more of those and I expect you to tell me what you're looking for in those papers."

"You mean your boys haven't already cased them to find out?"

"They've got other matters more pressing than the ravings of a junior-grade sadist who's thankfully passed from history. Now let's eat some food so we can drink another toast. That's the only reason we Russians eat."

He had made a mistake, André acknowledged silently, giving away his eagerness, an indication that there was something hot in those papers rather than something historic, but Gondrachov hadn't caught it. Maybe he was being too sensitive, too careful. After all, he had come from Paris to read this dossier. Even a dolt would know that there was something of significance in it. But significance to whom? Not everything of interest of an American television network would necessarily be of interest to the Russians. *Sois tranquille,* he urged himself. But be careful.

Gondrachov insisted that André try every dish. Every few minutes he would propose a new toast: "To peace . . . to the memory of John and Robert Kennedy . . . to your exclusive interview with the First Secretary." What did he mean by that one? André wondered. That the comrade would soon follow in the footsteps of Nikita Khrushchev? After the second toast, André had stopped drinking, simply lifting the glass to his lips and then setting it down again. "Come on, old man, that's not polite," the Russian said.

"Sorry," André said. "I can't drink a lot of brandy."

"Since when?"

"I really can't."

"I'm not going to pry any secrets from you. I was just kidding. Relax!"

"I'm relaxed."

But he wasn't at all. One of the great stories of his life might be sitting upstairs, and there was simply nothing he could do to stop the churning inside himself. He desperately wanted the dinner to end so that he could tackle that dossier. It was ten o'clock in Moscow but only eight o'clock in Paris, where he'd begun the day. He'd be alert for another four hours. If only Gondrachov would finish!

There had been chicken after the salads, and now there was dessert, blintzes with sour cream, and then coffee taken at the fire, all of this served by a woman in her early thirties whose heaviness, normal for Russian women, did not disguise her attractiveness. He wondered if the family to which Gondrachov had referred contained an on-the-premises husband; catching a look Gennady threw at the woman as she served their coffee, André was willing to bet that it didn't. When he pleaded exhaustion from jet lag and asked to be excused, and Gondrachov made no protest, he was convinced that his friend would be happily occupied for the rest of the evening.

Alone in his room at last, André sat at the table at once and began to read. Hoepner was scarcely a stylist; his writing was that of a man who had failed to finish high school. It was also self-serving in a poorly veiled way. There were no failures, only successes: so many Jews rounded up this week, so many Resistance fighters caught. An ambush of

German soldiers? Thirty Frenchmen are executed. A group
of suspects who will not be broken? He leaves the prison
door open and mows them down as they try to flee. There is
a certain cunning to his accounts. No challenge he ad-
dresses is ever a small one; the victories, as a consequence,
always seem large. The most serious challenge is the Resistance; that fact is emphasized over and over again, but he is
working on a solution. He does not even wish to speak of it
until he has it in hand.

At last Kurt Hoepner speaks:

Security Police (SD)   Clermont-Ferrand, 10.10.43
Einsatzkommando C l e r m o n t - F e r r a n d

Tgb.Nr. 563/89

To the
                Commander of Security Police
                and the SD - IV B
                Paris

Subject: Infiltration of the French Resistance in
                the sector of Clermont-Ferrand.
Reference: None

Leading *réseau* in this sector has now been successfully infiltrated by placement of sympathetic man of
military background, Camille Laurent, code name 'Felix,' in important leadership position. Information furnished by 'Felix' enabled us to meet and destroy American intelligence mission. Future successes likely as no
suspicions aroused.

                                Respectfully,
                                Hoepner
                                SS-Obersturmführer.

My God, André whispered, my God, my God, my God.

As he watched André through the other side of the one-way mirror he had used when combing his hair several hours before, Gondrachov easily picked up the American's soft exclamations on his earphones. He smiled and continued watching and listening until André rose from the table and began to undress. Then he went downstairs to a small study off the living room and dialed a number in Moscow. "Phase Three is completed," he said to the voice that answered.

There was a prolonged silence. "Very well," the voice said at last, "but remember, none of this is of any value unless he completes Phase Four."

12

Years before, just after André had joined the *Saturday Evening Post,* Phil Lewis, the magazine's West Coast bureau chief, had a sudden, desperate need to find a source on a story the magazine was about to publish. Certain assertions the source had made to Lewis had proved so troubling to the magazine's attorneys that they wanted the story pulled unless substantiation of the assertions was forthcoming. Lewis, normally unflappable, was frantic. It was a good story, he'd worked hard on it, and he didn't want to lose it. The problem was that his source, a motion picture executive named Stephen Kagen, was out of town and his secretary swore she didn't know where he was. The whole purpose of his absence was to get away, she said, which meant cutting off all business calls. Lewis had put everyone in the bureau but André, who was out of the office on an assignment, onto the problem but no one had been able to find a trace of Kagen.

It was four o'clock when André walked in. "Did someone die?" he asked after registering the funereal despair. He listened silently as Lewis explained the situation and then, because he was feeling good himself said, "You want me to give it a try?"

"Would you?" Lewis said. "I'd be grateful."

André called Kagen's secretary. "When was the last time you spoke to him?" he asked.

"Five days ago."

"And where was he?"

"In New York."

"And what were his plans?"

"He and Mrs. Kagen were going to drive to Los Angeles. They wanted a week by themselves."

"He was leaving that day?"

"The following morning."

"Thanks," André said. His next call was to the Automobile Club of Southern California, where he confirmed his suspicion that at this time of year—it was early March—the only real option for someone driving across the country was the southern route. Four days of driving at approximately five hundred miles a day, a likely target for a man driving recreationally with his wife, was two thousand miles. Which major city was two thousand miles from New York? The answer, he quickly ascertained on a road map, was Houston. André's next call was to the Shamrock Hilton in Houston, the one hotel in that city to which a man like Kagen would be most likely to go. "Stephen Kagen, please," he said to the hotel operator. There was a short pause, during which time everyone in the bureau fell silent. A moment later, André's voice rang through the office. "Mr. Kagen? Phil Lewis of the *Saturday Evening Post* would like to speak to you."

That kind of reportorial triumph, as small as it was, filled André with a special pleasure that couldn't be gained any other way. Of all such triumphs during his career, none matched the one he had just accomplished. He had penetrated the archives of the KGB, which not even the CIA would attempt. And yet, lying in his bed in Gondrachov's dacha six hours after discovering that Camille Laurent in all likelihood had been a Gestapo informant during World War II, André felt no pleasure whatever. What he did feel was a pain in his head so intense it had awakened him from a sleep that, given his travels, should have gone on at least two hours longer. That sort of pain for him was always associated with anxiety. It was the anxiety, he knew, that had to have annulled the triumph.

Always before, he had been a reporter of events and very often an interpreter of those events, but never had he been a perpetrator of an event as he would be the moment he broke his story. Camille Laurent would be so badly tarred by the disclosure that he might not even make it past the first round of the election to the runoff between the two leading candidates two weeks later. In that case, the Socialists were sure to win. And all because of an American journalist. For a journalist to perpetrate an event was not customary, not expected, and—according to the profession's unofficial canons—not desired. That an *American* journalist had been the perpetrator of an event sufficient in scale as to influence French history would heighten the shock considerably. Of one thing André was certain: he would be *very* sure of his facts.

"Did you find what you were looking for?" Gondrachov asked when André came downstairs. He was seated at the dining table, smoking a pipe, and reading a book. A coffee cup was within reach. The aroma of coffee mingled with the pipe smoke.

"Enough to hang him if he ever came back to France. I'm surprised the French never asked you for the file."

"They've got enough without this, don't they?"

"But not in his own words. Those memos are Kurt Hoepner's confession."

"Never thought of that. Well, they could certainly have them if they wanted them, I'd think. After all, we were allied against the Nazis." Gennady paused. "What do you do now?"

"That depends on whether your government is willing to oblige me with another favor."

"You have only to ask, old man."

In spite of himself, André laughed. "An exclusive interview with the First Secretary."

"After he retires. Seriously, what can I do for you?"

André willed his voice to stay calm. "How much trouble do you think it would be to take the original memos with me back to France?"

Gondrachov whistled. "That *is* asking for trouble. Whatever for?"

"The Hitler diaries hoax has everyone pretty gun-shy, particularly when it comes to German documents. I'd want to show the memos on the air, but I'd have to be able to say that they're the real McCoy."

"McCoy?"

"An expression. What I'd really have to say is that we had authenticated the documents beyond any doubt."

"How would you do that?"

"However it's done. The age of the paper, the typeface of the typewriter, that sort of thing."

"Can't we do that for you?"

"Things being what they are, Gennady, I'm afraid my people wouldn't go for that. They'd want confirmation from someone a little closer to home."

Gondrachov shook his head and suddenly looked unhappy. "What's the matter?" André said.

"Well, you know, old man, these things don't happen in a vacuum. If this were six, eight years ago, a request like yours might get favorable consideration. But with all your Cold Warriors back in power and talking about winnable nuclear wars I'm afraid nobody on our side is in a mood to do any favors for anyone from the West."

"But this isn't all that big a deal. I mean, forty-year-old papers written by a man you yourself described as a minor-league sadist."

"Precisely. Why should we bother? Just to do you a favor? I'm afraid that's not enough."

"You *owe* me, Gennady." The words were out before André could stop them. They were from the heart, but they were too edged with interest and even anxiety. If he wasn't careful, he could give the game away. And yet without the papers there was no game. He could feel the Russian's eyes on him, sense that mysterious mind at work, its almost mechanical processes stripping away the loyalties and due bills and even emotions that were a part of all human interchange to lay bare the spine of André's desire.

"What *are* you after, dear boy?" Gondrachov said. "I'm not sure I do owe you. After all, you got full value for what you paid. But supposing I did owe you, it's not like you to play such a big chip for such a small pot. Is there something you're not telling me?"

Once again, André measured his Russian friend. As much as they both enjoyed one another, he knew theirs was a friendship of convenience, designed for mutual gain. He was sure that Gondrachov had studied him and knew how to flatter his tastes. It was a compliment to his importance in Gondrachov's constellation of values. André had repaid the compliment. He thought now about the rumors surrounding the Russian, his role as an informant in the Siberian camps, his KGB connection. This was not a man to confide in, let alone trust. Still, André could not bring himself to lie. "I have a personal reason, Gennady. Is that good enough for you?" It was not a lie; if Camille Laurent worked for the Gestapo during the war, it was he who had given away the mission in which Charles Houghton was crippled. To all the reasons André could give for wanting to prove beyond a doubt that Laurent had been an informer, he *could* add a personal one: to be able to give the information to the father of Meredith Houghton.

The memory of Meredith suffused André so suddenly that for a moment he was immobilized. He knew then that he wanted desperately to get back to Paris as quickly as he could. He'd learned from the dossier everything that he needed, but unless he could prove its authenticity—just to be able to say he'd done so—he couldn't touch the story.

Years ago, just before moving to Paris to take up his new duties, André had called on Chip Bohlen, the veteran diplomat and an old favorite, to get some words of advice. Bohlen had once served as the American ambassador to Moscow and given an impeccable performance. He had been especially masterful in negotiations with the Russians. When André had asked him how he'd done it, he responded with a story of how foreign fur traders had learned to deal with the hard bargaining so characteristic of the Russian people. It wasn't enough to make a "final" offer, the traders learned; they had to pack up and leave. If the Russians really wanted to do business, they would stop the traders at the border and make the deal.

Three years later, in 1971, André had had occasion to test the fur traders' tactic. He'd gone to Moscow to do a story on Soviet youth. On his promise to do a balanced story, the Soviets had agreed to cooperate, but after several days in Moscow, André knew he was getting the runaround. His camera crew wasn't being permitted to get close enough to the young people to get decent footage. So André had told them to pack up and had scheduled their departure. Within hours, the restrictions had been lifted.

It was time to use the tactic again. André was an asset to Gondrachov; their history together proved that. Even a Russian knew that one didn't squander one's assets. "Look,

Gennady," André said, "I'm asking you as a favor. Find out if I can have the dossier—on loan for a couple of weeks. Do it today, if you will, because I need to get back to Paris. There's no point in my hanging around. Either they'll do it or not do it, and my presence here isn't going to persuade them one way or the other."

"You really need that dossier?"

"I really do."

"Whatever it is that you're working on, you wouldn't be able to proceed without it?"

"In all probability, no."

Gondrachov locked eyes with André, the first time he had ever done that, André realized with a start, and then slowly shook his head. "Ah, the things one won't do for one's friends," he said then.

"Then you'll do it?"

"I will try," Gondrachov said, holding up his hand. "Remember, it's not my decision." He smiled. "However, if the decision is yes, who am I to turn down a trip to Paris?"

"You'll bring it?"

"Of course. You don't think they'd simply make you a present of a historic document, do you? Your request will have a much better chance if I tell the authorities that the document will be in my possession at all times and will be returned to the archives as soon as the tests are completed. I assume such an arrangement would be satisfactory to you. Am I correct?"

"Of course," André said quickly. He hadn't had time to run it through his mind for reasons why the arrangement might not be satisfactory, but instinct told him that he had better respond affirmatively and at once.

Gondrachov sighed. "I will have to have the skills of a plastic surgeon on this one," he said.

"Why so?"

"Because your request will—how do you say it?—pull

their noses out of joint and it will be my job to realign them. They will not understand why you can't trust them to authenticate the document for you. Incidentally, which one do you need?"

"I didn't say I wanted just one. I need the whole dossier," André said.

"Ah! My mistake," Gondrachov said.

Had it been a mistake, or just an inadvertence? André wondered. Everything that Gondrachov said or did had to be carefully appraised. Or was he overreacting again?

"Tell you what," Gondrachov said abruptly, "why don't we drive into Moscow and put you into a hotel? Meanwhile I'll see what I can do and perhaps we can have this wrapped up one way or the other by tonight."

"Fine," André said. He knew then what a runner must feel like who has just finished a photo-finish race but must await the official result to learn if he has won. He couldn't remember feeling more tired. There was absolutely nothing he wanted to do in Moscow. He would spend the day sleeping—after telephoning Meredith, provided he could get through. "Tell me," he said, "have you fellows invented long-distance dialing yet?"

"Last week."

"Great. Next question: is there a hotel in Moscow from which I can dial direct to Paris?"

"I believe that can be arranged," the Russian said. Once again, he was smiling lightly, as though enjoying a private little joke.

13

There were no signs at 2 Dzerzhinsky Square advertising the presence of the KGB, but few residents of Moscow were ignorant of the nature of the business behind the doors of the heavy, ashen stone building, if only because it formed one side of a courtyard another of whose sides was formed by a Moscow landmark, the Lubyanka Prison.

Next to the headquarters building, which had belonged to a prominent insurance company before the Revolution, was a nine-story addition constructed after World War II by political prisoners and captured German soldiers. The office of the KGB chairman bridged the old and new structures. It was a massive office with a lofty ceiling and big, overstuffed sofas resting on a parquet floor covered here and there by Oriental rugs. Directly behind the chairman's high-backed desk chair, on a mahogany-paneled wall between two over-sized windows bordered with dark drapes, was a framed portrait of Lenin. The dominant impression was one of permanence; everything was as it had been for as long as anyone could remember.

The single exception was the chairman's desk. In spite of

the grand scale and heavy decor, it was the desk that dominated the room, not because it, too, was oversized, but because it was so covered with stacks of papers and cluttered
with telephones that it conveyed a sense of great activity in
progress.

To judge by the archaic black instruments, multiple-line,
push-botton telephones had never been invented; the reality
was that the chairman preferred to have a direct line to each
of his major clients—the Kremlin, the Politburo, and the
Defense Ministry among them. Other telephones linked the
chairman to major KGB offices throughout the Soviet bloc,
and to his six deputies, all of whose offices were on the same
floor as his.

All six of the deputies were seated at the table in front of
the chairman's desk, three on either side, their faces turned
to the end of the table, where Gennady Gondrachov sat. His
gaze, however, was on the chairman, Vassily Krylov, because regardless of what the others thought, it was Krylov's
opinion that mattered. He was a squat man, at least thirty
pounds overweight. The faces of fat people usually reflect
the enjoyment they've experienced in putting on their
weight, but Krylov's face wasn't like that. It had been cor-
roded by the acid of a thousand bitter moments, to the point
that Krylov, who had just turned sixty, looked more like
seventy-five. When to this result were added the ravages of
fear, it made his face almost painful to look at for anyone
with the least bit of compassion.

Compassion had never been one of Gondrachov's problems, a fact of which he was well aware and for which he
was exceedingly grateful. It would simply complicate trans-
actions that had to be made on the basis of hard facts and
cold reason, a point he had been attempting to develop for
the last half hour. "If the dossier stays here, Comrade
Chairman," he said in conclusion, "what good does it do
us? None at all."

"We can't send a document like this by pouch," Valery Yuryev, one of the deputies, a chain-smoker in a blue suit and white shirt whose collar hung loosely about his neck, said. "First of all, it's not secure from our own people, and secondly, we know from experience that the French secret service has been able to persuade the airport authorities to look the other way long enough to permit a pouch to be opened and its contents photographed. If the dossier goes, it would have to be sent by courier—and even then it's not secure because too many people are involved."

"Not if I'm the courier."

Yuryev looked at Gondrachov as though he could not believe what he'd heard. "You?" he asked incredulously. "You're a marked man. You'd be spotted by French intelligence. If, as you say, you wouldn't let the dossier out of your possession, then you would have to go with your friend Mr. Kohl to this authenticator. It would be nothing for the French, having followed you and seen you with Mr. Kohl and knowing something important is happening, to call on this authenticator and discover precisely what has arrived in France a month before the presidential election."

Gondrachov stole a look at the chairman and did not like what he saw. The chairman was not a gambler. For him, doing nothing was preferable to a course of action that could lead to great risks and uncertain consequences. "Please, Comrade," he said to the man in the blue suit, "I have no intention of entering through an international airport. I have other plans."

"We are making this more complicated than it needs to be!" Yuryev exploded, his voice weary with impatience and angry as well. He turned to the chairman. "The French journalists are not so meticulous as the Americans. Show one of their Moscow correspondents the dossier this afternoon and the story will be published tomorrow morning."

The chairman's eyes moved from Yuryev to Gondrachov,

the desire in them transparent to do as Yuryev proposed. Gondrachov knew that the moment had come to win or lose. "I beg you to believe me," he said. "The whole purpose of this exercise was to find a nonsuspect outlet for the story. No one will believe the story if it appears in *L'Humanité*— and the Communist paper is the only one that will print the story without verification. Before the Hitler hoax, perhaps. Not today, not even the French. But it's more than that. It's a matter of what would happen to the story once the dossier is produced. The right wing might sit on it, the left wing could be accused of partisanship and not be believed. That's the problem: belief. That's why I recommended Kohl. Yes, we are friendly, but that is my job, to know the members of the Western media. It's precisely because of this intimate knowledge that I chose him. He has never made a major error. His word is accepted worldwide. If he broadcasts this story, he'll have done our work for us."

"And if he doesn't?" Yuryev said.

"I know this man," Gondrachov said, his voice overflowing with conviction. "I have made a *specialty* of him. I was just as positive that he would suspect the story if I gave it to him directly as I was that the Israeli, Glaser, would go to him with the story. There are patterns, Comrades, that have to be acknowledged, that tell us what people will do in given situations. I am telling you now that André Kohl will broadcast this story. He cannot resist it. To him, a great story is more irresistible than a beautiful woman."

The chairman was silent. By the look on his face, Gondrachov could see that he was winning. He watched the chairman's eyes move to Yuryev, asking silently for any final rebuttal. "And what about this authenticator, whoever he may be? What kind of trouble could he cause us?" Yuryev said, pounding the ends of yet another cigarette on the table, his face a mask of frustration.

Gondrachov smiled faintly, knowing he had won. Images

of Paris danced through his mind. "I can promise you,
Comrades," he said. "The authenticator will not be a problem, no matter who he is."

André's last visit to Moscow had been marked by a hotel
accommodation far superior to any he had ever had before.
He'd stayed in a duplex suite at the Intourist Hotel. Furnished and finished as well in a rustic mode, its main floor
had a sitting room and dining room complete with dishes
and flatware and a set of wooden stairs that led to a comfortable bedroom. But the telephone service had driven him
wild. The Intourist Hotel had no switchboard. Each room
had its own private telephone, so that the occupant could
call any number in Moscow—including other rooms in the
hotel—just as he might have from a private residence. Theo-
retically, he was free to make long-distance calls, as well,
simply by dialing the operator. Reality was another matter.
There was the language barrier first of all—there *were* English language operators, but to get one you had to make a
non-English speaking operator understand what you
wanted. And then there was a four-hour or longer delay
before the operator could complete your call.
    So while André would have enjoyed staying in the In-
tourist Hotel once again, he was far more concerned about
being able to dial directly to Paris. On Gondrachov's assurance that he could do so at the new International Hotel
built by Armand Hammer, he had checked in there. The
manager had told him apologetically that the only accommodation left was a two-hundred-ruble-a-day suite. "I
couldn't care less," André had said. The moment the manager had left him in the suite he had made a dive for the
telephone and, following the instructions pasted to it, attempted to dial the Hôtel de l'Avenir in Paris. Each time he
dialed he got a recording in Russian. At last, in exaspera-
tion, he dialed the hotel operator. "I must be doing some-

thing wrong," he said. "I'm trying to direct dial Paris and all I get is a recording."

"You can't dial direct from your room, sir," the operator told him.

"But I was told that I could."

"You were incorrectly informed, sir. That's no longer the case. I'll have to get the number for you."

André hesitated before replying, trying to keep his temper in check. Every trip to Moscow was like that, filled with maddening contradictions, things that didn't work, the worst service in the world, nearly the worst cuisine, interminable waits for everything, shortages, dumpy-looking women, and a xenophobic populace. One simply had to bear up, to come as infrequently as possible, and to leave as quickly as one could. "How long a delay?"

"Six hours," the operator said. "There is trouble with the circuits."

"Never mind, operator," André said. He hung up, too tired to protest further. There was one alternative. He could take a taxi to the USBC Moscow bureau, where he could telex USBC in London with instructions to call the Hôtel de l'Avenir and give Meredith the number of the Moscow bureau. But by the time he got to the bureau and the circuit was completed, Meredith would probably have left the hotel for the day. Tired as he was, even that effort seemed worthwhile on the off chance that she might be in. But there was the matter of letting the Moscow correspondent as well as the London bureau know that he was at work again rather than on his leave of absence. The Moscow correspondent would be upset because André had come to his turf unannounced, and the London bureau would spread the word throughout the network, and there would be no way that André could offer a satisfactory explanation to anyone. No, he would just have to wait until he returned to Paris to talk to Meredith. André stretched out on the bed and fell asleep, fully clothed.

When he awakened to a pounding on his door, the room was semidark. It was Gondrachov. "I've been knocking on that door for two minutes," he said when André let him in.

"Sorry," André said. "I really passed out. Hey, I thought you said I could dial direct from here to Paris."

"You can."

"No way," André said. He summarized his experiences, including his talk with the switchboard operator.

"She doesn't know what she's talking about," Gondrachov said. He walked to the telephone and picked it up. "What's the number in Paris?"

André handed him the number. Gondrachov dialed and listened for a moment. "The circuits are busy, that's all. Keep trying, and you'll get through."

"Great," André said. "Now tell me what happened."

"I'm bringing you the dossier."

"You're kidding! That's terrific!"

"It will be a few days, maybe three, maybe four. I have some affairs to settle before I leave."

"No problem."

"I'm assuming that you still wouldn't want me to call you, so here is a number in Paris you can call to find out when I'm arriving. I would suggest you call from a pay phone. And when you call, ask for 'Boris.' "

It was too late to get back to Paris that evening, as André, tired as he was, would have vastly preferred to do. The evening flight left from Moscow at six o'clock, and it was almost that time now. So he was stuck in Moscow until the morning. Gondrachov had proposed a Georgian dinner at the Aragvi, the only decent restaurant in town, but André begged off on the grounds of jet lag, promising to make it up to Gondrachov when he arrived in Paris.

The door to his room had scarcely closed on Gondrachov when André rushed for the telephone. On his first three attempts he got the recording, but on the fourth there was a silence, followed by clicking noises. In a moment, he heard the reassuring ring of the French telephone system.

"Hôtel de l'Avenir, good day." It was a woman's voice. From the imperious tone of her response, he was certain that she was the owner, the hotel her tiny kingdom.

"I wish to speak to Meredith Houghton, please."

"I am sorry, sir, Miss Houghton has gone."

"When will she return?"

"No, sir, you do not understand. She has not gone out, she has *gone*. Left."

"She checked out?" He could not disguise his disbelief.

"Yes, sir."

"Did she say when she would be back?"

"No, sir. She did not say she would be back. She made no future reservation."

He tried to sleep but he couldn't. His mind was riven with doubts. Meredith had said she'd await his return. Why had she left so suddenly? Had the perspective of time, even a single day, persuaded her that there was no point in an involvement with an older man? Where had she gone, how would he find her, and what good would it do if he did?

He dressed and took a taxi from the hotel to Red Square and then walked through the gardens of the Kremlin. There was a concert in the hall that evening, but he knew he was too upset to be able to concentrate on the music.

He walked to the parapets and stared out at the city. As many times as he had stood there, the sight had never failed to stir him, not so much for its beauty as for the manner in which it locked him into history, to the Ivans and Peters who had stood exactly there, fashioning their fateful decisions. But he was not stirred tonight and not because he was tired. The experience was meaningless if it wasn't shared.

For years, he had fought off that admission, but he was defenseless against it now. Foreign corresponding, the most glamorous job in the business, could also be its loneliest. He was lonely now, lonelier than he could ever remember being. No one was waiting for him, not in Moscow or Paris or anywhere else. He was reeling from fatigue, but he would almost have preferred to spend the night on the parapet than return to his empty hotel room.

14

For forty years, ever since he'd been wounded, Charles Houghton had functioned on an almost exclusively rational plane. He could deal with his fate rationally; it had been the result of a conscious decision on his part to seek a vital war role. When he remembered it that way, the outcome seemed as logical as a syllogism. As long as he remained within the realm of logic, emotion couldn't get at him. In that manner he had passed those forty years without experiencing the futility and bitterness of anguish.

He was in the thrall of anguish now, he knew, as his daughter, Meredith, drove him down the Autoroute du Sud in a rented Peugeot. He had been operating on emotion since the visit of André Kohl. He didn't know whether what Kohl had told him made sense or didn't. But it raised the *possibility* that his all but useless legs and the life they had produced—so totally different from the one he had intended to live—were the consequence not of fate but of treachery. The very notion had crumbled his defenses, and he had been out of control ever since.

He shouldn't have gone to see Craig, not until he knew

much more. Craig's refusal to supply him with information forty years after the fact had apprised him of an unsolved mystery linked in some way to his own past, but it had also swept away the last remnants of his rational defenses, to a point that he could not process the intelligence as he should.

Nor should he have suddenly—and inexplicably to his staff, who knew him as a deliberate and measured man who never acted on a whim—announced that he was going to France for a week. His cover was that his daughter, with whom he went on annual art trips, had called from Paris and asked him to join her on a trip to the Côte d'Azur to see a cache of uncatalogued Picassos. Protocol required that he put an advisory out to the heads of various CIA departments to the effect that he would be away for ten days, vacationing in France. But if he had tripped any wires by his visit to Craig, he knew that his explanation wouldn't fool anyone.

Protocol also required that he notify the CIA's counterpart in France, the Direction Générale de la Sécurité Extérieure, or DGSE, that he was arriving in France, but not on official business. He had done that, too. Under the circumstances, another irrational move. Given the nature of his visit, he should have slipped into France, which in his case meant more than a false passport. Not that his face was instantaneously recognizable to the DGSE, but the eyes of the secret service men stationed at Charles de Gaulle Airport would be drawn to him in any case. His movements were simply too distinctive. Most quasiparaplegics dragged their feet through their canes or crutches or hobbled through by swinging their hips. Houghton, the once-gifted athlete, swung his legs through his canes, vaulting on a horizontal plane. The normal marching stride of a foot soldier, left heel to left heel, was six feet; each vault of the deputy director was ten feet. Healthy people had to jog to keep up with him. Even underlings in the intelligence business knew

about the crippled American who was now the top professional in the CIA.

Had he remained rational, Houghton would have given
no notices, feigned illness, driven to Canada, flown to Geneva—using a false passport—and then crossed by car into
France. Meredith would have met him in Geneva had he
asked her to do so.

Meredith. The truest measure of his irrationality. For all
these years, his love for her was the one emotion he had
permitted himself. (Even his divorce could be, and was,
handled rationally. A beautiful woman like Meredith's
mother should not be fated to a lifetime with a severely
handicapped person, as he had argued all along.) A com-
panion to that emotion was that he never involved her in
any way in anything he did for the Company, not even the
most benign trip, so that she would be protected at all times
from any accidents that might befall him. And yet here she
was.

He'd told her nothing about the purpose of his visit, and
she'd known better than to ask. He'd simply called very
early the previous morning from Washington, told her he'd
be arriving that evening and asked her to rent a car and pick
him up at the Crillon this morning. But the tension had
been palpable throughout the drive along the autoroute.

They'd been bantering, nothing more, since leaving Paris.
How inexpensive the city suddenly was for everyone but the
French. The steep drop in real estate prices. The terrible
morale of the moneyed class. Her own disappointment
about the contemporary art scene. André was right; all the
good French artists were in the States.

"You call him 'André,' do you?"

"What else do you expect me to call him?"

"I take it you've seen him."

"Of course."

"And it turned into more than a discussion of art?"

"You might say so."

He sensed that he should not pursue the subject, but he had to talk about something. "You like him?" he asked.

"I'm not exactly ready to elope with him. But, yes, I like him."

"And is it your impression that he likes you?"

Meredith's eyes remained on the road, but for the first time since they had started out a faint smile softened her face. "That would be my impression, yes," she said.

Another irrationality, putting Meredith in touch with a man twenty years older than herself. Had he thought for so much as a second, he could have figured out what would happen. But he hadn't been thinking at all in that moment; he had simply used the first idea that flew into his head to cover the panic he had felt as the emotions held behind the dam he had constructed had at last broken through and engulfed him.

"Well, I hope I haven't spoiled any plans you had by my sudden request for a chauffeur."

"With André?"

"Yes."

"No problem. He's in Moscow."

He shouldn't have been surprised. Surprise was the norm in intelligence. Yet he couldn't have been more shocked had she told him that she and Kohl *had* eloped. There was only one reason why Kohl had gone to Moscow: to try to get the file on Hoepner. That meant he believed there was something to the story, in spite of what Houghton had done to discourage him. You'd have to believe strongly in the story to justify such an effort with such a meager chance of success. To Houghton, his surprise was yet one more indication of how unprepared he was—forty years in espionage notwithstanding—to attempt anything surreptitious. He suddenly felt old and futile and foolish, a wounded spy on a fruitless quest.

They drove on in silence. Fifty kilometers from Clermont-Ferrand, he began to direct her onto secondary roads and then onto side roads. They were flanked on either side by farm fields and coming to a woods, when Houghton suddenly straightened. "Stop here," he said when they reached the edge of the woods. He turned to his daughter, smiled weakly, and said, "I'll be awhile." Then he got out of the car and began to swing toward the woods on his canes.

They left England at 2200 hours. They would cross the channel at an altitude of one thousand feet, drop to three hundred feet a few miles from the French coast, then hedge-hop across France with the help of their radar to the target ten miles from Clermont-Ferrand. At the last moment they'd rise to fifteen hundred feet for the jump. As their plane lifted from the runway, he gave a thumbs-up signal to the others and smiled. They signaled back, but only one of the five, Matt Kahane, the oldest at twenty-six, smiled back, and even he looked away like the others. They were all tight, Houghton knew, even though he could scarcely see them in the dim light. Little wonder; as exquisitely conditioned and superbly trained as they were—in stealthy movement and combat, the art of killing silently with knives and ropes and even their bare hands, the use of their own and German small arms, sabotage and communications—and as many times as they'd rehearsed the mission, the reality was overwhelming. The jump wouldn't faze them; they'd jumped a dozen times from even lower altitudes. But they would land in blackness on enemy soil and for the first hours, at least, their fate would depend entirely on the abilities of men they had never seen or even spoken to. Would the Frenchies have the area secure and be able to guide them in? The Americans had no way of knowing that; they would simply have to commit. They didn't even know for certain that the Frenchies would be there. The code had

gone out over the BBC French broadcast, which they knew
the Frenchies monitored: "The brown eagle screams ninety
times after midnight." There was no way for the Frenchies
to acknowledge; the success of Operation Screaming Eagle
depended, at the outset, on the Frenchies' correct use of the
code book smuggled to them on an earlier mission.

Houghton leaned back against the side of the plane and
let his body absorb the vibration, hoping it would relax him.
The adrenaline was flowing much too soon; if he didn't control it now he'd have nothing left when he jumped. He'd
always been able to control it, getting himself up for a game
so that he'd have that extra strength and reflex action.
Come on Jack Armstrong. All-American boys don't get
scared. You're here because you asked for it.

Slowly the vibration began to get to him. He closed his
eyes and took inventory of his body, starting at his toes and
working up to his head, commanding each part to relax.
Only when he let go of the tension around his eyes did he
realize how tight he had been. At last he felt entirely loose
and soon he was dozing. When he awakened, he had no idea
how long he had slept.

In the dim light, Houghton could barely make out the
time on his wristwatch. One-fifteen. Fifteen minutes until
the jump if they were on schedule. He rose and moved past
his men, three on one side of the aircraft and two on the
other. He could almost feel their eyes on him as he moved
forward to the cockpit. His legs were stiff from sitting so
long, and he could feel the cold through the cheap French
farmer's clothing he'd been issued for the jump.

The pilot nodded as Houghton put his head alongside his
and peered through the window. "Not much to see, is
there?" the pilot said.

"I can't see a thing," Houghton said.

"Neither can we," the copilot said, and he and the pilot
laughed.

"Don't worry," the pilot said, "we'll get you there. You'll have enough to worry about on the ground."

"Any idea how much longer?"

"Navigator says we're on the money. We'll start climbing in eleven minutes. When you see the red light, go."

"Right," Houghton said. He turned to leave, but felt the pilot's hand on his arm and turned again.

"See you in London," the pilot said.

"Yeah. Sure thing," Houghton said. He hoped his voice sounded natural.

Back in the body of the plane, he gave the thumbs-up sign again, and then held up ten fingers and pantomimed a jump. It seemed like only a minute later when he could feel the plane begin to climb and scarcely seconds later when the door opened and they rose to line up and the red light went on and they went out the door, each one getting a pat from Houghton, and then he was out the door and the night was so black he couldn't see the other chutes but he could feel the icy wind. When his chute opened he realized the wind was so stiff that he was moving sideways as fast as he was falling and he was sure that even jumping from fifteen hundred feet they would land at least a quarter mile from the target. It was then that he finally saw the chutes below him in a perfect line, the first man out the farthest down, each chute a little higher, but the space between them was much more than they had reckoned. In the wind he could hear nothing, not even the plane that had turned for home, which much later he would understand was why he couldn't at first identify those flashes of reddish orange suddenly bursting out of the ground.

He saw the ground about fifty feet before he hit it. He was out of his parachute in seconds and running for the woods. It would do no good to try to find the others. The instructions were to disperse if discovered. He was ten feet from the woods when he heard footsteps and labored breath behind him and just into the woods when he felt the bullet rip into his back and his legs go out from under him. Suddenly he was on the ground and seconds later a man in French farmer's clothes was leaning over him. It was several seconds longer before he realized it was Matt Kahane. "Keep going," he whispered. Matt hesitated for a moment. "Go!" he commanded, and Matt was gone, stumbling through the woods. Houghton tried to move his legs and couldn't. Using his arms, he pulled himself behind a tree. He could hear a group of men approaching. They were running and urging one another in German. They were almost at the woods when one of them shouted to the others and they veered away and entered the woods fifty feet from where he lay. He stayed where he was, trying to still his breath, trying to feel where he'd been shot. Then he heard a burst of shots and a few moments later another burst, and then another, and another and another, and soon it was still.

When he awoke it was daybreak, and he knew he had passed out. There was no sound at all now, not even the wind. He couldn't believe that the Germans were gone or that he was alive, but both facts were true. He reached behind him to feel his back. His shirt was stiff with dried blood. The effort was almost too much for him. It was all he could do to bring his arm around so that he could look at his hand. It was stained with blood, but the blood was dark and caked, which meant he'd stopped bleeding. He put his hands on the ground and tried to push away and to get his legs under him, but his legs didn't respond, and then he remembered and fainted.

The next time he awakened he was being lifted from the ground by what seemed like several men, but the pain was so intense he fainted again. When he opened his eyes, he was in the back of a truck. A man of forty was looking down at him.

"Do you speak French?" the man said.

"Yes," he answered.

"You are with friends," the man said, and pressed his hand on Houghton's shoulder.

"What about my friends?" Houghton said. For an answer, the Frenchman shrugged.

That night, they carried him into a farmhouse and then into a cellar. Each time they moved him he passed out again and he was always surprised to wake up. Finally, they came for him and one of them said, "We are taking you to a doctor."

There was the agony of the truck again and then another basement, this one with an extremely bright light above a table with a top that had once been a door and a hospitallike odor that told him even as he entered that other wounds had been dealt with there before. He never saw the doctor, but they smiled at him when he awakened from the anesthetic and showed him the bullet that had been taken from his back.

They kept him in the basement for more than a week. Finally, he was strong enough to be moved, and it was only then that he knew for certain what he had increasingly suspected. His legs were all but useless.

When he had been settled in an upstairs bedroom, a tall and extremely thin man a few years older than himself walked into the room and stared at him with steady blue eyes that seemed to sight down the barrel of his elegant Romanesque nose. The man did not even have to tell Houghton that he was the leader or that it was by his grace that Houghton had been treated and hidden. "When you are well you will teach us," he said. "We have much to learn."

"Was this where it happened?" Meredith asked. She had watched her father standing in the field at the edge of the woods for the last twenty minutes and then, seeing that he

made no move to return and sensing that something was
terribly wrong, had gone out to get him. His eyes were wide
and his face was white and drawn, as though a fever had
taken some years of life from him.

"Yes."

"How can you tell?"

"I was brought here after the Germans left and before I
was sent home."

"Why did you want to come again? Why all of a sudden?"

He turned to her, a look of misery on his face. "I can't
tell you now. I'll tell you when I can," he said. Then he
swung his way back to the car.

He would never tell her, he knew, because he didn't know
himself. What could he learn by standing in a French farm
field, at the edge of a woods, invoking a moment that was
already engraved on his brain? He had come because emotion had routed reason and he was out of control.

Only Houghton, had he been in condition to examine the
circumstances in a rational manner, could have appreciated
the magnitude of his indiscretions and how far they had
veered from his norms. How especially galling it would
have been for the nation's top intelligence operative to discover that his visit to Virgil Craig had indeed tripped hidden wires within the Company, wires that had been laid
forty years before and used discreetly ever since. Within
moments after Houghton's departure from Craig's smoky
and vaporish living room, a telephone call from the retired
intelligence agent had alerted a co-believer still on active
duty to the nature of Houghton's concern. Several days
later, that same person, having read a copy of the advisory
concerning Houghton's "vacation," had telephoned Craig
to say, "The person in whom you expressed interest last
week appears not to have been discouraged. He is on his
way to France."

Nor could Houghton, a master of operations and analysis on a grand scale, have taken comfort from the ineptitude a cold appraisal would have found him to be displaying as an agent in the field. The most basic activity of such an agent is to establish whether he is working unobserved or has been put under surveillance, but forty years of office work had deadened his sensibilities. So he had failed to notice the automobile that had followed his car from the moment he left the Crillon until he reached the outskirts of Paris or the series of observation planes that had tracked him since then. Nor had he seen the car that trailed him as he entered Clermont-Ferrand and followed him that evening and the next day, as he went calling on surviving members of the *réseau* that had sheltered him from November 1943, until V-E Day, the *réseau* of Camille Laurent.

Had Houghton recognized that he was under surveillance, it would have been elementary for him to have deduced that the notice of his visit sent to the DGSE as a matter of protocol hadn't provoked the action. One notified a friendly power of one's impending visit *precisely* so it would know that matters of security were not at issue. No, the action would have had to have been inspired by something else. A request from outside France. From Virgil Craig, perhaps, who knew something he didn't want Houghton to know, something connected to France and Germany and the Executioner of Clermont-Ferrand forty years ago.

At this point, Houghton would have had the option, on his return to Paris, to drive to La Caserne des Tourelles on Boulevard Mortier in the Twentieth Arrondissement, near Porte des Lilas—known to the cynical French as *La Piscine* (the swimming pool)—a converted women's prison, and pay a call on his old friend, Guy de Malesherbes, the director of the DGSE. He was not only exactly Houghton's age, but spoke American English, having been born to an American

mother. Because of his language proficiency, de Malesherbes had served as liaison officer between French and
American forces during World War II. He was that rarity, a
Frenchman who truly liked Americans. Knowing this, and
trusting in their long friendship, Houghton might have discreetly asked about the surveillance, at which point the
DGSE director would have persuaded his guest by his
astonishment and sincerity that he knew nothing of it. In
this manner, the two intelligence chiefs would have come to
recognize that actions were underway in their respective
departments of which they were completely unaware.

These actions were the product of informal organizations
within each of the agencies, groups of like-minded intelligence officers who believed that the best interests of their
countries could not always be achieved in official ways.
Even the clandestine efforts ordered by the agencies were
sometimes not enough to meet the Communist challenge,
these agents felt. If Soviet intelligence could act without the
restraint of law, then, in certain situations, it behooved their
own countries to do likewise. Extralegal efforts were their
domain, and they often accomplished their objectives by
calling on like-minded officers in friendly agencies. Willy-
nilly, a network had formed, linking certain layers of people, with certain attitudes, in a number of allied intelligence
organizations. At the moment, the network's principal interest was the election of Camille Laurent as the next president of France.

The DGSE's branch of the network had been organized
by one Pierre Gauthier, the number three man in the
agency, who years before had been a paratrooper in Indochina under Laurent's command and who had eventually
become his aide. Gauthier, noteworthy even then for his
large size—he stood well over six feet and weighed two hundred pounds—and for the perpetually quizzical look on his
round face, had been recruited by the DGSE while still in

the service. His rise in the agency had been meteoric. But all through the years he had maintained close contact with Camille Laurent. As far as Gauthier was concerned, there was nothing wrong with France that Laurent couldn't cure, particularly with Pierre Gauthier as director of the DGSE. Many special favors through the years had demonstrated to Laurent just how capable Gauthier was.

This latest favor had been initiated at the suggestion of an American friend. The report of Houghton's movements, plus the list of names of the men he had visited, left no doubt in the mind of Camille Laurent, to whom the evidence was shown, that Charles Houghton was looking into the circumstances surrounding his catastrophic wound.

There was one other important piece of intelligence in Pierre Gauthier's report. Friendly questioning of the people Houghton had seen, many of them supporters of Laurent, had elicited that Houghton had not been the first American in Clermont-Ferrand in recent weeks asking questions about Camille Laurent. The American reporter, André Kohl, had been there too.

So it was that when André returned to Paris from Moscow two of Gauthier's men were seated in a car parked on the Quai d'Orléans, twenty yards from his apartment building. They watched him leave the car that had met him at the airport and enter the building. When the lights went on in André's top-floor apartment, one of the men picked up the radio speaker and on a special frequency informed their boss, "Subject has arrived."

15

On Sunday morning, eight hours after his return from Moscow, André walked to a kiosk at Place St. Michel, bought several newspapers, and settled into a nearby café to read.

The coming election dominated the news. The biggest story was the surge of Camille Laurent. The polls had revealed widespread dissatisfaction with the Socialist government, even among those whose votes had initially brought it to power. The first round was the following Sunday; Laurent was gaining such strength he was virtually assured of a spot in the two-candidate runoff election two weeks later, and commentators were already assaying a future with conservatives once more in power.

The aching knowledge André had first experienced in Moscow—that, for the first time in his career, he might be a perpetrator of events rather than an observer of them—was magnified threefold now that he was back on French soil. He'd been close to danger many times, covering wars and riots, but none of it had produced the sense of personal jeopardy he was experiencing now. There were people in

France who would kill him if they knew what he was doing. Yet even the prospect of physical danger didn't worry him as much as the knowledge that it was within his power to change the political history of France. Journalists weren't supposed to do that, in France or anywhere else. Their job was to observe and comment, but never intrude. God help him if he erred.

The next several days were agony for André. There was little he could do on the story until Gondrachov arrived, and the Russian had not yet appeared. Each time he called the telephone number Gondrachov had given him, a woman would answer and the dialogue would be the same:

"Hello, yes?"

"I would like to speak to Boris, please."

"On the part of whom?"

"André Kohl."

"Ah yes, Mr. Kohl. Boris is not here. Is there any way I can help you?"

"Are there any messages for me?"

"No, Mr. Kohl, not yet."

"I'll call back. Thank you."

He asked around for someone who could authenticate documents and located an expert at the Bibliothèque Nationale with surprising ease. Then he called Mike Paul in New York to report on his progress, using the agreed-upon code name for the story, "Camellia." "I should know in a day or two whether 'Camellia' is real," he said. "I have reason to believe it is, but I still have to make some checks." He wanted to say more, but he had to go on the assumption that his telephone was tapped. The last thing he wanted at this point was interference from the French.

"Your two weeks are up," Mike said. "Are you willing to continue?"

"What two weeks?"

"You said in New York you'd give it only two weeks."

"Only if I had nothing by then. I'm pretty sure I have something."

"Enough to keep going?"

"You bet."

"And you're willing?"

Only then did André realize how entangled he had become in the web of this story. "For a while," he said, but as the empty hours passed after his New York call, he began to regret what he'd said. Because suddenly, the momentum had stopped. He was back in Paris, and yet not back, because he was not supposed to be there and he did not want to do anything that would involve him again in the life of the city. So he remained away from his office and fought down the temptation to call old friends. The toughest part was eating by himself. He couldn't remember the last time he'd had a lunch or dinner alone in Paris. To make matters worse, he deliberately chose unfamiliar restaurants because the restaurants he frequented were also frequented by friends. As to women, that was out. He simply had no desire to be with anyone he might call. The one woman he wanted to be with—desperately as each day passed and there was no call—had disappeared.

He tried to practice piano, but he had to resort to memory because he had taken all of his music to Varengeville, which meant that he was reduced to playing old standbys: the *Moonlight Sonata,* some Bach fugues, and a few Chopin preludes. Even with these he faltered at times and had to retreat a dozen bars in order to play his way through the errors and memory lapses. Each retreat served to underscore the larger retreat from his resolve to isolate himself for a year, to find that road not taken, and to walk at least some of its miles.

His reading was compromised, as well. Books never went onto shelves until he had read them, because he was sure they'd be forgotten. So there was nothing in the apartment

he hadn't read at least once. He tried some old favorites—
Trinity, by Leon Uris; *The Assistant,* by Bernard Malamud;
The Little Drummer Girl, by John le Carré—but as well as
they held up on second reading, he would have preferred to
be digging into the two cartons of books he had packed for
his sabbatical reading, most of them by authors he'd had to
neglect in order to stay current or had never read at all.

Except for his meals, he remained in the apartment, lest
he miss Gondrachov's call. He watched television, but
cringed at how bad it was. He started a letter to his son
Gene but abandoned it when he realized that nothing he
could say would truthfully reflect what he was doing. On
Tuesday evening, he retired at nine-thirty, the earliest he'd
been to bed in years.

At eight o'clock on Wednesday morning, there was a
knock at his door. Puzzled—not even the concierge knew he
was back—he peered through the peephole.

It was Meredith.

"Thank God," he said involuntarily as he threw open the
door. He wanted to take her in his arms, but instinct told
him not to. That, and the mystery she presented—by her
presence, her appearance, and the look on her face.

She had come unbidden and unannounced, not knowing
whether he'd be there or what she would find if he was. And
she had come, as well, as no woman ever had before, not
carefully dressed with face made up and hair arranged, but
in a sweatshirt and running shorts and running shoes, her
face glowing from the exertion and early morning chill.
Once again, as she had their first evening together, she
moved into the apartment with presence and self-assurance,
oblivious to what she looked like or how her appearance
would register on him. In spite of the emotions and questions racing through him, he could scarcely fail to notice
her lean yet muscular legs, which seemed to rise forever into

her brief and flimsy shorts. She struck him as the most desirable woman he had ever seen.

Then she turned, and he had to deal with what was in her face. "Where have you been?" he asked.

"Running in the Tuileries and along the Seine. When I realized how close I was I decided to come here."

"I mean where were you the last several days? You promised you'd be here when I got back. You left without a word."

"I'm sorry. Habit, I guess. You don't leave clues when you travel with my father."

"Your father's in Paris?" André asked, unable to mask his surprise.

"Yes, and because of you, I gather, although he won't tell me why. I want you to tell me, because he seems very troubled, and I'm very worried. I've never seen him like this."

He was totally unprepared and didn't know what to do. To tell her would be against every tenet he'd ever followed, both to protect sources and guard his story. But there had never been a circumstance remotely like this one. She had every reason to want to know and cause to be concerned. How could he satisfy her without violating his principles?

"It has something to do with your father's past," he said.

"That much I gathered." She locked eyes with André's. "You've dug up some sort of ghost. I want to know what it is."

"I can't tell you, Meredith," he said. What he read in her eyes he would have preferred not to see. They were suddenly cold and uncompromising.

"Did your trip to Moscow have something to do with my father's past?"

He couldn't tell her the truth, but he couldn't bring himself to lie. If he said once again that he couldn't answer, she would know the answer. He was trapped, and the only way out was to question her. "Why do you ask?" he said.

"Because when I told him you were in Moscow, I might as well have hit him over the head with a hammer." She looked at him in silence for a moment, her eyes steady and focused, as though they might penetrate his eyes and see inside his head. When she spoke, her voice was soft and her words measured. "I want to know what's going on. He's my father."

"Please, Meredith," he pleaded. "There are things I just can't do."

Once more she waited, breathing deeply now, seeming to make an effort to control herself. "My father would like to see you today. Can you meet him for lunch at Chez Tante Louise up the street from the Crillon?"

"Lunch will be fine."

"I'll tell him," Meredith said. She moved past him toward the door.

"You'll be joining us, won't you?"

"No," she said. She stopped and turned to him. "My father wants to see you alone. I didn't tell you about that side of my father, the one that requires you not to ask questions or be present at special times. I grew up in that atmosphere and I hated it. I never said anything to him, then or since, because I felt that, given what had happened to him, he was entitled to the benefit of the doubt. But that was the one reason I couldn't hate my mother for leaving him. He never gave us all there was to give." She paused. "I see you're more or less in the same business. That really bothers me a lot."

He would have sworn that, had she waited another second, tears would have spilled from her eyes. But she was gone before he could be sure.

Houghton looked even worse than Meredith had led André to expect. There were the usual signs of fatigue, red eyes and bags under them. But he also looked defenseless, a man who had received terrible news, expected more, and understood there was no way to avoid it. He spoke elliptically through lunch, asking André how his fishing trip had been, and whether he had caught his limit. André replied in kind.

An embassy car was waiting for them as they left the restaurant. "Do you mind walking?" Houghton asked, and before a surprised André had answered, he had waved the car away. "French driver," the deputy director explained. "I want to be sure no one hears us."

"Good," André said. They set out for the Place de la Concorde, Houghton vaulting with his canes, André racing to keep abreast. Finally, they stopped.

"You've seen the dossier?" Houghton asked.

"Yes."

"You're to be commended for your resourcefulness."

"Thank you."

"I don't suppose you'd want to tell me how you did it?"

"That's correct. I wouldn't be able to tell you that."

"Can you tell me specifically what you saw?"

"Of course." André described the contents of the dossier as fully as he could. When he got to the incriminating document, he took out a piece of notepaper on which he had written the text and read it word for word. When he finished, he looked at Houghton and was appalled at what he saw. It was as though the words had been bullets that had entered the deputy director's body and inflicted mortal wounds. His face was drained of all color. His head moved slowly from side to side. His mouth was open. The life seemed to be ebbing from him, and his eyes, fixed on André's, seemed to suggest that it was André who was somehow responsible. Was it Cleopatra who had ordered messengers slain when they brought her bad news? There was no such threat in Houghton's eyes, simply a question: "How could you?"

The answer was that he had to. As devastating as the

information might be to Houghton, personally, it was information that had to be broadcast. If the probable next President of France had been a traitor to his country during
World War II, it was imperative that the people of France
know that, and that France's allies know too. God only
knew what a man like that would do once in office.

And yet André had intruded, unbidden, into the life of
another man in a devastating way, and he saw with utter
clarity that he had been more than a mere messenger. Had
it not been for his enterprise, this knowledge and the damage it had inflicted would not have existed. He had no idea,
in this sudden rush of awareness, where his responsibility
lay, but his heart went out to Houghton, and his mind
searched for something to say or do that might somehow
bind the wounds. For the moment, he could think of nothing. The silence between them seemed endless. To break it,
he said, "Felix was Laurent's code name, is that correct?"

"That's correct," Houghton replied, his voice almost
inaudible.

They continued on in silence until they reached the
Champs Élysées and were walking in the direction of the
Arc de Triomphe. There were few pedestrians on this
stretch of the boulevard, but plenty of traffic to drown out
their words.

"This could be fiction, you understand," Houghton said
at last. "Those documents could have been manufactured
two weeks ago." It was obvious from the tone of his voice
that he hoped that was the case.

"The dossier had all the appearances of being genuine."

"There's an election coming up . . ."

"I'm very mindful of that."

"What do you propose to do about it?"

The question stopped André cold. He knew he should say
nothing to Houghton, and yet did he not owe it to the man
to reassure him that he was doing everything in his power to

make certain that the dossier, so personally devastating to
the deputy director, was valid? Perhaps such reassurance
would bind the wounds. "There's something I very much
want to tell you," he said at last, "but I have to have your
word that you'll keep it to yourself."

"All right."

Once more André faltered. "Am I being naive?" he said
then.

"You'll have to judge that for yourself."

"Okay," André said. "You deserve to know. The dossier's
coming into France. I'm going to have it authenticated."

Houghton took his time replying. "How's it being
brought here?" he said then.

"That I truly don't know."

"But you know for sure that it's coming?"

"Yes. I insisted on it."

"Insisted?"

"That's not the right word. 'Implored.' I really can't say
any more."

"Can you say who's going to authenticate it?"

He wanted to tell him. He wanted to give him all the
assurance he could. But he knew it wasn't prudent to give
him a name. Perhaps he could tell him obliquely. "I promise you that the dossier will be authenticated by the most
responsible man in France."

Houghton nodded, seeming to mull that information
over. "You'd better be sure he doesn't read German. If he
does, you could lose your scoop."

"He doesn't. I've already determined that."

At last, the deputy director stopped swinging through his
canes. André, breathing heavily, stopped with relief.
Houghton looked carefully at André, eyes probing his much
as Meredith's had done hours before. "You realize the implications if this dossier turns out to be real?"

"Perfectly," André said.

Houghton nodded and stared away. Then he looked back
at André. "If it does check out, I'd like a little warning
before you break it."

"That's no problem," André said. It was the least he
could do.

16

Charles Houghton left Paris at 12:45 P.M. the next day, Thursday, aboard TWA's flight 891. When he arrived in Washington at 3:15 P.M. Eastern Standard Time, he received yet another surprise. His boss, William Coughlin, the latest of the half-dozen political appointees he'd worked for, was waiting for him just outside the ramp, a storm on his round Irish face.

"What the hell?" Houghton said.

"I'll tell you in the car," Coughlin said crisply. He led the way through the corridors to the street, his gait and the stiffness of his retired admiral's posture belying his seventy years. Only after they had settled into the backseat of the black Cadillac limousine and the car had left the curb did he speak again. "We're going to the White House. The President wants to see us. I want to know what this is all about."

"How would I know?" Houghton said.

"Because you're what he wants to see us about. You're apparently up to something he doesn't like, and I want to know what it is before we're on the carpet. What were you doing in France?"

"Seeing my daughter."

"Horseshit, Charlie. Give!"

"It's a private matter, Bill. I've got nothing to tell you."

Coughlin's hazel eyes were malevolent. "Then I'll hear it from the President," he said. "He seems to know all about it."

The President was seated at his desk at the southern end of the Oval Office, in front of three lofty windows whose view of the South Lawn and the Washington Monument had been all but filtered out by curtains and drapes. Behind the President's right shoulder was an American flag whose standard reached almost to the ceiling. Every President Charles Houghton had ever come to see—there had been five in all, dating back to Lyndon Johnson—had risen at once from his desk at the sight of the deputy director swinging into the room with his canes, and ushered him to the arrangement of sofas and armchairs at the other end of the room. This President did not even greet his guests, nor at first let them sit down. His normally smooth and rosy cheeks were so mottled they might have been rubbed with sandpaper. "It's a goddamn good thing we've got some patriots left in your department," he began. "Otherwise, I might not have found out about this. Somehow, you gentlemen haven't seemed to receive the message. The one purpose of this Administration, the one for which it will be noted in the history books, is to attack and defeat world communism anywhere and everywhere it can. Ours is the superior system and, by Christ, it will prevail. One important means of doing that is to support the people who think like we do and embody good Christian values, wherever such people exist. We are particularly interested in seeing these people take power and maintain power wherever and whenever they can. Now is that concept too difficult for either of you gentlemen to understand?"

"No sir," Houghton and Coughlin replied in unison.

The President came in front of Houghton and stood a foot away. "Then what the fuck are you doing, Charlie, undermining the candidacy of Camille Laurent?"

Houghton did not have to look at Coughlin to know that the head of the CIA director had snapped in his direction.

"Who on earth told you that, sir?" Houghton said.

"Never mind who told me. I'm just thankful that they did. As I understand it, that network correspondent Kohl came to you with some crazy story about Laurent working for the Gestapo during World War II, and you put two and two together and figured he might have had something to do with your combat injury . . . ."

The President had it all: Houghton's investigation of the files, his conversation with Virgil Craig, his sudden trip to France, his visit to Clermont-Ferrand, his lunch with André Kohl. As he talked on, his anger simmering, Houghton did some further calculation. What had happened was all so clear. Virgil Craig had once been part of—and still had contact with—some supranational network of intelligence agents with interests precisely those just articulated by the President. His ill-advised visit to Craig had put that network on alert. His trip to France—he had been under surveillance from the time he'd stepped off the plane, if not by the DGSE then by some cell within it. They knew about André Kohl only because of him. They also knew what Kohl was up to—but not what he had.

"All right, sit down," the President said. He motioned them into chairs in front of his desk and took his own seat as well. As he did, his aspect changed. His features softened; his skin cooled. He looked at Houghton beseechingly. "I can understand what it must be like, Charlie. But what good would it do you if you did discover that Laurent had a hand in your injury? It's not going to give you your legs back. And what *if* Laurent worked for the Gestapo—for

God knows what reason? That was forty years ago. He was a kid then. Today he's the man we want to see elected President of France." The President straightened slightly. "It is not in the interest of this government to see any other outcome. There is no interest on our part in seeing a leftist government in power in France. That could change all sorts of things, beginning with the defense of Europe. We'd be unsure of France's commitment in Africa. The French could cause all kinds of trouble in the UN. And I don't have to tell you about the intelligence problems that are created when a friendly power becomes an antagonist."

The President's eyes bore into Houghton's. "Laurent is sure, Charlie. He'll be with us. We're not going to let you or anybody else torpedo him. As your commanding officer, I am ordering you to put this matter behind you. I not only want you off this case, I want you to help us repair whatever damage might have been done, or might still be done."

"In what way, sir?" Houghton said.

"By telling us what Kohl knows, so that we can deal with it in the appropriate manner."

A bare second passed before Houghton answered the President, because that was all the time he had. Any longer, and his answer would be suspect. But that one second was unlike any other that had passed before in his life. It was as though everything he had ever learned, as well as every moral reckoning he had ever made, had been processed by the computer of his mind and was waiting for that one impulse that would sort it all out and flash the answer. And the answer it flashed was a lie.

Lies were the currency of intelligence. In his forty years in the business, Houghton had been compelled to tell his share. Never in his most devious scenarios, however, had he imagined that he would one day be required to lie to the President of the United States. But the sum of all his personal intelligence had told him in that second of blazingly bright clarification that the long-term interest of the United States would not be served by telling its current President the truth. What this President did not understand and would never understand was that the network to which Virgil Craig belonged, and which Houghton's inadvertence had exposed, if only to the smallest degree, had not come into existence to protect the candidacy of Camille Laurent. It preexisted Laurent and would exist beyond his time. To what purposes? And with what personnel and techniques? What had it accomplished already? Were these accomplishments beneficial or inimical to the interests of the United States? The answers to these questions were worth whatever effort and subterfuges they required.

He had the feeling then that he had just emerged from an anesthetic fog, very much like the one he'd been in so many years before in a basement near Clermont-Ferrand. Then the anesthetic had been ether. This time it had been emotion.

His head was clear now. Reason was once more in charge. Reason told him he could handle what needed to be done far better than anyone else. Certainly better than Virgil Craig and his network, which would know everything he told the President within an hour of his disclosure. God only knew what the intelligence network would do to André Kohl. His way would protect Kohl from them. And it would answer what he needed to know about Camille Laurent. With any luck, it would also force the network to show its outlines more than it wished to do.

"There's been no damage, sir," Houghton said. "There's nothing Kohl knows that you don't already have."

The President eyed his deputy intelligence director for a moment as if deciding whether to believe him. Then, apparently convinced, he said, "There's one thing we don't know. Who got Kohl started?"

"The Israelis."

"I might have known," the President said.

17

Under normal circumstances, Gennady Gondrachov would have obtained a visa from the French Embassy in Moscow and flown directly to Paris. This time, although Paris was his destination, he obtained a visa to Italy and flew first to Milan and then on to Olbia, Sardinia. In Olbia, he rented a car, using a Czech passport and an alias of Milos Novotny, and drove at night to a tiny port on the north shore of the island. There he was met by a commercial fisherman, a member of the party, who put him aboard a Zodiac, an inflatable craft with an outboard motor, and set out across the Strait of Bonifacio, which separates Sardinia and Corsica. For a fifty-mile journey on a rolling sea, it was scarcely an ideal craft, but the motor was a powerful one and the fisherman competent. They made the passage uneventfully under a light cloud cover that filtered the moonlight. At 2 A.M. the fisherman cut the motor and rowed Gondrachov into a tiny Corsican cove, a mile from Bonifacio, an old fortress town on top of a hill that serves as the headquarters of the French Foreign Legion. Gondrachov slept until dawn, then changed into a fresh shirt

and slacks and, shouldering his satchel, walked into Bonifacio just as the cafés were opening. He ate a croissant and
drank a cup of espresso and then took a taxi to the airport
outside Figari, well in time for the second of four daily
flights to Paris by Touraine Air Transport. The flight landed
at Orly West; as it had been an internal one—Corsica being
a *département* of France—there were no customs or passport formalities.

Gondrachov had left Moscow with an ample supply of
French francs, so there was no need to change money. He
took a taxi from the airport to the Gare de Lyon, then rode
the escalator to the lower level leading to the TGV and
other Grande Ligne tracks. It was just as he remembered; a
bank of gray lockers was against the wall across from the
escalators. An orange marker with the word *occupé* appeared in almost all of the locker windows. Finally he found
a locker with a green marker and the word *libre* and a red
key in the lock and threw his satchel into the locker with a
feeling of relief. The chances were remote that he would be
stopped or, worse yet, recognized, but he believed in taking
every precaution he could. They were very close to achieving what they wanted; a misstep now would be inexcusable.

He found a telephone and dialed the same number he had
given André. The same woman responded. "I wish to speak
to Boris, please," he said in unmistakably accented French.

There was a pause at the other end and then a giggle, and
then the woman said, "Boris isn't here. I take messages for
Boris."

"My name is Novotny," Gondrachov said. "Please tell
Boris to meet me at Le Train Bleu at the Gare de Lyon at
2000 hours."

The woman giggled again. "Very well, sir," she said. "Boris will be there."

Then Gondrachov descended one more level to the
Metro. Having long ago committed the routes to memory,

he had no need to consult the Metro plan. His attention to such detail had not been exceptional; rather, Soviet agents were taught that subway stations were ideal locations for meetings with their local contacts and were urged to familiarize themselves with the systems in the cities where they would work. This trip was uncomplicated, in any case; it was a straight shot from the Gare de Lyon to the George V Métro station on the Champs Élysées. His first act on surfacing was to take a sidewalk table at Fouquet's and drink a double coffee. Thus fortified, he spent the next two hours visiting first the Mercedes and then all the other automobile showrooms on the avenue.

At ten minutes until eight, Gondrachov appeared at the entrance to Le Train Bleu. Seeing him, the headwaiter broke into a genuine smile. "Good evening, Mr. Novotny," he exclaimed. "So good to see you again."

"Good to see you, Pierre," the Russian said. "Have you a table for two by the window?"

"But of course." The headwaiter led him to a table overlooking the *quais,* and without asking, brought him a *Kir royale.* "With my compliments," he said.

Gondrachov saluted the headwaiter with his glass, sipped his drink and sat back to look alternately at the frescoes on the vaulted ceilings and at the crowds below, rushing to their trains. It was a Friday night; many in the crowd were skiers, wearing their ski clothes and carrying their skis and a small bag. They would sleep that night in their clothes on couchettes, six couchettes to a compartment, and in the morning, very early, they would be at their ski stations. They would ski for two days, board their trains once again on Sunday evening, and arrive in Paris early enough on Monday morning to go to their homes, change their clothes and arrive at work on time. For Gondrachov, every trip to Paris included a visit to Le Train Bleu; the food was scarcely the best in town, but he marveled at the organization of life such a tableau represented, and he never tired of watching.

At eight o'clock exactly, a woman of forty years was led to his table by the headwaiter. She wore a simple black sheath dress and a fur stole, which she slipped from her shoulders as she sat. She pressed her thigh tightly against Gondrachov's, turned her chiseled face to him and put her vibrant lips on his.

"Hello, my love," she said when she had finished kissing him.

"Hello, Boris," he whispered.

Her name was Paulette Jacques. She was extremely wealthy, the only child of an aircraft manufacturer who had died, along with his wife, in the crash of one of his planes. She had been part of the French equivalent of the fad known in America as "radical chic." Although by then she had been out of school for several years, she had fought alongside the students during the events of '68. A series of romances with young radical leaders had followed, but even they and what they espoused seemed tame compared to what Gondrachov could offer. They'd had their eye on her for several years, but it was he who had first recruited and then developed her. She did not seriously love him—she had never wanted a permanent attachment—but she did care for him, and she found the same allure in their intermittent affair as she did in her work for the KGB.

They ate a classical dinner: first a fish course, then a *steak au poivre,* then an assortment of cheeses, and finally a *soufflé au Grand Marnier.* They'd had two wines with their dinner; Gondrachov insisted on brandies with their coffees. By the time they reached her Avenue Foch apartment, collecting his satchel en route, Gondrachov—who had risen at dawn that morning—was nodding off. "Oh no you don't," she said. In less than a minute he had lost all thought of sleep.

They were making love again the next morning when the telephone rang. Paulette answered. She listened to the caller for a moment, then passed the telephone to Gondrachov. "You do call at the most inopportune times, old man," the Russian said without preamble. "Tell me, have you found your expert? Good! Do you think he'd mind working on the weekend? And you can arrange it? Excellent! Now listen closely. Here is what you're to do."

At eight-thirty that evening, a woman André had never seen before, a woman with chiseled features and vibrant lips, walked confidently up to him as he waited in the foyer of Maxim's and kissed him on the mouth. Rather than act surprised, he returned the kiss, put his arm around her and spoke to her with animation as the maître d'hôtel led them to their table. To anyone watching them throughout dinner, their rendezvous had the characteristics of a reunion of former lovers: a certain amount of fencing, a range of emotions, the locking of eyes, tentative caresses. Were such an observer to have followed them from the restaurant, he would not have been in the least surprised to see them disappear twenty minutes later into the woman's Avenue Foch apartment building, or to see lights go on in the woman's apartment and then go out again minutes later. What would have surprised the observer, as he took up his vigil outside the building, would be the knowledge that the man, once inside the apartment, had exited through a kitchen door and descended to the street via a circular staircase that wound its way past the servants' quarters attached to each apartment in the building.

André had not appreciated the need for this elaborate precaution contrived by Gondrachov, but he deferred to the Russian's superior knowledge in such matters. A minute after leaving the building by a rear entrance, he joined Gondrachov in a car parked on a side street. Twenty minutes later, the car pulled up at 58 Rue de Richelieu in the Tenth Arrondissement, the entrance to the Bibliothèque Nationale. As the two men moved from their car toward the building, a third man moved from the obscurity of the entry to greet them. He was short and thin and had a Gauloise in his mouth, whose smoke curled past his thick glasses. The odor of tobacco clung to him like perfume.

"Monsieur Montbrun?" André asked.

"Yes. Mr. Kohl?"

"Yes." André shook hands with Montbrun, who then shook hands with Gondrachov without bothering to ask his name. Nor did André offer it.

Without another word, Montbrun led them through the entry and down a flight of stairs to the basement, using a flashlight. Only when they had passed through a corridor and arrived at his office did he turn on a light, at which point, without a word, Gondrachov produced the dossier. Montbrun took it to his desk and placed it under an intense light and looked slowly through the pages. From time to time, he squinted at a portion of a page through a magnifying glass. As he worked, he hummed a melody that André recognized as being Brahms's *Variations on a Theme by Haydn*. Ten minutes passed before he spoke. "You realize that I can make no evaluation of the content," he said. "I was never able to learn German. Some kind of mental block." He touched his head and smiled and then looked apologetically at Gondrachov. "I mean no offense," he said.

"That's all right," André said quickly. If Montbrun had mistaken the Russian for a German, all the better.

Montbrun returned to the pages. When he arrived at Hoepner's memorandum about Camille Laurent he gave it no more time than any other page. A minute later he rose and went to a laboratory bench and looked at some of the pages through a microscope. When he finished his first act was to light a cigarette. Only then did he speak. "Superficially, the documents seem to be genuine," he said. "I have seen other documents from this era. These appear to resemble them. They are on the same size paper and appear to have been typed on typewriters in use at the time. But none of this is conclusive. If someone were intent on forging a document, the most rudimentary precautions he would take would be to find the proper typewriter and use the same size paper. If you really want to be certain, I will have to have chemical tests made on the paper, and I can't do that until Monday. The laboratory that does those tests is closed."

"I see," André said. He knew without asking Gondrachov that the Russian wouldn't permit Montbrun to hold the dossier. From his own point of view, André couldn't risk letting the Frenchman keep Hoepner's memo. "I'll tell you what," he said to Montbrun. "Supposing I were to give you a small piece from the bottom of one of the pages. Could you identify the age of the paper?"

"Of course."

"May I see the dossier, please?" André said. When Montbrun handed him the dossier, he leafed through it, coming in order to Hoepner's memo. To his immense relief, it was as he had remembered it, the writing confined to the upper half of the page. "Next question," André said to Montbrun. "Do you have a copying machine?"

"Of course."

"Supposing I were to give you samples from several of the memos. Would you be able to ascertain from the copies whether or not they had been typed on the same machine?"

"I think so," Montbrun said. "It wouldn't be ideal, but if you would be satisfied I see no problem."

"I would be satisfied," André said. He turned to Gondrachov. "What do you think?"

Gondrachov shrugged.

Once more André leafed through the dossier, as though making a random selection. He took the Hoepner memo about Laurent and two others, the first written just before the Laurent memo, the other just after. Montbrun led him to a copier in an adjoining office. He put a blank page over the last several lines of each of the memos so that the samples would be identical and the incriminating portion of the Laurent memo would not be copied. When he had finished, he tore off the lower portion of that page and handed it and the three copies to Montbrun.

"Very well," Montbrun said. "Shall I call you when I have the report?"

"Please," André said.

Montbrun led the two men through the basement corridor once again. At the street, they shook hands and parted. Twenty minutes later, André mounted the servants' staircase of the Avenue Foch apartment building he had left an hour and a half earlier. A few minutes later, he left the building for the second time that evening, this time through the front door.

18

André passed another miserable Sunday by himself in Paris. He wanted desperately to see Meredith and was on the verge of calling the Hôtel de l'Avenir several times if only to learn whether she was still in the city. But each time he came up against the same dilemma. What could he tell her that would satisfy her? Nothing more than he had. And that wouldn't be good enough for her.

Calling his friends seemed no more reasonable this Sunday than it had a week ago, so he was still compelled to eat by himself and in restaurants where he wouldn't bump into anyone he knew. He thought of inviting Gondrachov and his mysterious lady friend to lunch, but there was no response when he called. Other than his visit to the Bibliothèque Nationale, his dinner with Paulette had been the one bright spot of his week. Whatever game she was playing, she was clever enough to have resisted André's inquiries throughout a long dinner conversation.

At three in the afternoon—9 A.M. New York time—he called Mike Paul at home to tell him that the camellias would probably bloom in the next few days. Let the DGSE figure that one out, he told himself with satisfaction. At eight o'clock exactly, the election returns were announced: a runoff between the Socialist and Camille Laurent.

At 11 P.M., André went to bed, but he was still awake two hours later. His mind was filled with words and imagined pictures, mostly of himself doing a standup in the courtyard of the Élysée Palace, the residence of French presidents, telling the world of the sensational new development in the upcoming election, the disclosure that Camille Laurent had been a traitor during World War II. Supposing Montbrun came through in the morning, how much time would they need to get a piece together? A day perhaps, two at most. By midweek at the latest, the story would be out. After that, the real nightmare: he, André, would be in the news. How had he gotten the story? What were his proofs? Fair questions, certainly, but how could he answer them? Tell them about Shlomo? About Gondrachov? Impossible on both counts. He'd be hounded, attacked. He'd have no peace. And he'd certainly be attacked for interfering in the internal politics of France at the urging of a foreign government. They'd track him to Varengeville and ruin that sanctuary for good. It would almost be better if Montbrun were to call and tell him that the document was a fake. He'd have lost one of the great political stories of the century, but he would have regained his peace of mind.

André had been lying on his back. Now he turned onto his right side, an act that instantly brought to mind Meredith's remark about how, years after his divorce, he still slept on his side of the bed. What *did* that mean? That he really didn't want to be alone? If that were the truth, how much better it would have been not to have been awakened to it—just as it would have been better for Charles Houghton never to have known that the man he believed to have saved his life had actually destroyed it. How much better it would have been all around if he'd never been

called by Shlomo, which meant he never would have gone
to Washington to see Houghton, thus sparing the deputy
director all his subsequent pain, and sparing him, André,
the uncertainty produced by his relationship with Meredith
Houghton, whom he never would have met.

What good was the best story in the world if it didn't
produce peace of mind? Peace of mind came from answers
produced by deep introspection. Even if the answers weren't
readily forthcoming, the very quest provided a measure of
reassurance. That was what he'd undertaken in Varengeville
—which tonight seemed ten thousand miles from Paris.

Montbrun did report the next morning. His verdict was
unequivocal. Based on the samples he had been given, the
dossier was a fake.

For a moment, André was too stunned to ask questions.
"What's the basis for your verdict?" he said at last.

"The paper," Montbrun said. "All three of the samples
you copied were dated at the top. The first date was October
1, 1943, the last date October 26, 1943. But the sample of
paper you gave me could not have been that old and most
certainly was not produced during the war."

"Are you positive?" André said.

"Absolutely. The kind of paper in use during the war
contained mostly mechanical wood fibers and some chemical wood fibers. It most certainly never contained synthetic
fibers, which were not even introduced in Europe until the
1950s. The sample of paper you gave me contained synthetic fibers."

André waited a moment before speaking, unable to trust
his voice. "Anything else?" he said then.

"Something inferential, not conclusive."

"Go ahead."

"The dateline said 'Clermont-Ferrand.' Since the samples
were in German and the year 1943, the assumption is that

the paper would have been manufactured either in France or Germany. That does not appear to be the case."

"Do you have any idea where the paper was manufactured?"

"As we are relatively inexperienced in evaluating papers from the Eastern Bloc, we cannot be certain. But one of our chemists recalled seeing paper with the same characteristics that had been manufactured in Bratsk, a city in Siberia."

It took André fifteen minutes to calm down after Montbrun's call. His limbs tingled with adrenaline, and he paced back and forth to try to work it off. What was most surprising was the crudeness; he would have expected better of the KGB. What they'd done was obvious: they had the Gestapo files, no question. The memos and telegrams in Hoepner's file were genuine—with one exception, the memo about Camille Laurent. That one had been manufactured and slipped into the dossier.

Thank God he'd insisted on the authentication. What an unimaginable calamity if he hadn't. Had he gone with the story, the damage would have been done even if the dossier was suddenly exposed as a hoax. Denials and refutations never quite catch up to the accusation. Laurent would have been unjustly defamed, the election in all probability stolen from him. And poor Houghton! What unnecessary misery he'd already been caused.

But insisting on the authentication in no way excused André, in his own mind, for failing to consider, at any point, whether he was being run by the Russians. How was it that he had fallen into such an extraordinary story with such grave political implications—he should have asked himself—scant weeks before the French elections? He hadn't fallen into it; he'd been pushed. The Russians had gone through an elaborate charade to make him believe that he was accomplishing a great feat of reportage. How close he had come to serving as a tool of the Soviets! The thought was revulsive to him. He truly detested their system and its hopelessly unrealistic view of man, its self-righteous foreign policies, its cynical use of whatever means were required to achieve its self-serving ends.

There was only one piece to this Byzantine puzzle that couldn't be fitted: Shlomo. It was inconceivable to André that his old and good friend had run him. And yet it was he who had brought André the tip and set him on this chase. What was it Houghton had said to him that first day in Washington? That Shlomo might be playing games. That the Israelis needed friends. Laurent's views of Israel were decidedly Gaullist, whereas the candidate of the left was partial to Israel. But what was the connection between Shlomo and the Israelis on the one hand and Gondrachov and the Russians on the other? Ever since the state of Israel had been proclaimed the Russians had been its implacable foes, either because of an inherent anti-Semitism or out of a desire to court the Arab world and turn them away from the Americans, the Israelis' biggest supporters. It made no sense whatever that the Russians and the Israelis would suddenly cooperate in this venture, much as both wished for the defeat of Laurent.

That afternoon, André went to a section of the Bois de Boulogne known as *Le Paradis du Chiens* because it was a section of the park where Parisians could bring their dogs for a romp off the leash. There he met with the Israeli ambassador to France, David Lavi, who spoke English with an Oxford accent and twenty-two other languages as well. Three armed Israeli agents remained at a discreet distance, forming a protective triangle, as the two men walked among the racing dogs. André told Lavi about the German-born Israeli woman who had worked for the Gestapo, and gave him as much additional information as he needed to communicate what André wanted conveyed to Shlomo. Then the two men shook hands and parted.

At nine-thirty that evening, angry and miserable and out of patience, André finally yielded to temptation and called the Hôtel de l'Avenir. Meredith *was* registered once more. This time she had gone out, not gone away. Did *monsieur* wish to leave a message? No, no message. *Au revoir, monsieur.* Click.

At six o'clock the next morning, André's telephone rang. It was Lavi. "Sorry to wake you, old chap, but I figured you'd want to know right off. We can meet later for the details if you like, but I can tell you enough in the clear. They picked up that party last night. She finally broke an hour ago. Swears the information's true, but admitted she works for the rascals. We're not putting much stock in the report. I don't know what this does to your story, but we're bloody grateful to you. Your friend sends profound apologies and says he'll be in touch."

So, it was over. Both he *and* Shlomo had been had. It made him feel no better. He could accept the waste of time, the thousands and thousands of miles of travel, the lost sleep, the tension. Eventually, he might even overcome the knowledge that he'd intruded unnecessarily and cruelly in another man's life. What he would never get over was that a man he had once befriended, to that man's enormous profit, had used him.

If it had been ten o'clock, André would have opened a bottle of champagne. He had read somewhere that drinking didn't really change moods, as almost everyone thought, but rather perpetuated and deepened the mood you brought to it. Well, that was what he wanted: to get drunk and angry and ugly and, in his fantasy, at least, tear Gennady Gondrachov limb from limb. "You miserable bastard!" he shouted, not caring that no one could hear him.

He got up and made coffee and began to plot his revenge. He would do a story—the story of Gennady Gondrachov, the disinformation specialist of the KGB, the mystery man with the dacha and tennis court and swimming pool and Mercedes 450 SEL and two other cars. The story would ruin him, just as he'd said in Moscow when André had proposed it in jest. He'd do it and the doing would prevent Gennady from ever playing his dirty tricks again.

He thought about the story for ten delicious minutes. But then the idea began to lose its appeal as the practical problems of actually doing the story ran through his mind. It would mean at least one more trip to Moscow and trouble with the Russians, and then at least one more trip to New York. A month at the very least—a month when he might have been in Varengeville. Maybe *that* was the better revenge: to slip away to Varengeville without a word or clue as to where he had gone. Gondrachov might conceivably be able to get André's unlisted number, as Shlomo had, but André doubted it. The Russian wasn't in Shlomo's class. Oh, God, would that be marvelous! Gondrachov would be absolutely frantic! He'd have blown his assignment! He'd be summoned home and shot! "BANG! You're dead!" André shouted, raising his hands to hold an imaginary gun. And then he laughed aloud, as much from his own silliness as from relief that it was over.

One more day, he told himself, and he *would* be back in Varengeville. And *then* let someone try to drag him away. In the meanwhile, he would play out the charade.

At 8:30 A.M. André walked from his apartment to the Left Bank and settled into a café to read the papers. He shuddered to think of the headlines that might have appeared in these same papers a day or two hence had he done his story. And what would have happened to him? He hadn't even thought of that. Assuming Laurent could have disproved the charges, a reasonably safe assumption, his own career would have been ruined.

At nine o'clock, André telephoned Gondrachov from a pay phone. When Paulette told him that the Russian was out, he did not know whether to believe her. Never mind, he told himself. With great effort, he told her as calmly as he could that he needed to meet as soon as possible with Gondrachov.

"He won't be back until evening," Paulette said.

"Is he reachable somewhere?" André asked, knowing it was a foolish question.

"I'm afraid not. He's road testing a Porsche."

At any other time, André would have laughed. Not this time. "I'll call this evening," he said.

The two men finally spoke at 6 P.M. Gondrachov was obviously in high spirits. "Are we celebrating your triumph?" he asked when André said that they must meet.

"Oh, indeed," André said.

Gondrachov hesitated for a fraction of a second. "Very well," he said, "then it should be someplace appropriate. Meet me at the Crazy Horse Saloon at 11:30 tonight. Ask for Mr. Novotny."

Thirty seconds later, acting on an impulse, André telephoned the Hôtel de l'Avenir. This time Meredith was in her room. "Can I have another chance?" he said.

"You can have all you want," she said.

He did not want to read more into the remark than he should, but he thought that she sounded as relieved as he felt. "Tell you what. Let's start over. Meet me at my apartment, and we'll go to Chiberta."

They never made it to Chiberta. She was in his arms the moment she stepped through the door, and there was never any question about what would happen after that. He had imagined that their future, whatever form it would take, hung on his willingness to disclose everything to her, and now that the story was as good as dead, he'd been prepared to do just that. But the intimacy would have seemed like a quid pro quo if they'd waited until he'd told her. Was this Meredith's way of expressing her trust in him? Whatever the reason, they were in bed five minutes after she arrived, in the center of the bed, and an hour later he had the feeling that ten years of his life had been given back to him.

He told her the story as he prepared a supper of soup, omelettes, salad, and cheese. Telling it was like having a poison leeched from his body. He spared no details, held nothing back. The more he told her, the closer she seemed to draw to him, each revelation weaving yet another strand of trust between them. They finished dinner just as he finished the story. She rose, held out her hand and led him back to bed.

To André's astonishment, they made love twice more before he had to leave. "I hope you don't mind that I can't take you," he said as he dressed.

"I won't mind if you let me stay here until you come back."

He looked at her for a long time before responding, feeling himself being carried across some invisible and undefined boundary into territory he had never treaded before. When he spoke it was in a deliberately ambiguous manner, giving her the choice. He said, "You can stay as long as you like."

19

The Crazy Horse Saloon at 12 Avenue George V has been a Paris institution since 1951. For many young foreign males, Americans particularly, it is the first place they visit after checking into their hotels. It is a small and uncomfortable cabaret, with minuscule tables jammed together on tiers built around a tiny stage. There is a bar at the back of the room for those who want to avoid a cover charge. The air is rank with smoke and the drinks outrageously overpriced. No matter; Le Crazy Horse, as it is known in French, continues to pack them in. The reason is a simple one: in an era characterized by the demystification of the female anatomy, the Crazy Horse restores its allure by draping it in shadows. Young women with perfect bodies wear the scantiest costumes, as at other shrines; the difference here is a masterful use of lighting, which adds mystery to their overtly sensual movements.

André had last been to the Crazy Horse a decade before, when he'd taken the then president of the network, Frank Dudley, and his very young second wife, who had come to Paris on their honeymoon. The suggestion for going had

been Dudley's, whose fascination with sex was a fact of life
that had to be taken into account by USBC's correspondents whenever he showed up in their cities. At some point
during the show, as one of the dancers held onto a bar
above her head and performed her half of an imagined act
of intercourse, André suddenly felt his shin being stroked by
a stockinged foot. Very carefully, he turned his eyes in the
direction of the Dudleys. Both of them were looking raptly
at the show. Whether the foot belonged to Mr. or Mrs.
Dudley he couldn't tell. The probable answer was that Dudley had simply missed his target. On the other hand, Mrs.
Dudley had been making eyes at André all evening. He
would never know what had really happened. His only con-
solation was that he could dine out on the story for months.

Going to the Crazy Horse had never been at his suggestion, he reflected, as he entered precisely at 11:30 P.M. But a
Russian proposing a visit to this epitome of Western deca-
dence—that was a first. It would be a treat to see how his
Russian friend would act.

Five hours earlier he would not have believed that he
could ever again think of Gondrachov as a friend. But the
lovely interval since than had detached his emotions from
the problem. He saw it now for what it was: a conspiracy, a
manipulation, a game of political poker with the highest
possible stakes. It would be a mistake to take it personally.
He would chide his friend, oh would he ever, but he
wouldn't lose his temper, not now, when what had seemed
to have wound up as an unlucky story had turned out to be
the luckiest. What was the Laurent story, or any story,
however great, compared to the affection of a beautiful
woman?

As instructed, André asked for "Mr. Novotny," and was
immediately led to Gondrachov's table. He was not surprised to discover that the table was in a corner of the room,
against a wall, as far from the stage lights as possible.

"Ah, André, my friend, sit down! The show is about to start," Gondrachov said, directing André to a seat. "Here, have some champagne—or would you like a Scotch?"

"Champagne is fine," André said.

Gondrachov filled André's glass, then raised his own. "To your success," he said.

They touched glasses. As if that had been a signal, the lights dimmed in the flowered lamps above the tables, and the scratchy sound of a Louis Armstrong recording evaporated, replaced by the upbeat tempo of a piano player, electric guitarist, and drummer. Moments later, the bright red-sequined curtain across the stage went black, the drummer began a drumroll, and a sign in English, French, and German flashed on the curtain announcing that the show would start in thirty seconds. Exactly thirty seconds later, the curtain parted to reveal a row of women wearing black German World War I helmets, black leather ribbons crisscrossing their bodies, black fingerless gloves, black garter belts holding wilted silk roses, and high black patent leather boots, their heels adjusted to make all of the women appear to be the same height. Bright red bicycle reflectors covered their crotches. Their breasts were bare. Their bodies were uniformly slim and perfect; their smiles displayed perfectly even teeth. But the smiles were not convincing and neither were their efforts at mouthing the words, in German, French, and English, to the music accompanying their dance, a marching song celebrating the wonders of Paris and its dedication to love. When the number ended, the curtain closed and reopened at once to reveal a movie screen and a film in which three blondes danced nude. Over this the credits rolled, each name more contrived than the last: Moona Contralto, Diana Sensation, Sassy Staccato, Melba Parachute, Sherri Rainbow, Tricia Boogaloo. One by one, or in pairs of threes, the women did their numbers, each number an improvisation on the same theme, the enduring allure of the female form.

Throughout, Gondrachov remained raptly attentive, laughing appreciatively and shaking his head in admiration. When Tricia Boogaloo's name flashed on the curtain, he turned to André and said, "Wait'll you see this one. She's my favorite."

Suddenly there were sounds of thunder and rattling chairs. When the curtain parted, not even Tricia Boogaloo's makeup and wig of long, wild hair could disguise the spectacular quality of her beauty, her full lips and flared nostrils and high cheekbones the perfect complement to the illusion she was creating. She was a prehistoric woman, naked except for two tiny patches, more an animal than a person, caught behind the bars of a cave. To the accompaniment of "Working On a Chain Gang," she spun and slid and finally slithered her way through the bars.

Gondrachov turned to André. "Profound, eh? Would you believe she's American?"

It took Gondrachov only a moment after the lights went up to catch the eye of the waiter. He spent the next few moments flirting with an incredibly pretty photographer who was moving through the tables taking group photos. "You should be in the show, not out here taking pictures," he said in his heavily accented French when she approached their table.

She smiled. "You're very kind. Would you like a photo?"

"I'd like your phone number."

"I'll have to think about that. What about the photo?"

"No, thank you."

"I'll have it printed in twenty minutes. You don't have to pay if you don't like it."

"I fear for our future together," the Russian said with a smile. "I don't want a photo, and you won't give me your phone number."

"Alas!" the photographer said with a smile and moved away from their table, just as the waiter brought a fresh bottle of champagne.

"You seem to be feeling no pain," André said.

Gondrachov nodded his agreement. "I use Paris in a constructive way. It affirms for me what kind of decadent creature I might have been without my Marxist-Leninist upbringing. Now, my friend, tell me all about it. There's so much noise in here that you can't possibly be overheard."

"I'll put this as gently as I can, because I know how disappointed you're going to be. Your little game is over, Gennady."

It took the remark at least two seconds to penetrate Gondrachov's alcoholic fog. His brow wrinkled. He looked at André through half-veiled eyes. "What do you mean?"

"The dossier's a fake, as you well know. Now I know it too. Montbrun called me yesterday morning. That paper with the Hoepner memo on Camille Laurent is only ten years old." André shook his head. "I'm disappointed in you guys. I thought you were better than that."

Gondrachov said nothing. He simply stared at André. Then he put his hands to his face and massaged his forehead with his fingers. When he dropped his hands he stared at André once again, as though hoping to find some answer to his dilemma in André's eyes. No answer was there for him, but what André saw in the Russian's eyes and face, as well, set uneasy tremors coursing through him. There was nakedness, to begin with, which he had never seen before. There was also earnestness and conviction and genuine pain, all of them strangers to his repertoire. What made André so uneasy was that Gondrachov didn't look at all like a man who was acting.

"I have told you some lies in the past," he said at last. "I won't deny it. But I am not lying to you now. André, listen to me. *The dossier is real.* It turned up in a routine computer search on Laurent after we realized we had to take him seriously. Our people called me in to ask how they could get the information into the Western press under credible auspices. You were the first person I thought of. You can believe this or not, but I thought I was doing you a favor by giving you a great story. I'm sorry now that I didn't come to you directly. I played it too—how do you say?—cute. But I'm telling you again, André, the dossier is real. You've got to believe me. You're missing the greatest story of your life. Let me ask you: if I could prove to you beyond any doubt that the dossier is real, what would you do? Would you sit on the story, knowing that Camille Laurent had been a traitor?"

André had been listening to Gondrachov with mounting panic. He had the terrible feeling that the Russian might not be lying. For one of the few times in his life, he didn't know what to do. Whether the dossier was real or not, the fact was that he had been run by the Russians, which—whether he allowed it to anger him or not—he profoundly resented. "Gennady, do me a favor," he said. "Go peddle your story to *France Soir*."

He felt a vise close around his arm. "Don't duck me!" Gondrachov said, his fingers tightening until André could feel his arm go numb. "Would you ignore the story if you knew the dossier was real?"

He didn't want to answer, but he had never seen Gondrachov like this. The man seemed fevered. His face was an open wound. Besides, the question was theoretical; in spite of the Russian's earnestness, in spite of his own uneasiness that he might be telling the truth, André still didn't believe him. "I probably wouldn't ignore it," he said finally.

"Then I must prove it to you," Gondrachov said, almost to himself. "Tell me, who sent you to Montbrun?"

"No one. I found him myself."

"Did anyone know you were going to him?"

`"Absolutely not."

"You said nothing to Houghton?"

The Russian's question hit André like a punch. "How did you know about Houghton?"

"Because we've had you under surveillance ever since you got involved. Now tell me, did you or didn't you say anything to Houghton?"

Under surveillance! Another punch—even harder than the first.

"Well?" the Russian demanded.

"I said absolutely nothing to him about Montbrun."

"What did you tell him? Tell me exactly what you told him."

Blood surged to André's head. "Why the hell should I?"

"For God's sake, old man, we both need to know whether or not you've been had. No, I'll change that. I know you've been had. I'm trying to figure out how. I would think you'd want to know that, too."

He was right, and André knew it. "The man was devastated. He asked me if I intended to authenticate the dossier . . ."

"So you told him about the dossier?"

"Yes, of course."

"Did you tell him it was coming to France?"

"Yes."

"And I suppose you reassured him that you would do everything in your power to make certain the dossier was real?"

"Yes, exactly."

"Did you spell out what you would do?"

"I told you. No!"

"What did you say? I need to know exactly what you said."

"I don't remember."

"Of course you remember. You're a reporter, damn it. You're trained to remember quotes."

"For Christ sake, Gennady."

"Think!"

André shut his eyes. In his mind he could see himself with Houghton, standing on the street. He could hear Houghton's questions, but not his own replies. Why not? Was it that he couldn't hear them, or that he didn't want to hear them? "I can't remember what I said exactly. But I know I reassured him. I probably told him I'd gotten the best man I could find."

His voice trailed off as he spoke the last six words, until it was no more than a whisper. He didn't need the stricken look on Gondrachov's face to tell him what had happened. He didn't need to hear the Russian say, "Oh, André, that's all the clue he needed." In a devastating moment of clarity, André knew exactly what had happened. Charles Houghton had found Montbrun just as André had found him, by asking about for the leading authenticator in France. He'd then gone to Montbrun and either persuaded him or bribed him. In God's name, why? Because it was in the interest of his government to see Laurent elected. Loyalty had triumphed over self-interest. Houghton had undoubtedly kept his word: he'd told no one that the dossier was coming in. He'd simply taken care of the matter himself. And André had made a colossal blunder. He couldn't have hidden his pain from Gondrachov now if he'd been the best actor in the world. "I blew it, Gennady. I'm sorry," he said at last.

Gondrachov sighed. "It's not all your fault, old man. I've been too cute, too cute."

"You've really had me under surveillance?"

Gondrachov hesitated for a moment, as though debating with himself. Then he said, "I think you'd also better know that the DGSE has had you under surveillance ever since Houghton went to Clermont-Ferrand."

It wasn't a poker game, after all. It was a chess match. And he, André, was a pawn. Had Houghton put him under surveillance, as well? Probably so. He felt a sudden sense of sheer physical menace, imagining himself in the center of a struggle between the three services. He looked nervously about the room, trying to see who might be watching him.

"Don't worry," Gondrachov said. "No one's here. The DGSE followed you, but they're waiting outside."

"How do you know?"

"Because I've got a man at the door. If they'd have started to come inside, I would have given you a new rendezvous and left at once."

André sat back, trying to digest his situation. "You planned this whole damn thing, is that what you're telling me?"

"Not the whole thing, old man. We didn't plan on Houghton going to Clermont-Ferrand."

"But Shlomo? My own trip to Clermont-Ferrand? My visit to the baker?"

"We weren't positive Shlomo would call you, but it seemed worth a try, given the history between you two. Your trip to Clermont-Ferrand was automatic, once Shlomo got in touch with you. How else do you check out the story? As to the baker, we found him when we made our own check into Laurent. He's a member of the party, so he agreed to help us. Hates Laurent."

"So you truly believe that Camille Laurent informed for the Gestapo during the war?"

"There's no question about it, old man." Gondrachov smile lightly. "The big question is what you're going to do about it, now that you know, too."

"What happens to you if I do nothing?"

The Russian shrugged. "I'll get a slap on the wrist, I suppose. Maybe a little worse. There are people in the office

who don't like me, but I have friends in high places, shall
we say. I won't be badly hurt."

It dawned on André then that for the first time since he'd
known Gondrachov, the Russian had dropped his cover. He
was no longer pretending to be a free-lance journalist for
hire by the Western press. The "friends in high places" had
to be the present First Secretary and several members of his
entourage.

"Well?" Gondrachov said. "What's the verdict?"

It galled André to think that an act of his would directly
serve the purposes of the Soviet Union. Try as he might, he
could not work around that obstacle. But if the story was
valid, what alternative did he have?

"Don't torture yourself, old man," Gondrachov said, as
though he had just read André's mind. "There had to come
a point where you and we would agree on something. I
think we can both agree that the Nazis were no good. You
lost your share of people putting them away. For our part, it
was the greatest calamity ever to befall the Russian people.
Twenty million dead, André, twenty million dead. Is it so
reprehensible for us to agree that anyone who helped the
Nazis was evil?"

André closed his eyes. The sounds of the room poured
into his head, the rumble of voices, the tinkling glasses, and
over this, the disco beat. The smell of tobacco smoke mixed
with that of the disinfectant from the men's room. What a
putrid environment. He would have given anything in this
moment to have stepped outside his study in Varengeville
and filled his lungs with the sweet channel air and the fragrance of apple blossoms. He could drop the story and be
there tomorrow and take Meredith with him.

Meredith! Oh, God, what would he tell *her?* He'd con-
fided in her earlier on the assumption that it had all been a
hoax and that the story was dead. Now, in all probability,
the story was very much alive again. More than that, her

father was not only part of the story, he was also part of the problem.

Never in André's life had he been more at sea. As he sat in the Crazy Horse, unable to make up his mind, he had a sudden, powerful urge he had never felt before, to unburden himself to another person.

He opened his eyes and looked at Gondrachov. "I've got to get home," he said. "I'll call you in the morning."

What a fool he'd been, Gondrachov told himself after André left. How could he have been so stupid as to take the outcome for granted. His mistake had been in believing that André, a tested professional, would tell no one about the dossier in order to protect his story. Not only does he fail to keep silent, he tells the deputy director of the CIA! Ah, God, these sentimental Americans! They'd be the death of him yet.

It was one of those expressions Gondrachov had learned in his study of American English. This time, he knew, it was not a mere expression. The stakes had just risen, and he was to blame. He should never have counted on André's silence. Of course he would confide in Houghton, the most interested party to the proceedings, who, if he chose, could throw an entire intelligence-gathering apparatus at the problem.

He'd made an even worse mistake, Gondrachov knew. He'd met in public with André before the case was closed. The celebration had been premature. Blame that on his weakness—he did love a good time—and blame his weakness on the corrupting influence of the West. He'd taken normal precautions, but they might not have been enough. He'd have to be doubly careful now. How did they say it? No more fun and games.

Gondrachov might have taken some grim satisfaction in knowing how right he had been: his precautions *hadn't* been sufficient. The French agents following André hadn't come inside, not wanting to be so obvious in a place where they were well known. What they'd done instead was to locate the beautiful photographer, who regularly worked the Crazy Horse as well as other *boîtes* in the neighborhood, shown her a picture of André and asked her to photograph André and his party. The photographer, who had done the same thing dozens of times for the DGSE, had had no difficulty in fulfilling the assignment in spite of Gondrachov's expected refusal to let her take his and André's pictures. She had simply made certain that they were in the background of several of her group shots, and then made an extra exposure of each of the several groups, focusing instead on the background.

Half an hour after the photographer had given the agents their prints, Gondrachov's photograph was up on a screen in a special office of the DGSE, his description being matched to thousands on file in the DGSE's computers. In another thirty minutes, the Russian's identity had been established. Minutes later, Pierre Gauthier, the DGSE's number three man, was conferring with Camille Laurent.

20

It was after two A.M. when André got home. He slipped into the apartment as quietly as he could, then removed his shoes and walked slowly into the bedroom. Meredith was asleep on the right side of the bed.

He undressed quickly and got in bed beside her, close enough to feel her warmth. He wanted to awaken her, to hold her in his arms and even more, he realized, to be held by her. He needed the reassurance that he was not alone. What puzzled him as much as the need—which he had never experienced before or at least had never acknowledged—was that he would want this reassurance from a woman who was not only almost twenty years younger than he was but also a virtual stranger.

In the Navy, he'd fallen overboard once in heavy seas while helping to lash two ships together prior to a transfer of men and supplies. That was nearly forty years ago, but he could still see those large gray shapes bumping together over his head and he could still feel the sharp pain in his lungs as he swam underwater away from the boats, trying to avoid being crushed. The sensation now was not dissimilar:

he was in over his head, being pressed from all sides, not quite at the point of panic, but well within its range. For so many years, he'd been the one in pursuit of others; suddenly, he was the one being pursued. It was like those movie cartoons he used to laugh at as a child, first hunters chasing animals, then animals chasing hunters. Only this was not a cartoon and not funny.

Yet he'd been upset and even frightened before, but never felt this irresistible need to spill it all to another person. What was it that Meredith had said about her father? He'd never given what there was to give. It reminded André of a splendid novel he'd read once, *The Tears of Autumn,* about a CIA man who loved his woman a very great deal, but only when he was with her; when he was in the field working, she ceased to exist for him. Was it possible that he, André, had been like that? Secretive, yes, because that was a requirement of the profession. But removed? Had that been the trouble with Katie—and, God help him, with the children? Had he really been there even when he *was* there? Or was he no better than those married bachelors who populated the foreign correspondents' ranks, family men who were never happier than when they were off alone in some foreign capital working on an assignment? "I see you're more or less in the same business," Meredith had said, comparing André's remoteness—the distance he had placed between them—to her father's. "That really bothers me a lot," she had said, meaning that if anything was to come of their relationship it would have to be on other terms.

What kind? What did she want? Not information, he was sure. Trust. All of him, or none of him. No half and half.

Not since his mother had André known a woman as strong. Yet their strengths were used to completely different purpose. His mother was domineering; she had to have her way. Meredith wanted equality. She was strong but she was feminine, like those women about whom *Time* had done a cover story, the ones who aerobicized and lifted weights but turned out lithe instead of muscle-bound. "The new ideal of beauty," *Time* had trumpeted. Was it not also the new ideal of equality? A woman who could resist a man, if necessary, to make a point: that she would be her own entity, not the man's reflection. And now that he was involved with such a woman, he had to ask himself whether he had ever offered such a proposition to a woman, including his wife. It had been *his* life that had defined *their* life. Was he prepared to have it any other way? What had happened since Katie's departure? He'd been a bachelor, active, true, but seemingly unable to find anyone who could permanently occupy the other side of the bed. And Varengeville! What was one to make of a man who would take himself out of circulation for a year to live by himself in a country home, regardless of the purpose? How was an empty apartment or country home different from an empty hotel room? Had he been afraid of something all these years? Was that something called "intimacy"? Was he ready for it yet? And could he accept an independent woman?

When he awakened, Meredith was watching him. He reached out for her and she came to him. "Just hold me," he said.

He held her, as well, very tightly, listening to her breathing, smelling her fragrance. It was five minutes before he thought to move his hand along the still unfamiliar contours of her back. When they made love it seemed to go on forever. There was nothing else for him during this time except this woman and their physical connection. His climax shook him, and she seemed shaken, too. He looked down at her, locking his eyes to hers, trying to think of something to say that was worthy of the moment.

"That was fun," she said.

He burst into laughter, and it was only after he had

stopped that he wondered if she had said what she had to keep him from being as solemn as he must have looked.

He was dressing twenty minutes later after his shower, when she emerged from the bathroom naked, toweling her hair, her skin pink from the hot water. The sight of her transfixed him. She was thin without being skinny and firm but not muscular. She caught his gaze and smiled, letting him look at her. At last he shook his head, thinking of how they compared.

"What's the matter?" she said.

"I don't understand what you're doing here."

"I'm working on a relationship with a fascinating man," she said, moving to him and putting her arms around him.

"Look, you don't know anything about me."

"I know that you're considerate."

"How do you know that?"

Meredith smiled and stroked his cheek. "The world, my love, is divided into two kinds of men, inconsiderate ones who leave the toilet seat up after they pee, and considerate ones who replace it for the women who follow. I could never be serious about a man who would leave the seat up, but you, I was relieved to find, fall in the latter category."

He laughed again, loving that she could make him laugh, and he held off telling her about last night until after breakfast so that he could experience her presence in a normal way. They took their croissants and coffee to a little table by the window and watched the barges move along the Seine, flower pots next to the cabins, dogs aboard, laundry flying— each one a tiny, self-contained world. He wanted a world like that for himself, a world of familiar patterns, one of them sitting by this window each morning with this beautiful young woman, sipping coffee and watching the barges.

He told her then about last night. She listened silently and without emotion, even though the facts indicated that her father and her new lover might be pitted against one another in a struggle of enormous consequence. "And now there's you," André concluded.

Meredith held up a hand and shook her head. "No, no. You should do what you would do if we had never met."

"Thank you," he said. He was silent for a moment. "I'm still not sure what that would be. It's a real moral quandary."

"Why?"

"Because in a sense I'm working for the Russians."

"Would you have done the story if the Russians weren't involved?"

"Of course."

"Then it's a valid story—assuming the dossier is real."

"No question."

"Then I don't see the moral dilemma. Whether you want to continue is another matter."

"Do you think I should continue?"

"That's not a question for me to answer."

"Do you *want* me to continue?"

"Is that important to you?"

"I think so."

She was silent for a moment. "Yes. I want you to continue—if that's what you want to do."

"Even though your father seems to be working at cross purposes?"

"You don't know that for certain."

"I have a pretty good idea."

"Now there's a moral dilemma," Meredith said. She chewed on her lip for half a minute. "Daddy wasn't himself when he was here. I'm sure you saw that, too."

"I don't really know him."

"But didn't he seem different from when you saw him in Washington?"

"Completely."

"It's possible that this revelation unhinged him. He's near retirement, you know."

"I figured he might be. What do you think he would do if he knew the truth?"

"Why?"

"Because if he got to Montbrun, then Montbrun has told him the truth, regardless of what he told me."

"Daddy would do his duty. The country would come first."

"But is his duty what he's told to do, or what he construes it to be?"

"That's the question, isn't it?"

André shook his head. "The other question is how do I get the dossier authenticated by someone I can trust?"

"Maybe I can help you," Meredith said.

He looked at her in surprise. "How?"

"If you want me to, I could ask around and find out who authenticates works of art. Whoever that is would know someone who deals in old books and letters. Wouldn't such a person know how to authenticate the dossier?"

"I'm sure he would. Even the art expert should know. The big question is the age of the paper. Wouldn't an art authenticator deal in watercolors, and wouldn't watercolors be on paper?"

"Yes on both counts."

"Can you do it today?"

"Of course."

It was so very tempting, such a good solution to the problem. He was being followed, but Meredith was free to move about. Suddenly, he froze. *Was* she free? Would the DGSE follow her, not just because she was involved with him but because she was Houghton's daughter? They would know that because they had followed them to Clermont-Ferrand.

"What's the matter?" Meredith said.

"I don't want you getting into trouble on my account."

"What kind of trouble could I get into? I'm just going out to do what I do every day, make the rounds of the galleries and seek out young artists."

She was right. If she made enough stops, the DGSE wouldn't suspect that she was after something special. "It might work," he said.

"Of course it will work."

"And you'd be willing to do that?"

"Why wouldn't I be?"

"In a sense you'd be working against your father."

"We don't really know that. We don't know what he's up to."

"That's true."

"Then let's find out the truth about this matter and deal with the consequences later."

He watched her from the window as she walked along the Quai d'Orléans and across the bridge from the Île St. Louis to the Left Bank, with Notre Dame on her right and the memorial to the victims of the Holocaust on her left. Her strides were so long and fluid that he thought he could pick her out in a crowd of pedestrians at a hundred yards.

Two men were seated in a car forty yards from the door to his apartment building, undoubtedly agents of the DGSE, but neither of them moved to follow her after she passed by. They'd had a good look at her though and could be alerting a colleague by radio to pick up the tall, obviously American woman, blonde and slender and beautiful—the French would elaborate the description—with the long and fluid strides. André had a brief premonition that, in wanting to include her to gain her trust, he'd done a selfish and unwise thing. If anything happened to her on his account, he would never forgive himself.

He quickly shook the thought, however, because he had his own work to do. On the assumption that Meredith

would be successful in finding an authenticator, he needed
to contact Gondrachov to make arrangements for the delivery of the dossier.

He crossed the bridge to the Left Bank and walked to a
telephone booth he used whenever he was uncomfortable
about making a call from his apartment. A man was in the
booth, but he hung up and left the booth just as André
arrived. André removed the telephone from its cradle and
was about to deposit a coin when he realized that a piece of
paper was covering the coin slots. It was a note, written in
English, and with a chill André realized that it was meant
for him:

> One of the lessons you'll have to learn if you intend
> to be successful in this line of work is that you must
> never use the same pay telephone more than twice, par-
> ticularly if there's the remotest possibility that you've
> been put under surveillance. A public telephone can be
> tapped just as readily as a private one. Please pretend
> to make a call, then hang up as though the line is busy
> and go to a café a few blocks away, order a coffee and
> call the usual number from there. Destroy this note.

André followed the instructions, convinced that he had
entered another world. There was no turning back or
thought of abandoning the effort; if Meredith was working
in his behalf, the least he could do was carry through his
part.

If Gondrachov was under any added strain, he did not
betray it. His voice was as measured as always, his tempera-
ment as even. "Have you a paper and pencil, old man?
Good! I'll be moving after this call, so we'd best get our
signals down. Now, assuming Miss Houghton is successful
in finding someone to do the work . . ."

"Wait a minute!" André interrupted. "How did you—?"

"It just made sense that she'd help, old man, given her expertise."

They knew where he made his surreptitious phone calls. They knew he was seeing Meredith. They knew all about her. What *didn't* they know? And what was he doing, working with them? All of the doubts resurfaced once again, and he had a sudden impulse to hang up, find Meredith, and disappear with her into Normandy. But Gondrachov's even tones and confident voice were somehow reassuring as he continued with his instructions.

"At ten tomorrow morning, Miss Houghton should go to American Express on the Rue Scribe as though she is picking up some mail. Then she should go to the Café de la Paix, having instructed your expert to meet her there. They should have a coffee. Afterward, they should go to the lobby of the Grand Hôtel next door and visit their respective WCs. Just before parting, she should give the gentleman a room number: 522. Each of them should go separately to that room after leaving the WC, the gentleman first, Miss Houghton, five minutes later."

"What happens in Room 522?"

"Your expert will discover that the dossier is authentic."

"With what? He'll need microscopes, chemicals, special lights."

Gondrachov's tone was like that of a teacher chiding a slow pupil. "It will all be there, old man."

André did not miss the inflection. "What about me?" he said after a moment. "Don't I come?"

"Impossible, unless you want to give the game away. You're being followed very closely."

"Isn't she being followed?"

"Not as far as we can tell. The several stops tomorrow before the hotel are just to make sure. We'll have counter-surveillance on both her and the expert. Incidentally, we'll need to know his identity as soon as you have it. You can communicate it to Boris. Any questions?"

"I'm to learn the verdict from Miss Houghton, is that it?"

"Correct. I trust that will be good enough for you."

"Temporarily. I'll need an attestation eventually."

"That's between you and your expert."

"Next question: what will happen to the dossier?"

"Ah ha! That will have to remain a mystery for the moment."

"Will it be available if and when I need it?"

"I'll see to it that it is."

Everything seemed in order. It wasn't perfect, but it would do. Yet André was uneasy. "Gennady, I'm going to ask you a question, and I want you to tell me the truth. Are you capable of doing that?"

"Try me."

"Is Miss Houghton in any danger?"

"Perhaps," the Russian said without the slightest hesitation. "I have every belief that it will proceed as planned, but one can never be sure. I gather you care for the young woman."

"Let's just say I don't want anything to happen to her."

"I can't promise that, André. That's something you'll have to sort out with her."

He knew he'd received an honest answer. He couldn't ask for more. A sudden feeling of concern for the Russian caught him by surprise. "Are you in any danger, Gennady?"

There was the slightest pause. "It comes with the territory, old man."

On his way back to the apartment, André decided he had better do some shopping. In case Meredith returned before lunch, he wanted to have something for her; if she didn't, he could remain at home to receive her call. His first stop was at a *charcuterie,* that wondrous French version of a delicatessen, where cooked game birds and poached and decorated fish and *oeufs gelées* are sold along with twenty versions of pâtés, terrines, salads, cheeses, and desserts. Waiting his turn amid these dizzying aromas, André could feel the tension within him ebbing, as though the food was functioning like a mantra, focusing his concern on this one primary need to the exclusion of all others. For the first time in all his years in France, he understood what a meditative effect the preoccupation with eating had on the French.

When his turn came, he purchased some *pâté de campagne,* cold chicken, and *chèvre,* the goat cheese which none but the French seem capable of producing successfully. Then he stopped at a *boulangerie* for some *pain de campagne,* that rough-textured country bread that went so well with the pâté. Once again, the good smells overpowered him, but this time with a reverse effect. They reminded him of his hunger, which made him anxious, which reminded his body, in turn, of the tensions under which he was operating.

As soon as he returned to the apartment, he set out the lunch. Then he waited, fighting his hunger, hoping Meredith would appear. When she hadn't returned by two o'clock, he succumbed and ate alone.

He was almost frantic at five o'clock when she finally appeared. But one look at her face told him she had succeeded; a mask could not have concealed her pleasure.

The authenticator she had found, one Jules Roget, fit the task exactly. His specialty was paintings—he had been the expert used by insurance companies to validate Van Goghs, Dufys and Gauguins after a number of works allegedly by these artists had been stolen and the owners had collected, leading the companies to suspect that the paintings might have been fakes. But Roget also appraised rare books as well as old manuscripts and letters. He would be happy to evaluate what André had, no questions asked, and he would expect a call that evening.

André called at once. "Do you speak German?" he asked after the pleasantries were out of the way.

"Unfortunately not," Roget said, his voice cordial but matter-of-fact. "The material is in German?"

"Yes."

"Then perhaps you will want to find someone else."

"Only if you feel that you couldn't tell me how old the document is without knowing what it says."

"What it says has nothing to do with the age of the paper it is written on."

"Then I'm sure you'll do fine," André said, convinced now that the content of the document was secure. He explained the arrangements to Roget, as much as he had to know, and they agreed on a fee of twenty-five hundred francs.

At nine the next morning, as they sipped their coffee and ate their croissants and watched the barges slip along the Seine, André said to Meredith, "You're sure you want to go through with this?"

"Why wouldn't I?"

"God knows what could happen."

She took his hand. "Nothing will happen, my love."

She was right. The arrangements had been flawless, she reported on her return shortly before 1 P.M. The meeting in Room 522 of the Grand Hôtel had taken place as scheduled (which told André that she hadn't been followed, because Gondrachov would have aborted the meeting if she had been). Jules Roget had done his work in silence and discreetly asked no questions. Rather than announce the verdict, he had written it out, sealed it in an envelope addressed to André, given the envelope to Meredith and departed at once. A few moments later, she had left as well. "I don't think your Russian friend was very happy with all the secrecy," she said as she handed André the envelope.

"We'll worry about him later," André said. His hands were shaking slightly as he opened the envelope, even though he was almost certain he knew what it would say.

Dear Mr. Kohl:

Analysis of the documents indicates that the age of the paper corresponds to the dates of the documents. A portion of one of the documents, dated 10.10.43, was missing but further analysis indicated that the paper of this document was identical to the paper of similar documents written just before and just after this date.

J. Roget

André handed the letter to Meredith without comment. "Could you understand it?" he asked when she had finished reading.

"Of course."

"What it means is that Camille Laurent was a traitor—assuming Roget is right."

"Do you have any doubt?"

'I have to doubt everything connected with this story. Montbrun said it was a fake. I'm assuming your father got to Montbrun, but I don't know that for sure. Montbrun would never tell me, and I can hardly ask your father."

"Do you *think* the dossier's real?"

"Yes. But what I think isn't good enough. I've got to know beyond the proverbial shadow of a doubt."

"What can you do?"

André walked to the window and looked down to the Quai d'Orléans. The DGSE car was still there, two men inside. He stood there, listening, thinking, then turned back to Meredith. "There's only one man who really knows whether that memo's authentic."

She looked at him intently for at least ten seconds. "I hope you're not thinking what I have a feeling you're thinking."

In spite of himself, André laughed. "What do you think I'm thinking?"

"That you should go to Bolivia and look up a certain Mr. Hoepner."

He shook his head in admiration. "You're right."

She sat then and stared at him again. "Do you think he'd see you?" she said at last.

"I have no idea. And if he saw me I don't know if he'd tell me what I need to know. But there's only one way to find out."

He sat at the piano and absently played several bars of Bach. Then he turned to Meredith. "Look, do you have plans for the next few days?"

"At some point I have to face reality and think about getting back to New York."

That wasn't the answer he wanted. He didn't want to even consider the prospect of her leaving. "Isn't someone taking care of the gallery?"

"Of course."

"Then come with me to London this evening." Before she could answer, he was explaining. "I've got to have a long, long talk with New York. I suppose I could figure out some way to do it from here, but being tailed by all these spooks has given me the jitters. I'd like to be able to make my call without worrying that they'll figure out some way to listen in. And then there's this woman I've met, and I'd like to take her to London and show her a good time."

Meredith studied him for a moment. Then she smiled. "Life in the fast lane," she said. "Sure. Why not. Do I have time to go to the hotel and pack?"

He was about to answer "of course," but the words caught in his throat. Everything he did now had to be examined in terms of the knowledge that he was under surveillance. Anything Meredith did that bore on his movements had to be examined in that light, too. Forget the KGB and the CIA, if they were on the case; it was the DGSE that mattered because the DGSE had power in France: power to bug, tail, harass, detain, arrest, or at least arrange for an arrest. Two of these powers had already been invoked; the rest could be brought to bear at any time.

Suddenly, he laughed.

"What's funny?" Meredith asked.

"I'm trying to figure out how I would do this if I were a spy."

He walked to the window again. The DGSE car was still there, the agents still in it. "I've got it," he said. He turned and smiled. "Sure, you can pack your bags. As a matter of fact, I'd suggest that you check out, because I honestly don't know when we'll be coming back. And then, instead of London, how would you like to spend tonight in Varengeville?"

Meredith frowned. "Is there time for that?"

"There's time," André said. "And, incidentally, while you're in your hotel room, call Air France and make two reservations, one in my name and the other in yours, on the Concorde to New York tomorrow morning. Ask for two seats in the first cabin."

"I'm thoroughly confused," Meredith said.

"Excellent," he said. He was beaming.

21

At seven o'clock that evening, Pierre Gauthier, the tall, hefty number three man of the DGSE, still in his musty and cluttered office at La Caserne des Tourelles, the women's prison turned secret service headquarters in the Twentieth Arrondissement, received a telephone call from a police lieutenant with whom he had served in the army in Indochina in the early 1950s. The lieutenant, one Jean Faust, explained to Gauthier that he had received a visit from an art appraiser named Roget, who was under investigation by his department for his part in a counterfeit ring that produced phony French identity cards and sold them to foreigners wanting to remain permanently in France. Roget had described an unusual encounter earlier that day with an American woman named Houghton who was acting in behalf of the American journalist, André Kohl. The woman had taken him under mysterious circumstances to a meeting with a man he took to be Eastern European or Russian to examine a set of documents in German. Roget did not read German, but the titles and dates on the documents indicated unmistakably that they pertained to the Gestapo's ac-

tivities in Clermont-Ferrand during the occupation. On one
of the documents, Roget had told them, he had seen the
name of Camille Laurent. Knowing that Gauthier had been
Laurent's aide-de-camp in Indochina, Faust said, he had
decided to give him a call.

Roget, Faust went on, could describe the man and tell
them the name of the hotel and the number of the room in
which the man had been staying. In exchange, he wanted to
be dropped from the investigation into the counterfeit identity papers. His department would be willing to do that if
the information was worth anything to the DGSE, Faust
said. Was it?

Conceivably, Gauthier said, without a trace of excitement
in his voice.

Then they should make the exchange?

If it would not be a great inconvenience, Gauthier said.
And he might as well wait on the line for the information,
so that Faust would not have to go to the trouble to make
another telephone call.

Fifteen minutes later, Gauthier, himself, and two of his
men appeared at the Grand Hôtel. The man who had been
in Room 522 that morning had checked out at 1 P.M. He
had registered as Milos Novotny and given an address in
Prague. He had used a Czech passport.

Gauthier showed the desk clerks a picture of Gondrachov. Was this the man? Yes, the desk clerks answered.

By the time he reached his car, Gauthier had decided that
it was time to confront André Kohl with some questions.
But since André Kohl was who he was, it would not do to
pick him up and bring him in. Far better for Gauthier to
call on the journalist at his home.

Using the telephone in his car, Gauthier learned that
Kohl had left his Île St. Louis apartment several hours before with the American woman, Miss Houghton, driven in
his car to the Hôtel de l'Avenir in the Sixth Arrondisse-

ment, waited for Miss Houghton while she packed and
checked out and then driven to his country home in
Varengeville-sur-Mer. According to the surveillance team
on the scene, Kohl and Miss Houghton had been greeted by
his housekeeper, changed into more comfortable clothes,
and then sat down to dinner.

It would not be wise to alarm Monsieur Kohl, Gauthier
reflected. Rather than telephone him or have someone pre-
cede him, he would simply show up there in the morning.
Although he didn't think it was really necessary, he decided
to play it safe and maintain surveillance through the night
and so instructed his men.

That done, Gauthier returned to his office, where he
made a direct dial call to a private residence in Virginia. "I
believe you assured us that you had taken care of Monsieur
Houghton," he said without preamble to the whiskey-
voiced man who answered.

"We certainly have," came the reply. "The President
himself ordered Houghton off the case."

"Then why is Houghton's daughter working with André
Kohl?"

Craig was silent for such a long time that Gauthier wondered if he had lost the connection. "Hello?" he said.

"I'm here," Craig replied. "I must tell you that the moment is fast approaching when Mr. Kohl will have to be
dealt with with extreme prejudice. Do I make myself
clear?"

"Perfectly," Gauthier said.

Once again there was a series of lightning telephone calls in
the vicinity of Washington, and once again they ended with
an irate call from the President of the United States to the
director of the CIA. The President was shouting so loudly
that William Coughlin, the director, had to hold the phone

away from his ear. "You get that son of a bitch in your office and you fire his ass, do you hear me?"

"I hear you, Mr. President. But shouldn't I make an investigation? Houghton's been with the service his entire professional life. Isn't it possible that he didn't put his daughter up to it and doesn't know what she's doing?"

"I don't give a shit what's possible. If a man can't control his daughter, what the fuck good is he? Now are you going to fire him, or shall I?"

"I'll take care of it, Mr. President," Coughlin said.

He'd do it next week, when Houghton got back. The deputy director had left the office abruptly that morning as sick as a dog.

At nine-thirty the next morning, Gauthier arrived at the gate to Le Pré Ango, André's country home. His men, tired and stiff from a night spent in the car and needing a shave, saluted. "Any activity?" Gauthier said.

"Only the housekeeper. She went on bicycle to the village for some bread and returned fifteen minutes later."

"Excellent," Gauthier said. "Let's go inside." A member of the surveillance team opened the gate, and Gauthier's driver pulled into the gravel driveway and parked alongside André's car. Two Bedlington terriers, barking furiously, raced up to Gauthier as he emerged from the car, but stopped suddenly fifteen feet from him and kept their distance as he walked up the path to the house. He did not need to knock; Madame Cartet opened the door and came outside to identify the commotion.

"Good morning, madame," Gauthier said. "I would like to see Mr. Kohl. I am Inspector Gauthier of the DGSE."

"I am sorry, sir, but Mr. Kohl is not up yet."

"Then would you please awaken him? I have driven from Paris to see him." For emphasis, he showed Madame Cartet his identification.

Madame Cartet excused herself. She returned a minute later, with a puzzled frown. "I am sorry sir, but Mr. Kohl is not upstairs."

"And the lady?"

Madame Cartet's frown deepened. "Not there, either."

"Perhaps they've gone for a walk."

"Perhaps."

Ten minutes passed, during which time Gauthier became increasingly restless. At last he asked if he might use the telephone. Within another minute, he had instructed his aides to check all airlines and railways at once for reservations in the name of André Kohl and Meredith Houghton. He said he would wait on the line. Three minutes later, one of his aides came on to report that there were reservations in those names for today's Concorde flight to New York.

Amateurs! Gauthier muttered to himself. He'd had enough of this silliness. "Pick them up," he ordered. He'd figure out some charge.

An hour later, as his car was speeding him back to Paris on the autoroute from Rouen, Gauthier, lost in a delicious fantasy involving himself and two of his younger women agents, was interrupted by a telephone call from *La Piscine*. The agents sent to pick up Monsieur Kohl and Mademoiselle Houghton had just reported that they had failed to report for their flight. *"Merde!"* Gauthier muttered, feeling as foolish as a professional can feel who's just been outsmarted by an amateur. "Call the frontier police. Find out if they've left the country," he ordered. In less than a minute, he had the answer he'd expected. Monsieur Kohl and Mademoiselle Houghton had sailed to England that morning. What was even more galling was that they'd used their own passports and names.

Late the previous evening, having turned out the house lights as if they were going upstairs to bed, André and Meredith had slipped out of the house through the French doors in the study and made their way through the apple orchard in a fog so dense it dampened their clothes. Within a few minutes, they were on a small country road, little more than a lane, that ran along the back of André's property and led eventually to the house of Madame Cartet's brother. The brother, three years older than his sister and with a face made rosy as much by apple brandy as by the coastal winds, was a bit nonplussed at the sight of André and the strange young woman, but as he was also in André's employ, being charged with the apple orchard as well as the grounds, he could scarcely say no to André's request for lodging. At six the following morning, he had driven André and Meredith to Dieppe, where they had boarded the morning ferry across the channel to Newhaven, with railway connections to London. At the moment Gauthier discovered what they had done, André and Meredith were in sight of the English coast. Because the boat was French, Gauthier had the option of preventing André from debarking, thus compelling him to return to France, but what he had initially envisioned as a quiet little chat would, with a few modest turns of the screw, have escalated to an international incident, and he was not prepared to risk one.

Besides, he had a more fruitful possibility to pursue: the capture of Colonel Gennady Gondrachov of the KGB, who had come into France illegally—there was no record of his entry—and who had with him some kind of document that, when all the pieces were put together, related to a chapter in the life of Camille Laurent that had to be suppressed at all cost.

Gondrachov didn't know it yet, but he had been trapped in France, Gauthier reflected with satisfaction. There was no way he could get out.

Even if he had known it, Gondrachov would not have had time to think about it. He was too busy dealing with a more immediate calamity: André Kohl's capricious conduct.

The American hadn't telephoned since the previous morning. All of his past conduct had assured Gondrachov that he would call to inform him of the authenticator's verdict, if for no other reason than professional courtesy. In all of their previous dealings, Kohl had been unfailingly courteous. Not this time. Had the failure been deliberate, or had some unforeseen circumstance intruded? Why had he suddenly and inexplicably left Paris yesterday afternoon? That much his countersurveillance team had affirmed; they had followed him from his apartment to his car and then to the young woman's hotel and finally to the outskirts of the city. But there they had stopped, mindful that any further pursuit would alert the French surveillance team between them and André. The assumption was that André had driven to his country home, because he had left Paris going in that direction. But a call by Boris had raised only a housekeeper, who said he wasn't there. There was no immediate way to check whether he was or wasn't, no time to turn a housekeeper or gardener, or to get a party member in the area to look in. At home we do these things better, he thought.

His superior would interpret this turn of events as a blunder—his blunder. He hadn't blundered. He had promised the dossier would be authenticated, and it had been. But how could he have imagined that the moment the story had at last checked out André, instead of doing his broadcast, would flee the city?

There was no longer time for any other plan, even if another plan had been possible. Those thickheads in Moscow simply didn't understand that no Western journalists, not even the French, would use a story like this without first checking into it. Everything he had learned in three decades of cultivating the Western press had told him that their best chance lay with André Kohl. He hadn't been wrong. He didn't know anyone who could have accomplished what Kohl had in this short a time.

But why had he left Paris?

And what to do with the dossier until André's return?

Until his mistakes—his erroneous assumptions about André, his appearance with him in public—Gondrachov had felt reasonably comfortable in moving about Paris as Milos Novotny, a Czech. No longer. He could take nothing for granted now, least of all that the French weren't aware of his presence. So he would have to find a cache for the dossier. A locker in the Gare de Lyon wouldn't do; after two days, a little white sign with red letters popped up, saying *"S'adresser à la consigne,"* meaning that the locker had been emptied and the contents taken under custody. Should he play it very safe and take the dossier to the Russian Embassy? If the French knew he was in town and even suspected what he was up to, he would never make it past the embassy gates. And once in, how could the dossier be brought out when the time came to put it to use? The embassy could not risk the charge of interference in the domestic affairs of a sovereign power. However erroneous his other assumptions about André had been, Gondrachov was absolutely certain that his American friend was still on the story and that there would come a time when the dossier would need to be put to use. What if he, Gondrachov, was picked up? No one, not André, not anyone, could get the dossier out.

Could Paulette, his adventuresome "Boris," who was once again sheltering him now that it had become too risky to remain in a hotel, provide a solution? Surely she had a strong box in a bank vault. The dossier would be safe there. But if something happened to him *and* Paulette—if they were picked up and detained—then how would André get the dossier? Besides, Paulette knew nothing of the dossier; if it were in her strong box, she might succumb to temptation, and all kinds of mischief could result. No, Paulette was out: too bright and feisty. What he needed was someone equally devoted but not as bright, who would help him without asking questions or caring what he had, someone with access to a cache that no one would ever suspect.

Suddenly, Gondrachov threw back his head and let out a laugh befitting a Cossack. The perfect hiding place. Even André would be amused.

22

André didn't relax until passport control had stamped its mark in his book. Then, in the few minutes before the train departed for London, he called Jean Hedley, the public relations director of the St. James's Club in London. "Terribly sorry for the short notice, but I'll be in town in two hours. Can you possibly fix up a suite?"

For an answer, he heard a little scream. "Oh, André, you are *awful*. Couldn't you have called last night?"

"If I could have, I would have."

There was an audible sigh. "Oh, come along. We'll fix it somehow."

The St. James's Club is in a refurbished five-story turn-of-the-century building, painted a striking terra-cotta and trimmed in white, on Park Place, a short cul-de-sac off of St. James's Street and two blocks below Piccadilly. It is neither an old club nor an exclusive one; it is simply very special, offering low-keyed elegance and superb service in an extremely comfortable setting. There are beds for only eighty-four guests, most of them filled by people possessing well-known faces or names. Turned-down covers, choco-

lates on the pillows, heated towel racks, newspapers outside
the door in the morning—these were just a few of the
touches that had persuaded André to choose the club over
the Connaught or Montcalm hotels, two other favorites, for
his unexpected visit to London with Meredith. The restaurant on the bottom floor was another reason. Like Chiberta
in Paris, where they had spent their first evening together, it
was furnished in art deco style, the colors coral and brown.
The crowning touch was a skylight above the bar, level with
the street.

Jean Hedley was at the bar with friends when André and
Meredith walked in. She came up to them at once, a small,
pretty, intense woman with a savvy look about her. *"There's*
that awful man," she said.

"My favorite magician," André said, first returning her
hug and then introducing her to Meredith.

"I trust the digs are suitable?"

"Excellent."

"Hm. Better be. It's the best bloody suite in the house. I
won't burden your conscience with what I did to get it."

"I wouldn't want to know."

Jean laughed. "You both look bushed, if you don't mind
my saying. Go to your table and have a drink. Lunch is on
me, love."

In their suite an hour later, they both undressed for an
under-the-covers nap. For the first time in days, André had
the feeling that no one could get at him, not the French or
the Russians or even the Americans. It would all change
when he telephoned Mike Paul in New York, but for the
moment there wasn't even a plane to catch. Meredith was
here, her head on his shoulder, his arm around her. He was
in a hotel room, but it wasn't empty. He slept.

They awakened almost simultaneously at four o'clock.
He drew her to him and began to caress her. After a mo-

ment, she said, "Before we get something started, I'd better remind you that I came to this town with nothing to wear."

They had left *Le Pré Ango* with only the bare necessities, packed into an overnight bag. He had told her she could get what she needed when they got to London. But now that they were here, he wanted to prolong that feeling of being out of everyone's reach. "Tell you what," he said, "why don't we have dinner tonight in the room? That way, you won't have to shop until morning."

"Will there be time in the morning?"

"We'll make time in the morning."

"That's a deal," she said, reaching out for him.

As they made love, he tried to discover what it was that made the experience so singular. Certainly, her youth and vitality had something to do with it; he had never before made love to a woman in such superb condition. He knew he would never laugh again at assertions that sex was a fitness event. Their bouts of sex were much more prolonged than any he had ever before experienced and left him physically exhausted. And certainly, technique had something to do with it; Meredith's mouth was soft and pliant and expressive, her hands loving and provocative. But there was nothing especially exotic about the way in which she made love. There were no special moves or positions; on the contrary, her approach, which she made known to him through subtle encouragement, was almost classic. And yet he knew —even now, as they brought one another along—that their loving had another dimension.

Of course! The dimension was time. Not duration, necessarily. Simply a sense that their period in bed together existed in its own dimension, independent of other time. Nothing, absolutely nothing, pressed them, not the need to climax or the need to be elsewhere. They existed for this moment and what was happening in this moment, apart from all other considerations. They were suspended in time, perhaps even in another level of consciousness, because as his climax finally neared, André knew it would happen only when he decided to move out of this special state.

Could he possibly communicate this experience to Meredith? Did he need to? Watching her, seeing her smile, and the way her eyes opened wide as though to absorb as much of him as she could, he knew there was nothing to say.

When he called Mike Paul, it was after five o'clock—after twelve noon in New York—but he wasn't worried about missing him because he knew that Mike didn't go to lunch until one-thirty. He was right. Mike was in and bursting to talk. He always was when a big story was developing. After thirty years in the business, he was as excitable as a cub reporter. André could understand that, because he still felt it himself—never more keenly than when he had exciting news to convey.

"God, am I glad to hear from you!" Mike said. "What have you got?"

"First, let me explain that I had to come to London because it's getting very uncomfortable in Paris."

"That tells me the story checks out."

"Hold on. I've got to give this to you play by play, because it's very involved."

It took André half an hour to tell the story. "Good God!" Mike exclaimed half a dozen times, but otherwise he was silent. "What's the risk if you go to Bolivia?" he asked when André had finished.

"That Gondrachov will give up on me and go to somebody else. But I can't see anyone using the story without checking it out. The Russians want the story out before the runoff election. I don't see that as our objective. It's as good a story after the election as before."

"What's the risk if you don't go to Bolivia—and go with what you've got?"

"The risk is that we're wrong. If we are, it's a disaster, as bad as the Hitler diaries hoax. Worse, maybe. Laurent's alive."

"What are the odds that we'd be wrong?"

André exhaled. "That's tough! Everything suggests that I was set up by Houghton, but I don't know that, and there's no way I *can* know it. Right now, I'd bet a year's pay that the second guy was right and the dossier is authentic. But I sure as hell wouldn't want to gamble the reputation of the network, no matter how good the odds were."

"I agree."

"And there's one other possibility. This one's really far out, but we have to think about it. Let's say we knew absolutely that the dossier was real. Simply no question that the Laurent memo was written in October of 1943 and that Hoepner wrote it." André took a deep breath. "Suppose Hoepner was puffing? Making himself sound more effective than he really was? Laurent was a big man in the Resistance. Turning him might have gotten Hoepner a promotion. But did he really do it? There would have been no way for Hoepner's superiors to check."

There was a long silence at the other end. "I guess you've got to go to Bolivia," Mike said at last.

"I guess so."

"What are you going to do when you get there?"

"Damned if I know."

The two men laughed.

"Is there any way we can help you?" Paul said.

"You bet," André said. "First, get a file on Hoepner to me as fast as you possibly can. Put half a dozen people on it if you have to. Put it in the pouch to London no later than tomorrow night. I won't leave here until it arrives. Next, find out whether any of the correspondents have been to Bolivia, I don't care how long ago, and what, if anything,

they might have heard about Hoepner. His alias and his
address would be gold."

"Wouldn't the embassy in La Paz have those?"

"That's out, Mike."

"God! Of course."

"Incidentally, strict instructions to the researchers: no
calls to any government agencies, least of all State or the
CIA."

"Got it."

"Okay. I'll call you from La Paz."

The next day was heaven—just a lovely spring day anywhere else in the world, but a miracle for London. The sun
warmed the earth, unfiltered by clouds, fog, or smog. A
light breeze freshened the air, and millions of spring blossoms perfumed it.

André's mood matched the weather. For the first time
since his telephone call from Shlomo the day his leave of
absence officially began he seemed to be giving himself permission to enjoy what was happening and be grateful it had
happened. He had a tremendous story going; of that much
he was certain, but for good measure Mike Paul had now
confirmed it. And he had discovered a thrilling woman, and
she was with him in London.

There was an aspect of London that André didn't like: its
pervasive concern with class. At moments, the city's mer-
itocracy struck him as a kind of ultimate Ivy League. Born
in the western United States and educated there, he was
especially sensitive to attempts to convert the place of one's
formation into special status. Apart from that, he loved
London and its people—their sense of proportion, their
style, their whimsical attitude, their unflagging politeness,
their seemingly inexhaustible spirit, even their much ma-
ligned sense of humor.

London changed him. He never went there without responding to its rhythms, without feeling almost British. He never ate big breakfasts except when he was in London, and then he devoured them. He never went to bars just to be going to a bar, except when he was in London; if he had to name his favorite luncheon spot in town, it would be the Audley, the pub down the street from the Connaught. It was the traditions of the British that André liked so much, traditions locked into their history yet accessible to outsiders. You could live in Paris for twenty years and still feel like an outsider; no one felt like an outsider in London for more than a week. André loved to tell the story of the American who brought a newly purchased bowler and umbrella to the final fitting of his custom-made suit at his tailor on Savile Row. Gazing at the ensemble in the mirror for the first time, he burst into tears.

"What's the matter?" the alarmed tailor asked.

"We've lost India," the American sobbed.

In the morning, André and Meredith went on a shopping spree of their own. They each bought clothing and sundries with the other's help. It was a compressed lesson in one another's values and tastes. Meredith's purchases were restrained, as much by predilection as by the knowledge that André, at his insistence, was paying the bills. He took her to S. Fisher in Burlington Arcade, where she selected a black twin cashmere sweater set and a black, tan, and cream tartan kilt. They continued through the arcade and were almost immediately at Ferragamo, where she found some tan Italian pumps. "That should do it," she said.

"Oh, no," André said, and they went by taxi to a boutique near Harrods in Knightsbridge, which had a beige Chanel-type suit that fit as though cut to her measure.

"Your special knowledge of this city is raising certain questions," Meredith said as they walked from the boutique.

André laughed. "No comment," he said, as he led her to

Harrods, where he quickly bought some shirts and ties and a pair of tan cavalry twill slacks to go with his blazer.

It was like that through the day, a gathering of information about one another by two people whose emotions had raced ahead of their knowledge. They went to the Audley but it was hopelessly crowded, so after drinking a pint of lager, they went to the Surprise, a restaurant frequented by expatriate Americans hungry for fried chicken and barbecued spare ribs. After lunch, they went to see the Turner Collection at the Tate. It had been years since Meredith had been to the gallery; as they walked through the rooms and rooms of paintings she clutched his arm and gasped at the explosive skies in those oils, skies that foreshadowed the later world of nonrepresentational modern art.

They returned to the St. James's Club and made love for two hours, André once again marveling at the force she aroused in him, once again feeling that years had been given back to him. That evening, they went to the Royal Festival Hall for a concert conducted by von Karajan. This time it was André who was carried away, not simply by the music and the way it resonated through the hall, but by his consciousness of this young woman with whom he was sharing the experience. Tomorrow they would separate. Would she return to Paris or go on to New York? If Paris, would she wait for his return? Did he *want* her to wait? He would be devastated if she didn't, and yet little warning flags were posting themselves along the route of his reveries.

Another commitment had not been on his agenda; a commitment to an American woman had been the furthest thing from his mind. Suppose they became deeply involved? Forgetting the difference in their ages, was Meredith adaptable to Europe, or would she hate it? And what of *her* feelings about involvements? When you became involved with a European woman and it eventually ended, she understood that and there was no tearing of hair and going to court. It was a part of life. How would Meredith react, if it came to that? It struck him suddenly that he was being terribly parochial and terribly male and he didn't like the idea at all because it told him how much of a throwback he was.

He forced his mind back to the music. A moment later, Meredith took his hand, making him wonder how he could ever again go to a concert alone. He was being whipsawed by conflicting emotions, he knew; he could feel the tautness in his body. Relax, he told himself. Enjoy the moment. You have permission.

They went back to the club for supper. There were only half a dozen tables occupied when the waiter served them their fettuccine with smoked salmon. "Oh, God," Meredith said after her first bite. "Thank you."

He smiled. "You're welcome," he said.

"You'll be leaving tomorrow."

"Probably."

"Is this the way it is all the time—Moscow one day, London the next, La Paz the third?"

"You forgot Paris. I do spend a lot of time in Paris."

"But isn't Paris just a glorified staging ground? I mean, do you really think of it as home?"

"I suppose not. Home is wherever I am. If I didn't think of it like that I'd go nuts."

"America isn't home?"

"Not really. Not anymore. I call France home now because that's where I live, but I'd have no difficulty living anywhere and adjusting to the differences."

"Don't you miss America at all?"

"Is there something I should miss?"

Her head tilted, and little lines appeared in her forehead, and she looked at him in a way he didn't like. It wasn't a critical look, simply one of surprise tinged with enough discomfort to remind him that they really were still strangers to one another, despite their intimacy. Who knew what discoveries, even the smallest ones, might disrupt the flow for either of them, or both?

"What an odd thing to say," she said. "You sound bitter, like someone who's been jilted."

"I've never thought of it that way, but that's not exactly inaccurate."

"Tell me."

For a moment, he decided not to go on. It was the wrong subject for a time and a setting like this one. But she was looking right into his eyes in a way that told him it was important to her, a key to her understanding of him. So he told her about leaving the United States in the sixties because he couldn't understand why his country seemed to be self-destructing and he wanted to distance himself in the hope that he could see it better. But as he spoke he knew that the explanation, which he had given so many times before, really wasn't adequate. He *had* felt jilted. He had loved America as only those who aren't born into its mainstream can love it, as though the fervent and faithful exercise of this love could make up for what the mainstream would identify as their shortcomings: their relative newness to America, their ethnicity, their nonhomogeneous appearance. He was not certain that blacks could love America like that because they knew that no amount of loving would cause the mainstream to let them forget their blackness, but Jews could love it that way, and so could Catholics, and so could the sons of French and German immigrants, and he was all of these, his father being German and Jewish and his mother French and Catholic. It was more than identity, however. It was history. History had been his passion and his academic major, and history had taught him that in all the world and in all time, America really did have the best chance of any political enterprise to realize the objectives of liberty and justice for all. And it was more, even, than history. It was his own belief in the perfectibility of man, not because of any objective evidence, but out of his faith that it must happen.

All of these things he told Meredith, as surprised to hear them as she was because he had never said them before, not even to himself. At last he recounted the end of his romance with America. "Something was going out of American life that had initially caused me to love it—the sense of the possible, the belief, which I shared, that it was all going to happen the way it should. I'd always believed in the basic goodness and decency of my countrymen, and suddenly I found that I couldn't believe in that anymore. I could see America moving very rapidly toward something I didn't like at all, as though its true nature, a profoundly malevolent nature, had suddenly been exposed, and I didn't know how to deal with it. The assassinations broke my heart. So, yes, I guess you could say that I felt jilted."

She was silent when he finished. He was suddenly aware that they were the only ones left in the restaurant, except for their waiter and the cashier. He motioned for the waiter. "I'm so sorry," he said.

"That's quite all right, sir. I'm glad if you had a nice time," the waiter said. André judged him to be Portuguese.

He tipped lavishly to make up for his thoughtlessness. Then they took the lift in silence to their suite. Meredith sat on the couch with her legs crossed. "I was part of that generation, you know."

"Which generation?"

"The one that was making all the noise, organizing the marches and the sit-ins. I wasn't all that active, but I was sympathetic. I'm sorry we scared you. We must have scared a lot of people." She looked at him imploringly, as though asking to be understood. "But those were good questions we were asking. They were questions that had to be asked. And I think they served their purpose."

It was after one A.M., but it was obvious to André that

Meredith didn't want to stop. It was important that she tell him how she felt about America. What a strange subject for what, in effect, was a honeymoon. But as she spoke, he understood why she was saying what she was, and why it needed saying now. They would be parting soon, and she needed to know before they did whether there was sustaining substance to their relationship. Opposites may very well attract in physics, but they seldom did in love, and when they did, it wasn't for long.

She was not a woman who married the values along with the man, as many women had in the past. She had her own values, along with her own ideas, their core being that what had driven him away was, in fact, the clamor of a country confronting its reality in an honest way for the first time. That was an occasion to celebrate, not flee. She spoke quietly, intensely, about the changes she had witnessed, the increased consciousness and open-mindedness, attitudes you almost never read about or heard about because they weren't as dramatic as their counterparts; the laws that were on the books now, laws that didn't translate into practical equality for women and minorities but at least gave them a better shot at it. Look at the crowds, she said, if you want to see what's happening to America, the crowds at the ballgames and in the corporate cafeterias. There are kinds of people there who just weren't there twenty years before. There's so much still to do, she said, but if you see only the dark side nothing ever gets done. The art is to see all sides.

"You're an eclectic," André said.

"You better believe it."

She was dead serious, and he didn't want her to be. "How do eclectics feel about nightcaps?" he said.

She looked out the window, across the rooftops to the sky, lightened by a near-full moon. "If I talk much longer, maybe morning tea would be more appropriate."

André chuckled. "How about it?"

"Are you trying to jolly me up?"

"Heaven forbid," André said. He went to the telephone, called room service, and ordered a split of champagne.

"What time is it?" Meredith asked.

André looked at his watch. "A little after two."

"And they still have room service?"

"Wait," André said. In less than a minute, there was a soft knock at the door. The waiter, a smiling young red-head, came in, set the champagne bucket on a coffee table, opened the bottle, filled two glasses, got a signature from André, said, "Goodnight, sir, goodnight, madame," and departed.

André raised his glass. "To the eclectics," he said. "May they save our hides." They touched glasses, but she didn't smile. "Go on," he said, regretting now that he had interrupted at all.

She looked away again and then finally back at him. "There *is* something else," she said. "It has to do with the future. Not a long time from now, maybe another twenty years. It has to do with women and how they'll change the country. You people haven't reported this, and you might not even understand it. What we've read about or seen on television has been, first, the bra-burners, and then the first woman justice and the first woman in space and the first woman weight lifter, and of course ERA. I'm for ERA and political power for women and women legislators and justices and presidents. But whether a woman ever becomes President of the United States doesn't matter as much as what women will do to the *thinking processes* of the country within another twenty years. In the past, what women thought and felt never counted for much. Now it counts, believe me, and even more important, women value what they think and feel. And what they think and feel is different from what men think and feel. They're *not* as aggressive. They absolutely detest wars because they carried the people who fight them. And forgive me for sounding like a female chauvinist pig, but women *are* more sensitive and caring and humane. They *do* have a more sensitive emotional register, which means that they're more aware of others' thoughts and feelings . . . Do you hate me?''

"No," André said, afraid to smile or laugh.

Meredith rose and walked to the window and put her back to it and perched on the sill. In the dimness of the lamplight, he couldn't read her face, but the thrust of her jaw told him all he needed to know.

"So here's what I think will happen," she said. "When the values that women carry come more and more to influence their sons—as these women gain the *confidence* to influence their sons—then the sons are going to change. They won't be so aggressive. They won't like wars so much. *They'll* be more sensitive and caring and humane and maybe a little less competitive and a little less willing to devastate the competition." Her voice dropped to a near whisper. "Then America may have a chance to become the kind of place you envisioned."

He had listened to her arguments and descriptions and knew that he didn't recognize anything she had described, even though she was talking about a country and a people he had thought he knew very well. They were very tired when she finished and there were no signals about making love. Nor were there any in the morning; she had showered and dressed before their breakfast arrived. She ate sparingly and swiftly and then moved to the door.

"Where are you going?" he asked.

"Downstairs to check the airline schedules and see if the hall porter can book me on a flight."

He hesitated for a moment. "What kind of a flight are you getting?"

"London–New York."

"You're not going back to Paris?"

"I'm finished in Paris."

The way she said it chilled him. Had that been deliberate? Was he imagining or was she implying that their affair was finished, in addition to her work? If so, what had happened? "I'll be back in a week," he said.

"You don't really know that. Besides, I've got to get back to my gallery before it dies of neglect."

As soon as she left, he called the USBC bureau. The pouch from New York had just arrived, a desk assistant informed him. If he would like to hold, she would open it and see if there was anything for him. As he waited, he thought about the distance Meredith seemed to have suddenly placed between them. Their conversation of the night before—had the flow been interrupted for her by the discovery that, whatever they felt for one another, an ocean still lay between them?

The desk assistant came back on the line. "There is a packet for you. Will you pick it up, or shall I have it sent?"

He asked her to send it, then called the hall porter to find out how to get to Bolivia. Varig could fly him to Rio de Janeiro at nine forty-five that evening, and he could fly on to La Paz aboard Cruzeiro Airlines at nine-fifteen the following morning.

The packet arrived in half an hour. It was very thick. He couldn't bring himself to read it. It was a long flight to Rio; he'd read it on the plane. Instead, he read the covering memo. There was no address for Hoepner and he had an unlisted telephone. The only lead was the alias under which he had lived for thirty years: *Wilhelm Kurtz.*

A few minutes later Meredith returned. She had reserved a seat on TWA's 4:25 P.M. flight to New York and then gone for a walk.

"I'll need your address so I can send your bag as soon as I

get back to Paris. Or if you need it sooner, I can have Madame Cartet send it from Varengeville.''

"It can wait. I brought the vital ingredients with me.''

She began to pack. André watched her for a minute. "Don't go to New York,'' he said suddenly. "Come with me to La Paz.''

23

This time there had been no errors, Charles Houghton reflected with satisfaction as he sat waiting for his first caller in his Watergate apartment. No impulsive visits to total strangers. No advisories to the heads of the various departments. No reliance on anyone, not on Meredith, who was in all probability still in France, not even on Billy, his loyal assistant, whom he would normally trust with his life.

Nor, most importantly, did any emotion whatever attach to what he had determined to do. He had willed himself out of the problem. It was the national interest that concerned him; for this, he could offer only his best, his reason. Once again, he was functioning where he had ever since his injury, on that exclusively rational plane.

For all the gimmickry that attached to his profession, reason was its essential tool. The gadgets helped but they didn't figure out the essentials of most intelligence problems: *why* were people acting as they did?

Why had the Russians planted this particular piece of information on André Kohl? That was elementary. It served their interests to do so; they wanted Laurent defeated.

Why had Virgil Craig acted as he had about a piece of information more than forty years old? That was not so elementary, yet it, too, could yield to reason.

The possibilities:

What had happened was somehow deeply embarrassing to Craig. Not a good possibility, because Craig had instantly involved all sorts of people, Frenchmen and Americans, all the way to the President of the United States. Besides, Craig could scarcely be embarrassed by an episode in which his role had been minor, indirect, and after-the-fact.

What had happened related to something more current than forty years ago. That would explain why so many active people had become so immediately involved. The superficial answer was what the President had said it was: it was in this country's interest to see Laurent elected. Craig himself had told him, that day at his home, that it wasn't in the national interest for him to know what he had come to find out. But somehow that answer didn't satisfy. It was all right as far as it went, but it didn't go far enough. Virgil Craig, several years past retirement, was not likely to get so passionately worked up over a future election in a country not his own.

What had happened was not only current, it related to matters in which Craig had a personal concern. That answer satisfied. This seemed eminently reasonable. What were those matters? If he could find that out, Houghton might have his first lead to identifying this curious network he was now certain existed within the CIA, the DGSE, and God knew what other intelligence agencies.

Now that the problem had been defined, the next step was to acquire information. That process, too, had nothing to do with gadgetry; it was accomplished with simple, old-fashioned digging.

The first important piece of information was gained through a re-reading of Virgil Craig's file. There had been a brief period after the war when the Office of Strategic Services was disbanded and the Counter Intelligence Corps took up the slack. Craig had transferred to the CIC. It was during this duty that he had interrogated Hoepner, along with a number of other Nazis.

The second piece of information was gained by reading the files on these other Nazis. There were half a dozen of them, men of the Gestapo's second rank, each charged with a district in one of the conquered countries, each compiling a record no less comprehensive or sickening than Hoepner's. As he read, Houghton felt increasingly disquieted, something apart from his revulsion. He couldn't for the life of him figure out what was causing it, but the feeling persisted. It had to do not with what he was reading, but what he wasn't reading.

And then he knew. Not one of these men had been tried for their crimes against humanity. Like Hoepner, they had all escaped—*and all to South America.*

How? Why? Could Virgil Craig have had a hand in these escapes? It was too farfetched to consider. And yet it had to be considered.

Reason told you that these men could not have escaped alone. They had to have had the help and protection of powerful friends. Which friends? Reason supplied the answer—as incredible as the answer was.

He would need proof. Proof like that was never in files. He would have to find it.

And so, the previous Tuesday, having made all his arrangements, he had put five .6-milligram tablets of atropine sulfate under his tongue just before the morning staff meeting with the heads of all the CIA departments. Five minutes after the meeting began, Bill Coughlin had looked over at him and said, "Jesus, Charlie, you look awful." In truth, he did. His face was flushed and his skin was clammy. A doctor summoned hurriedly to the conference room reported his temperature at 101.5 and his pulse at 120 beats per minute, double his normal rate. A redness covered his chest. The doctor proposed Walter Reed Hospital, but Houghton insisted on going home. Four hours after arriving at his apartment, he was normal. The next morning, the first of his guests arrived.

Like the others Houghton would be seeing at carefully staggered intervals during the next several days, a period when he would presumably be recovering from his sudden illness and when his absence from the office would be unquestioned, the first guest had worked in the CIC at the same time as Virgil Craig. There was a risk in seeing these people—they might have been involved with Craig in whatever he'd been doing—but it was a risk Houghton had to take. He had told each of the men he'd called that this was top secret; his great hope was that they'd all be so flattered by this summons from the nation's ranking intelligence professional that they would keep the confidence entrusted to them. And tell him what he needed to know.

They did. And as they did, a story began to emerge that seemed consistent and plausible and held up under his persistent questioning. It was a time, they said, when they were groping in the dark. They'd been assigned the job of learning everything they could about the Russians and their agents throughout Europe. As far as they were concerned, every Communist everywhere was an agent or potential agent of the Russians. With help like that the Russians could run through Western Europe. The only force against them was the Americans. It was a terrifying prospect and, for the men in the CIC, an overwhelming assignment. They knew next to nothing about the Russians, what they had or how they operated, and the pressure on them to gather information was enormous. So they did what they had to do:

they enlisted the help of men who did know something—or, at least, professed to.

Out of all the former intelligence agents he might have summoned, Houghton had selected five whose work not only spanned the spectrum of what such agents did, but who also lived along the Atlantic seaboard, so that coming to see him was not a major undertaking. And all five of these men struck him as well-meaning, dedicated Americans who believed at the time that they were doing the patriotic thing. They knew that these Germans had been Gestapo; of course they knew. But they were under orders to gain information to counter a sudden massive peril, and they felt that the benefits outweighed the costs. Besides, they said, they hadn't known exactly what these Germans had done.

It was the job of others to try war criminals, they said. It was their job to acquire intelligence. Everyone, not just the Americans, was using Nazi war criminals in intelligence operations after the war—Britain's MI-5, Russia's KGB, even the French internal intelligence agency, the DST.

Had they ever suspected that the former Nazis were inventing information in an effort to make themselves credible? They had no way of knowing that at the time. They took whatever they could get.

There finally came the time when the efforts of the war crimes prosecutors intersected with those of the intelligence community. A prosecutor looking for Hoepner found him registered as an informer—under the protection of a CIC operations chief who had initially issued a warrant for his arrest. In less than a year, the CIC chief's assignment had been changed from chasing Nazis to chasing Communists.

"We treated him very well. We went overboard to be nice to that guy," a former major in intelligence told Houghton. He was in his seventies now, a frail man with a goatee who looked like he wouldn't last more than another year or two.

His voice was worn with age. "We put him and his family in
a nice little home in Augsburg and used one of our trucks to
move them in. We gave him good leather suitcases for his
travels in our behalf. We went out and had a few beers now
and then. He was totally at ease."

How could this be? Surely Hoepner knew that others
were trying to arrest him. "He knew. But he wasn't worried.
He knew we'd protect him because he was producing. We
had a lot of respect for his ability and a lot of confidence in
his material. He was very useful."

Houghton never judged. He simply listened. He could
understand how it must have happened: the escalation of
the Cold War; the increasing pressure for information, the
genuine *need* for information; then the blockade of Berlin
by the Russians, which seemed to validate America's worst
fears about Russia's aggressive intent. The Americans
wanted to penetrate the Bavarian Communist Party.
Hoepner said he could help them do that. And he did. His
standing among Americans rose: "Very shrewd, extremely
intelligent, very capable professional who knew how to extract information through interviews and interrogations,
who could single out strengths and weaknesses of certain
individuals. In short, a really competent, experienced professional."

Listening to this evaluation forty years after the fact,
Houghton only nodded. What good would it serve to say to
his informant, "This professional gained his experience, his
very competence through the brutal interrogation of four
thousand persons whom he subsequently killed"?

The French went looking for Hoepner, but he had disappeared. They asked the Americans if they knew where he
was. The Americans said they didn't. Hoepner had to be
protected. They needed his help.

Hoepner became increasingly friendly with his American
employers. Encounters became more frequent, some social,

all occasions for talking shop: "He told me his war stories, I
told him mine. He talked about some of the atrocities that
were committed against German troops and the reactions
that resulted from them."

"Did he talk about his methods?"

"There was a mention of forced interrogations, and he
expounded a little bit around the point that there are times
when forced interrogations are imperative because you have
a deadline to meet and unless you have positive results the
consequences can be disastrous."

"And did you agree?"

"Yes."

"Who were Hoepner's sources?"

"They were almost exclusively former SS-men."

"How did you feel about that?"

"The type of information that we wanted quickly sometimes could only be had from somebody that had a thorough knowledge of police techniques and procedures."

The French persisted, ever eager to find the man who had
murdered Jacques Ferrer, the president of the *Comité National de la Resistance*. The Americans repeated that they
didn't know where he was.

"We were damned certain that the French intelligence
agencies had been thoroughly penetrated by elements of the
Communist Party and by the KGB. If they got Hoepner,
they would break him and discover everything about our
operations and the sources he had recruited for us. We
couldn't let that happen."

But the pressure mounted. The French sent an interrogation team to Germany to look for Hoepner. They almost
found him. After that, the word came down, "Don't surren-
der Hoepner, but get rid of him." Hoepner had become too
grave a political problem.

And so Hoepner and his family were put aboard the Rat
Line, a secret escape route organized by U.S. Army intelli-

gence to get its friends out of Europe. By truck and train, they were moved first to the Austrian border, then through Austria to Italy and finally to Genoa. They traveled with false passports and each had a cover story: Hoepner was a watchmaker; they were moving to Bolivia where relatives had sponsored them. The papers had been arranged with the American consulate in Munich. On the papers was his new name: Wilhelm Kurtz. An American escort accompanied them all through the Rat Line, until they went aboard ship. Whenever officials had to be dealt with, it was the American who did the talking. It was an easy trip, without problems of any kind; all of the officials along the line had either been helped in some way by the Americans, or bribed.

So now Houghton had the story. Only it didn't tell him what he needed to know. From an intelligence point of view, it was ancient history. How, if at all, did it connect to *now?* And to Virgil Craig? He knew the answer was there somewhere. It had only to be reasoned out.

When the answer finally came—a theoretical answer, until checked out—it was as much a product of hunch as it was of reason.

Late Friday evening, several hours after his last guest had left, Houghton made a call to Annapolis, Maryland, to a man named Dick Sexton, who during the late 1950s had run a small airline called Air Congo. It was supposedly a privately owned company; in reality it was financed and staffed by the CIA to facilitate its work. In particular, the CIA was eager that the rule of Patrice Lumumba, premier of the Republic of the Congo, be a short one. It was. Lumumba was assassinated in 1961. Sexton had been the general manager of Air Congo throughout that operation. He had remained with the agency for another ten years, always dealing in African affairs. Then he had taken early retirement to do the same work on a free-lance basis. His clients were governments, corporations, and even the CIA itself—whoever needed a job done through unofficial channels. Two years ago, Sexton had returned to the United States for good and settled in Annapolis, where he ran a boatyard. En route, he'd called on Houghton to pay respects, express thanks for the business, and assure the deputy director that he was always available for a special assignment if the need arose.

"Dick, we're getting ready to move into Latin America in a very big way," Houghton said on the telephone.

"Check."

"We're going to be needing a lot of help very soon. The kind you were able to provide as an independent contractor in Africa."

"Check."

"I was hoping you might be able to recommend someone."

"Check. The guy you want is Virgil Craig."

24

They were two hours out of London in the middle of a sumptuous dinner in the first-class section of a Varig Airlines 747, when Meredith said to André, "The only question I have, other than what am I doing here, is how you're going to get this Hoepner man to see you?"

André smiled. "First, I'm going to find someone who knows him very well. Then I'm going to tell this gentleman to whisper two magic words to Hoepner."

"The two words being?"

"Camille Laurent."

"Why should that open any doors? Their last contact was forty years ago."

"True. But whether Laurent wins the presidency is literally a life and death matter to Hoepner." André tapped the file on Hoepner sent him by New York, which he'd finished reading just before dinner. It lay now on the armrest between them. "However Hoepner got to Bolivia, the French found out he was there. They've been trying ever since to get the Bolivians to repatriate him. As long as Bolivia was ruled by dictators, there wasn't a chance. But a few years

ago a political upheaval began, and when the dust settled a
relatively progressive regime was in office. Since then, the
French have been pressing, and there's some indication the
Bolivians might cooperate, even though Hoepner's now a
Bolivian citizen. But if Laurent's elected, you can bet that
the repatriation demand will be quietly dropped."

"Ah."

"So Hoepner will see me because he'll understand at once
what I know and he'll want to know what I intend to do."

"Hey, wait a minute," Meredith said. She looked at André carefully. "This could be dangerous."

André finished his wine. "I intend to tell Hoepner right
off that if anything happens to me it will signal New York to
break the entire story. I also intend to tell the Bolivian police that I'm here—they'll know that anyway, once we register at the hotel—and tell them who I'm going to see."

"A lot of good that will do you if Hoepner kills you."

André squeezed Meredith's hand. "I'm not a hero. I
won't take needless chances."

She studied him for a moment. "Aren't you afraid?"

"Not now. At the appropriate moment, I'll be terrified."
He squeezed her hand again. "Let's not worry about it now.
Let's talk about that other question of yours."

"Well, what *am* I doing here?"

"You don't know?"

"I thought I had it all figured out this morning. Talking
last night finally awakened me to a few realities about this
relationship."

"Such as?"

"Such as you're a famous man with a fixed position in
Europe. I'm a fledgling art dealer trying to breathe life into
a gallery in New York. That doesn't make for a great future."

"You could open a gallery in Paris."

"Not bloody likely. The gallery owners there are well

entrenched. They've got the older artists all sewn up. As to
the younger artists, you were right, their stuff is really second-rate. So there's nothing for me to acquire that I'd really
like to sell."

"What about those Eastern European artists?"

"Very tough. They may be great, but they're all
unknowns. I'd have to create the market. That takes time
and time takes money, and money I haven't got."

"I have money."

Meredith shook her head. "That's the other reality I saw
last night. When I was explaining to you why I was so
excited about what was happening in the States, how
women were going to change the national mentality, I had a
strong feeling that you didn't believe me. I realized then
that you'd been away during a period of profound change
and that maybe you don't really understand what American
women like me are about. What we want is our own identi-
ties."

"I understand that."

"But do you *feel* it? Do you *want* it?"

A stewardess was coming along the aisle, offering more
wine. She was so stunning that they stopped talking to
watch her—a lush, dark-skinned woman with black hair
and brown eyes. As she filled their glasses, she smiled at
André. When she had moved on, Meredith said, "See, *that's*
your image of woman . . ."

"Not fair."

"Okay. It's the image of your generation."

"And *that's* not kind."

She squeezed his arm and that same feeling shot through
him, the one he'd felt when she'd touched him their first
night together. "I didn't mean it the way it sounded. I
promise you that your age and mine have nothing to do
with it. That just doesn't bother me. You're very young in
your ways, and you look young, too. You could use a few

good workouts, but that's something we can fix. What I'm talking about is what's up here." She touched his head. "Twenty and thirty years ago women didn't think like we do today. They might have wanted what we want, but they didn't know how to go about it or even talk about it. I'm sure without even knowing her that your wife was like that."

"My wife wasn't liberated, if that's what you mean."

"Then my point's even stronger. I *am* liberated. Completely. What are you going to do with someone like me? You're not going to compromise. Why should you? You're this famous man who flies all over the world in the front of airplanes. What I'm saying is that you and I are worlds apart—and that's what finally hit me last night and this morning."

"I knew that something had happened."

"So what am I doing on this airplane?"

André leaned over and kissed her. "You're flying down to Rio. So why not relax and enjoy it?"

He turned back to his food then, but his appetite was gone. He hadn't answered her question, and he wasn't sure he could.

They landed in Rio at 6:45 A.M., ten minutes ahead of schedule. The cool air surprised them, until they realized that they had crossed not simply an ocean but the equator as well. It was early May, and winter was approaching.

It was four hours earlier in Rio than in London, which meant that they had traveled for thirteen hours. "My body doesn't know where I am," Meredith said. She regarded André. "On the other hand, you look like you spent the night in your own bed." In truth, he did. His narcotic—motion—had produced its usual adrenalizing effect. In addition, he had shaved and changed his shirt, a ritual on long trips. Whatever problems existed for him personally had been repressed by his anticipation of the denouement to what, by any measure, had been the toughest story of his career.

At 9:15 A.M. they were aboard Cruzeiro Airlines. Six hours later, they were over La Paz. The city seemed to have been scooped out of the surrounding mountains, with buildings as far as the eye could see in neat and precise patterns, reaching from the altiplano into the canyons. Above the canyons and below the snowcapped peaks the beige earth, cracked and hollowed, looked like the surface of the moon. The sky was a vivid blue, the light intense and clarifying. Here and there the clouds cast purplish shadows on the city and surrounding mountains, dominated by Mt. Illimani, which hovered over the city like a giant snowbird.

The research packet André had received from the network had advised him that at fourteen thousand feet El Alto Airport was the highest commercial landing field in the world. "Take it easy," he said to Meredith as they stepped from the plane onto the field and began the walk to the terminal, a one-story building with a tower. His carry-on bag felt like a suitcase. His head began to pound, and he found it difficult to breathe. He looked at Meredith, who smiled. "Oxygen deficit," she said. "It doesn't exactly make you feel like jogging, does it?"

The research packet had also included a warning to André that if he didn't want company in his taxi on the ride in from the airport, he would have to so specify. He did and they were soon on their way. Descending from the airport, they seemed to be entering a vast amphitheater with high rises at its center and adobe houses on steep tiers carved out of the mountain sides. There were silver flashes from the tin roofs and orange flashes from the tiled ones. Clumps of tall, straight trees reached upward, their foliage like thin elongated fans. Every few hundred yards they passed Indian women making the descent into the city, leading packs of llamas burdened with bundles secured with ropes. Some of the women had infants wrapped in rebozos tied to their backs. A coat of dust covered the city, but the streets, maintained by men with short brooms that required them to stoop, were clean. In a few minutes they were at their hotel, the Crillón, on the Plaza Isabel la Católica. A young assistant manager escorted them to a suite overlooking the plaza. Five minutes later they were asleep. When they awakened, it was 10 P.M., but neither of them felt like eating. They slept fitfully through the night, still bothered by the altitude. In the morning, Meredith complained of tunnel vision and André found it hard to move.

At 9 A.M., just as he was about to leave to call on the police, the telephone rang. They looked at one another, perplexed. André answered. "Here is Hoepner," a voice said in German-accented English. "I understand you want to see me."

There were so many questions they collided with one another in his mind. Who had told Hoepner that André was coming to La Paz? Who *knew* that he was coming? How had they figured it out? And how had Hoepner known that he had arrived and where he was staying?

The last question was the easiest. Either the immigration service or the police had notified Hoepner of André's arrival. The police, with their passport control, would have known at which hotel he had registered. This told André that Hoepner was well connected and that there was no point in his going to the police.

As to his coming to La Paz, since no one but the network knew his plans, that had to have been figured out by deduction. If he wasn't in France working on the story, there was a strong possibility that he was following the story to its conclusion. But to deduce that he had come to La Paz required the knowledge that Hoepner was involved. Who knew that beside the CIA and the KGB? It had to be the DGSE. But would the DGSE alert Hoepner? Never, no more than the CIA or KGB. So the only possibility was that someone *within* the DGSE who was sympathetic to Laurent had informed the general. Because the only person who could have conceivably alerted Fritz Hoepner was Camille Laurent.

So they knew what he had. How they had learned about it he would probably never know. All that mattered was that they knew it. And they were prepared to deal with it. André hadn't needed to do a thing; Hoepner had come to him. He had even used his given name, rather than his adopted one. And he wanted to see André—for lunch at his club, the Club La Paz, today. "Ask for Señor Kurtz," he said. "That is how they know me."

"Be careful," Meredith said at one o'clock as he was going out the door.

"There's nothing to worry about," he said. "If Hoepner intended to engage in hanky-panky, he would have set up something with blindfolds and switching cars to be sure they weren't being followed on the way to some hideaway. I'm just walking to a club for lunch."

"When will you be back?"

"Four-thirty. Maybe five."

"If you're not back by five, I'm calling the American Embassy."

He turned back and went to her and took her head in his hands and looked into her eyes. "You still don't understand what you're doing here?"

"I'm afraid I'm beginning to."

"Why 'afraid?' "

She was silent for a moment. "You don't need to clutter your mind with that kind of stuff. We can talk about it tonight. Now go on. The sooner you leave, the sooner you'll be back."

"Will you think about something while I'm gone?"

"What's that?"

"Think about the fact that I love you."

He kissed her lightly and left.

The dining room of the Club La Paz was yet another attempt at art deco, the walls mirrored, the furniture done with chrome. Hoepner stood when André reached his table, but he did not put out his hand. André was grateful for that. The German, short and heavy, indicated the seat he wished André to take. The maître d'hôtel immediately pulled it out. André sat, grateful, too, for this moment in which to compose himself. His heart was beating rapidly, the altitude reinforcing his anxiety. Throughout his walk to the club, he had wondered what his reaction would be to sitting at the same table with a mass murderer. If he had had a choice, he wouldn't have done it. But Hoepner was directing the encounter.

He didn't want to look at the man he had come to see. In the hours between Hoepner's call and the luncheon, André had read through the file again. He had always tried to keep an open mind about the people he interviewed, but in this case it was impossible. The evidence was too conclusive. Thousands of persons had attested to the bestiality of the Executioner of Clermont-Ferrand.

Finally, André had to look. If he had not known the man and someone had pointed him out as a kindly grandfather, he would have accepted the description. He was at least seventy and looked it. No older, no younger. His hair was very thin on top. He had the sad look of a bassett hound, the eyes pinched together in a perpetual frown.

"Would you like a drink?" Hoepner said. "They make all the American drinks. Or perhaps a rum sour? Or a beer? The local beer is Paceña. Very good."

He was desperate for a drink. "No thank you," he said. "I'll pass."

Hoepner nodded. "Do you speak Spanish?"

"No."

"Then let me order for you. What do you like? The food is excellent."

André had been prepared for anything except this: the man was charming. He could not have been more gracious. He was looking solicitously at his guest, waiting for an answer. "Something light," André said. "Perhaps an omelette."

"Very wise," Hoepner said. "At this altitude, it's best not to eat heavily until you have become acclimatized."

Hoepner summoned the headwaiter and gave his order in Spanish. It was more than just an order; it was a set of instructions, complete with gestures as to how whatever he had ordered was to be prepared. He could have done the same in English; his was accented, but otherwise excellent.

"So," he said, turning back to André, "judging by your name, you are the son of a French mother and German father. Am I correct?"

"You are," André said, realizing with shock that if Hoepner hadn't been who he was he actually would have liked him. What he said next wasn't prudent in terms of what he had come to do, but he couldn't help himself. "My father was a Jew."

Hoepner inclined his head in André's direction, a small bow to his point. "And you?" he asked.

"I was raised in my mother's faith. She is Catholic."

"In German we would call you a *Mischling*. But perhaps you speak German?"

"Your English is as good as my German."

Hoepner bowed his head again. "Now, would you like to tell me why you came all this way to see me?"

"Perhaps you would tell me first how you knew I was coming and when I had arrived."

For the first time since André had joined him, the German smiled. It was a sly and devilish smile, complete with a dimple in his right cheek. His teeth were white and even and had obviously been well cared for. "The second part is easier than the first. This is a hardworking but poor society. Almost everyone must have a second job to survive. There are men in special places who help me to be informed, shall we say, about what I need to know. As to the first part, I can only tell you that I had heard you might be on your way."

"There's only one man in the world who could have told you."

Hoepner shrugged. "You may believe as you wish." He turned his head. "Ah! Here is our first course. Have you ever eaten sea urchins?"

The waiter set them down, round spiky shells with holes in the middle, inside of which was a pink, gelatinous meat.

"They taste better than they look," Hoepner said with a laugh. "And they're quite fresh—flown in daily from Lima."

He attacked his portion with relish. André hesitated. He did not wish to eat with this man, let alone sit at his table, but he had no other choice. It wouldn't be the first time he had acted a role contrary to his feelings in order to get a story. With great reluctance, André extracted the meat of the sea urchin from its shell and put it into his mouth. It tasted surprisingly good, like a mild, fine-textured caviar.

When they had finished and the plates were cleared, Hoepner said, "Now, perhaps you can answer my question."

"I believe you know the answer."

Once again, Hoepner bowed. "Yes. Of course. Do you

think a discussion between us would be at all profitable, or have you already made up your mind?"

"I'm always willing to listen."

The waiter brought their main courses. "Wild boar, with a special sauce: green peppercorns, cream, mustard, and just a touch of sugar," Hoepner explained. He began to eat with gusto, his meal accompanied by a Paceña beer. André picked at his omelette, simply for appearances, so that the sight of an untouched plate wouldn't cause Hoepner to break the flow of his talk.

Hoepner did not speak of atrocities. He spoke of a war and actions to win the war, of French provocations, the murder of German soldiers, acts of sabotage, all of them requiring a response. An eye for an eye, he said. Surely you're familiar with that? Yes, there had been killings, but only as reprisals. If only the French had understood the real menace, not the Germans but the Russians. "We should have all joined forces—the Germans, the Americans, the French, the British—and turned on the Russians. What a different world we would live in today."

There was a silence when he finished, and André realized that the German was waiting for him to speak. Nothing he could say would in any way approve of this man or his version of history. The moment he'd both anticipated for so long and dreaded so greatly had arrived. From the wallet pocket of his blazer he drew out a piece of paper, unfolded it and showed it to Hoepner. It was a copy of the memorandum Hoepner had written to his superiors about Camille Laurent. "Do you recognize this memo?" he asked.

"Yes. It's mine. I wrote it. It was imperative that the occupation forces be informed so that Laurent would be dealt with appropriately in his work, or in the event he was captured."

For a moment, Hoepner, the table, the room, even the noise, all seemed to spin out of focus. The Executioner of

Clermont-Ferrand had just confirmed that the dossier was real. Camille Laurent, the Resistance hero, the respected general, the favorite to win the French presidential election five days hence, *had* been a traitor to his country during World War II.

In more than thirty-five years in journalism, there was, for André, no moment that remotely compared with this one. It had been, far and away, the toughest assignment of his career, covering three continents and thousands of miles, accomplished at great speed, utilizing sources with access to the highest level of governments, all in behalf of a story that was, quite simply, a sensation. And now, at last, he had it. There was just one more step, the payoff: broadcasting the story. He was quivering with eagerness to do that and desperate to leave this man, this butcher. "Thank you," he said, folding up the paper. He began to rise.

"Just a moment," Hoepner said, reaching out his hand. He grabbed André by the arm and pushed him back into his seat. André shuddered involuntarily. Hoepner smiled. "So, now you will go back to France and broadcast your story?"

"I would think so."

"Mr. Kohl, perhaps you have wondered why I have spoken to you so freely."

"Yes, I have."

"I have two very good reasons. The first is that I hoped, by my candor, to persuade you that it was in your interest, as a patriotic American, to pursue a different course from the one you intend. Yes, of course, Laurent worked for me, but you must understand to what end. He and I shared one single objective: to defeat the Communist menace. Laurent saw that the Communists were taking over the Resistance. He believed that they would translate their wartime preeminence into postwar preeminence. He couldn't stop them alone; he needed my help. And I needed his. Together, we were able to accomplish many things that we might never have achieved independently."

A waiter put a cup of espresso in front of Hoepner and another in front of André. Hoepner put a lump of sugar into his cup, stirred it methodically, and then sipped his coffee. André didn't touch his.

Once again, Hoepner looked at André. "Let us admit for the sake of argument that the Camille Laurent of forty years ago was technically guilty of treason. My own belief is that he was a great, farseeing patriot who was attempting to save his country from eventual enslavement by the Communists. That postwar events did not transpire exactly as Laurent foresaw them in no way diminishes the long-term validity of his vision. Today, the danger is far greater than it was forty years ago, because the consequences of Communist domination are so much more dire. Camille Laurent can arrest that danger. He is the only Frenchman who can. Are you, Mr. Kohl, all by yourself, willing to make it impossible for him to do that? Is what a man did forty years ago, good or bad, as important as the great good he can accomplish today? Are you, Mr. Kohl, willing to assume responsibility for the calamitous series of events that will surely follow the defeat of Camille Laurent?"

For a moment, André was speechless. He was being lectured on responsibility and morality by a butcher of human beings. More, he was being given a guided tour of a spiritual wasteland by one of its principal inhabitants. It was a wasteland that resembled a battleground over which men of indestructible certitude had marched for centuries, believing that their vision must prevail at whatever cost to humanity. The wreckage of this vision was strewn across the landscape. Kaiser Wilhelm had said that those who did not wish peace must be destroyed, and he had attempted to destroy them. An American army lieutenant had said that a Vietnam village had to be destroyed in order to be saved, and he had destroyed it. What would Camille Laurent do to "save" France—employ the techniques he had learned from the Executioner of Clermont-Ferrand?

None of this could André say to Hoepner. He knew it would do no good. All of the training he had brought to this moment told him he must guard his rage and answer the German with great care. "I don't agree with your analysis of the condition of France or of its future with or without Camille Laurent," he said. "I *have,* however, asked myself questions about my responsibility in this matter. And my responsibility—my obligation—as I understand it is to report the facts, and let the people decide what to do."

"The 'facts,' as you call them, initially came from the Russians, isn't *that* a fact?"

"I won't comment on that."

"You don't have to. We know all about it."

A sliver of fear pierced André's heart. Suddenly, Hoepner's voice and manner had changed. The change was almost imperceptible, yet it was there, iron in the voice, ice in his eyes. "Does it mean nothing to you, Mr. Kohl, that these so-called 'facts' came from the Russians?"

"Facts are facts."

"You fool!"

For just a second, André caught a glimpse of the man he had read about. There was a flash of rage in his face and a readiness to kill. And then, just as suddenly, the rage was gone, and Hoepner was once again the kindly, grandfatherly host he had been at the outset of their encounter.

He sighed and spoke with seeming regret. "Now, unfortunately, I must tell you the second reason why I have spoken to you so frankly. It's because I know you will never broadcast your story."

"Is that a fact?" André said, trying to keep his voice steady. His body was shaking.

"Yes, it is a fact, because I believe you to be a sensible

man. And a sensible man would not sacrifice the woman he loves for the sake of a cheap story."

"What?" André rose from his chair and started for Hoepner.

"Sit down, Mr. Kohl," Hoepner said. "There is a man within twenty feet of me who will kill you if you touch me."

André sat, mouth open, eyes wide, waiting helplessly for the blow he knew was coming.

"Half an hour ago, this gentleman signaled me that a program we had arranged for Miss Houghton had been successfully accomplished. She is now in our custody."

André rose again and started for the door.

"Listen carefully," Hoepner said, in a voice that made André freeze. "If you wish to see her alive again, you will not broadcast your story or give it to some other information outlet. Nor will you broadcast the story of Miss Houghton's abduction—or, for that matter, discuss it with the Bolivian police. If you go to the police, I beg you to believe that I will know of it within fifteen minutes. If you do as I say, Miss Houghton will be released after the French election. If you then broadcast your story, I will find her and kill her, no matter where she is."

A scream of despair issued from André. He raced through the dining room toward the exit, past startled Paceño gentry. In a moment, he was in the street, running to the hotel. His heart was pounding and his lungs were on fire. The sounds from his throat were like a death rattle as he gasped fruitlessly to draw enough oxygen out of the rarefied air. He welcomed the pain as expiation, but he knew that even if he were to drop dead in his tracks it would not make up for the terrible thing he had done. Meredith was in mortal danger and all on his account. Worse yet, he didn't know how to help her. He was an amateur, a bungler, a child in a grownup's game. He had never known such people and hadn't the least idea how to deal with them. He had never felt more helpless. He was in a strange country, didn't speak the language, knew absolutely no one, and didn't dare go to the police.

The hotel was in sight now. He was lurching instead of running, the forward thrust of each leg keeping him from falling, his gasps so loud they were the only sound in his ears. Pedestrians made a path for him and gazed at him in concern and wonder, as if to say that a man of his age had to be crazy to exert himself like that. He was crazy, out of his head, not only to be racing his body, but to hope that Hoepner's story had been a bluff or a ruse, and that Meredith would be safe in their room at the hotel.

He rushed into the lobby, got his key, and stumbled to the elevator. He had to brace himself against a wall to keep from falling down. He was heaving so loudly that everyone turned to stare. An assistant manager came rushing over. "Are you all right?" he asked. André had no breath to speak, and there was nothing he might have said, so he simply nodded yes.

At last he was in the elevator, and the elevator was at his floor. He ran down the corridor to his room and flung open the door. "Meredith!" he screamed.

She was gone.

He sank into a chair. "Oh God," he cried, "oh God, oh God, oh God!" It was not simply the anguished entreaty of a totally devastated man. It was a plea for divine guidance from a lifelong professional spectator who had watched thousands of human dramas from a special box, who was suddenly himself the drama, and did not know how to act.

25

A room service table told the story. The lunch Meredith had ordered lay upon it, untouched. Hoepner's men had arrived with it. They had either bribed or terrified the waiter. Then they could had drugged Meredith or taken her at gunpoint down the stairway, or the service elevator.

A new wave of remorse engulfed him. Not only had he left her alone, he hadn't even thought to warn her about the possible danger. She'd warned him, he hadn't warned her.

He sat where he was for another minute, unable to move. Then, at last, he roused himself. As inadequate as he feared it would be, there was one thing he could do. He picked up the telephone. "Do you speak English?" he said when the operator answered.

"Yes, sir."

"Give me the American Embassy." In less than a minute, he had been connected to the ambassador's office. "This is André Kohl of USBC . . ."

"Well! Mr. Kohl! This is Ambassador Curtin's secretary. Welcome to La Paz. We didn't know you were arriving."

"I need to speak to the ambassador. It's an urgent matter."

"I'll see if Ambassador Curtin can speak to you."

Seconds passed. Then Curtin came on the line. "Mr. Kohl," he began, but André cut him off.

"Mr. Ambassador, I need to speak to your station chief on a matter of life and death."

There was the slightest pause. "I'm sorry, Mr. Kohl, I don't quite understand. What station chief?"

"Please, Mr. Ambassador, let's cut the crap. I've got to see the CIA. I'll be there in however long it takes to get from the Hotel Crillón."

He hung up, then jiggled the disconnect button for the operator, and asked for the concierge. "I need a car with an English-speaking driver right away. Can you do it? The name is Kohl."

"Just come down, Mr. Kohl. The car will be at the door."

He raced to the elevator, grateful to be moving. It gave him the feeling that he wasn't entirely helpless. In the lobby, he walked rather than ran, knowing that he had already attracted too much attention, certain that his every movement would be reported back to Hoepner, realizing too late that his calls might be reported as well. Nothing lost yet, he told himself as he sank into the backseat of a gleaming, twenty-year-old Chevrolet. Hoepner would figure that he'd rush to the CIA.

A marine was waiting for him at the door to the embassy. "Mr. Kohl? Follow me, sir." The marine, lean and blond, brass and shoes gleaming, not a wrinkle in his shirt or trousers, led André down a hallway, then up a flight of steps to a door with no name on it. He held open the door. André walked inside. A sixty-year-old man with salt-and-pepper hair as short as the marine's rose from a chair beside a conference table. He wore a white shirt, a black knit tie, and gray trousers. He shook hands with André but did not offer his name. "The Ambassador said you had a problem," he said, resuming his seat and signaling André to sit.

"Are you the station chief?"

"Are you André Kohl? You sure look like him."

André slid his passport across the table. The man in the white shirt looked at it briefly, then slid it back. "Okay," he said, "what's up?"

"Are you the station chief?" André repeated, an edge to his voice.

The man fixed his narrow eyes on André. "Mr. Kohl, I'm not going to tell you a goddam thing until you tell me what this is about."

It took André three minutes to tell the story. The man said nothing throughout. Nor did he display any emotion, not even when André identified Meredith as Charles Houghton's daughter. When André finished, the man said, "If I were you, I'd do exactly what Hoepner told you to do. He's one mean motherfucker."

For a moment, André was without words. Then he said, "Maybe you didn't understand me. This woman is your boss's daughter."

"I understood you perfectly, Mr. Kohl. My advice is still the same. There are half a million structures in La Paz. She could be in any one of them. Hoepner is protected by around-the-clock bodyguards. What the hell do you expect us to do?"

André rose without another word and walked to the door.

"Incidentally, for what it's worth, Charlie Houghton isn't my boss anymore. He was fired two days ago."

He would have traded years of his life to be suddenly awakened and told this had all been a bad dream. However this waking nightmare turned out, he vowed, he would find out why he'd been cold-shouldered by his own embassy. There was no time to think about that now. First, he had to elude his surveillance. Then he had to find help.

In the car, he told his driver to return to the hotel. As they pulled away from the curb, he turned around slowly to see if they were being followed. As he did, a car parked down the block pulled out from the curb and fell in behind theirs.

"What are you going to be doing after you let me off?" he asked the driver.

"I'm going home, sir."

"How would you like to help me solve a little problem?"

Their eyes caught in the rearview mirror. The driver's eyes were clear and steady. God help him if he read too much in another man's eyes, André thought. But the face went with the eyes: young, smooth, composed, a face one could look at with comfort. "Whatever you wish, sir."

"Okay, here's what I wish."

Ten minutes later, the driver let André off at the hotel. He took the elevator to his room, looked up an address in the telephone directory, praying that the classifications and proper nouns in Spanish would be similar to those in French. They were. He copied down the address he needed, then took the elevator to the lobby and walked into the hotel dining room, where high tea was being served. He asked the maître d'hôtel for a table near the kitchen. As soon as he was seated, he looked back to the entrance. No one had followed him. In another second he was through the kitchen door and racing past startled cooks and waiters to the delivery entrance at the rear. Then he was through that door and across a loading pier to the street, where he jumped into his hired car and gave the driver the slip of paper on which he'd written the address. As the car raced away, he looked back. No one was following. Thanks for the inspiration, Gennady, he thought. For the first time in days he wondered about the Russian. If Camille Laurent and whoever was helping him in the DGSE knew that a Gestapo dossier had arrived in France, surely they also knew that a Russian had brought it in. Had they caught him? God help him if they had.

The driver moved skillfully from the downtown area, avoiding the main thoroughfares in favor of small, often hilly and sometimes angled side streets. In ten minutes they were at the Israeli Embassy.

He had to talk his way in, first past the Bolivian soldiers at the gate, then past the Israeli guard at the door. At the gate, his driver interpreted for him. At the door, he made himself understood in German. Once he was with the ambassador, credibility, not language, was the problem. The ambassador spoke perfect English, but he had never served in the States. While he had read André's book on Kennedy, he'd never seen him on television. He was interested but suspicious, until André mentioned Shlomo Glaser. "I beseech you to call him," André said.

"It's the middle of the night in Israel."

"I promise you he won't mind."

The ambassador excused himself. Five minutes later he returned and beckoned André to follow. "He wants to talk to you."

They went down to a basement room and through a thickly padded door. The walls and ceiling were padded, as well. The room was filled with communications gear. The ambassador gestured toward the telephone. André seized it. "Shlomo!" he said.

"My God, André, what are you doing down there?"

"I came to see Hoepner."

"But you told us the story was phony."

"It's *not* phony, Shlomo," André said. He told him as much as he could without giving the story away. And then he explained what had happened in La Paz.

"How can we help?"

"I need to call the States on a secure line."

"That's all?"

"For the moment."

"Let me talk to the ambassador."

André gave the telephone to the ambassador. As the ambassador talked with Shlomo in Hebrew, André realized that he hadn't even asked his name. Ambassador what? It was Eshel, the ambassador said when he was off the line. "We are at your disposal."

"I'll need to make some calls," André said. His first call was to Saul Geffin at USBC in New York to get Houghton's number. "Don't ask, Saul," he said when Geffin pressed him for details.

The next call was the hardest André had ever had to make. He had to tell a father that his daughter had been kidnapped—and all on his, André's, account.

Mercifully, Houghton did not lose his poise. When he spoke his voice was calm. "I wish I had known she was going," he said. "I could have predicted this would happen."

"I don't understand," André said.

"There are things you don't know about. There are things *I* still don't know about. I'll explain what I can when I see you."

"You're coming?"

"Of course." Houghton paused. "Do you happen to know if you were followed to the Israeli Embassy?"

"I'm quite sure I wasn't."

"How did you arrive?"

"With a car and driver."

"Then I'd advise you to give your driver enough money to take a brief vacation."

"That's already been taken care of. He's on his way to Lake Titicaca."

"Do you think you could stay where you are until I get there."

"I believe so."

"Good. While you're waiting, see what the Israelis have on Hoepner. It should be substantial. We'll need a thorough plan of his domicile, as well as a list of people who work for him, their hours, and any special habits. The most important information we'll need is on Hoepner himself; where he goes each day, how he gets there, who guards him, and so on. Now, most important, no matter how desperate you get, don't contact the police. You have to believe that Hoepner will do what he says he will . . ."

"Do you believe he'll release Meredith after the French election if I haven't broadcast the story?"

"I wouldn't want to count on it."

André shivered. "Anything else?" he said.

"Yes. Don't talk to anyone at the American Embassy again, not even if they call you and offer help. Do you understand?"

"What the hell's going on?"

"I can't tell you now. I'll contact you tomorrow."

André hung up reluctantly, feeling that he was surrendering his hold on the only hope he had.

In Washington less than a minute later, Charles Houghton dialed Dick Sexton in Annapolis. "I have a sudden, desperate craving for hard-shell crab," he said.

Sexton hesitated for only a fraction of a second. Then he gave Houghton the address of a restaurant near his boatyard. An hour later a taxi delivered Houghton there. It was on the water, a home that had become a restaurant, its rooms decorated with the paraphernalia of the sea—lines and buoys and steering wheels and compasses. The smell of seafood had seeped into its walls.

They drank dry martinis. "Still interested in work?" Houghton asked Sexton after his third swallow.

"You bet."

"I haven't the vaguest idea how we're going to do this, but the first step is to assemble the right people and equipment and get ourselves to La Paz."

Sexton drew back and regarded Houghton through suddenly narrowed eyes. "La Paz? That's Virgil Craig's home away from home. Why didn't you call him?"

"Because I'm almost positive he's part of the problem, Dick," Houghton said. He watched Sexton closely for a reaction. It was one of simple and genuine surprise.

"May I know more?"

"When I know more. In the meanwhile, do you know anyone who's had experience in Bolivia?"

A waitress came to take their order. She exuded good cheer, smiled and spoke with a rich, Deep South drawl. Sexton looked questioningly at Houghton. "We'd better eat," Houghton said. "I don't know when we'll get our next meal."

They ordered sautéed crab because it could be eaten more quickly than hard-shells. "Y'all want another drink?" the waitress asked.

Once again, Sexton looked at Houghton. "How soon do you want to leave?"

"As soon as we can."

"Tonight?"

"I hope so."

Sexton turned to the waitress. "We'll pass," he said. He was silent for a moment. "Okay, I've got just the guy. He was the station chief in La Paz fifteen years ago, but it can't have changed that much. Now if you can tell me just a little bit about the nature of the problem, it will help me figure out the kind of people and equipment we're going to need."

"Okay. First, we have to get into Bolivia undetected."

"Check."

"Then we have to capture a man who's probably well guarded."

"Check."

"Then we have to make him release a woman he's holding prisoner."

"Check."

"And, finally, if necessary, we're going to have to threaten to fly him out of Bolivia."

"Check. One question you'll have to answer: is the Company picking up the tab?"

"Why do you ask?"

"Because a little birdie told me you've just been fired."

Houghton nodded. "Okay, you deserve to know. Yes, I've been fired and, no, the Company's not paying for the trip. I am."

Sexton frowned. "This could cost a hundred grand. Do you have that kind of money?"

"I have whatever it takes." Before Sexton could speak again, Houghton added: "The hostage is my daughter."

Sexton whistled and stared at Houghton in astonishment. "I'm a son of a bitch," he said. "You're going to explain that to me when we're airborne?"

"Absolutely."

"Then let's get going. Incidentally—my part's on the house."

26

Patience, patience, Pierre Gauthier, the hulking third in command of the French secret service, had counseled himself ever since Camille Laurent had received the first warning from Virgil Craig. Sooner or later, the trail will open up. Sooner or later, the target will be in the sights. But counsel patience to Camille Laurent! The man had been possessed from the first moment. Could he blame him? So close to the presidency, only to have a campaign carefully orchestrated over a lifetime ruined by a forty-year-old secret. It had to be some secret, to judge by the man's reaction, once they had learned of the Gestapo file and its presence in France: "Get that dossier, no matter how, and bring it here! And you are on your honor not to read it. I am sure it's a pack of lies." How would the general know that? And could he *really* expect the man who would be his intelligence chief not to establish what was in the document if and when it fell into their hands? Not realistic, not at all.

Soon they would both be satisfied, Gauthier reflected with satisfaction as he sat in his musty office at *La Piscine*. Because at last the trail had opened up and the target was coming into range. For this, Laurent had Gauthier's patience to thank. Despite all the signs that every clue in Clermont-Ferrand had been uncovered and there was nothing of value left, Gauthier had kept a man in the city, sifting, sifting, and last night—how appropriate—whom does he turn up but a baker, a baker who had served with Laurent in the Resistance and who was a member of the Communist Party *and* who had seen the American, Kohl. The baker was brave but he was old and he'd been broken overnight.

So then they had a telephone number, which in moments translated to a name and an address. Avenue Foch: how quaint! And now, with just a little more patience, the target would be in the sights.

You've really mucked this one up, old man, Gennady Gondrachov told himself as he walked the streets of Paris. He'd left Paulette's apartment at dawn because he couldn't stand being cooped up any longer. Seven days now since André had fled and not a clue as to where he'd gone. Far, far worse, no story, not a breath of one, provoking long harangues from Moscow, passed to him, via Paulette, by agents from the Paris *rezidentura*. Do something! That was what they boiled down to. Do what? All of the reasons for taking the direction he had were no less credible today, four days before the election, than they were four weeks ago when the plan had been set in motion. It had been an excellent plan. It should have worked. It could still work. If only André would materialize!

He had walked for more than two hours, through this most beautiful of cities, first over to Trocadéro, then down the long steps behind the Palais de Chaillot, then across the Seine in the shadow of the Eiffel Tower, then along the Left Bank to Boulevard St. Germain, then to the Rue des Saints Pères and up that narrow street to pause for a moment in front of the Hôtel du Pas de Calais, where he had had his first-ever dalliance with a Frenchwoman, God, so many years ago. Then a few blocks further until he had reached his destination, Poilain, the bakery with the best croissants and *tartes aux pommes* in Paris. He intended to buy some of both. He stood in the line that had formed outside the bakery, inhaling the devastating scents, his stomach in turmoil, as much, he judged, from the strain of all the waiting he had done as from the anticipation of the food. When he had been served, he cradled his package in his arm and reached in for an apple tart. It was gone by the time he reached the taxi stand on Boulevard Raspail.

In the taxi, he gave the driver the address on Avenue Foch and then offered him a tart.

"Ah no, sir, it's too early for a dessert," the driver said with a laugh.

"Then have a croissant," Gondrachov said, handing one to him.

The driver smiled, shrugged, took the croissant and ate it.

They were a block away when Gondrachov saw the stakeout.

"Don't turn," he said, "go straight."

He sank back in the seat, covering his face with a hand. A block farther on he had the driver turn left and then left again and left a third time onto Avenue Foch. By the time they had gone a hundred yards past Paulette's building, he had counted five more stakeouts. "Gare Montparnasse," he said to the driver.

"Yes, sir. By the time we get you to your destination it may be time for dessert," the driver said, again laughing at his own joke.

The driver let him off at the main entrance to the station on the Place Raoul Dautry. He climbed the center stairs to the first level and then took another staircase to the arrival area for the Grandes Lignes, where he stood as though waiting for a train, meanwhile checking the giant board over the

tracks that listed all arrivals and departures. There was a
train for Dreux leaving at 9:26 A.M., fifteen minutes from
now. It would stop in Montfort L'Amaury thirty-five minutes later. From Montfort L'Amaury it was a twenty-min-
ute taxicab ride to a farm that had served the *rezidentura* in
Paris as a safe house for as long as Gondrachov could remember. He had been given the key while on a job in Paris
years before and had carried it on his key chain ever since, a
memento of all his fond memories of France.

The ticket he bought was to Dreux. An extra precaution,
on the remote chance that the vendor would be questioned
later. Then he went to a telephone and dialed Paulette's
number.

"Allo, yes?" she answered.

"I would like to speak to Boris."

"This is Boris," she said.

He hung up at once. So the DGSE had found her. Even if
she had answered correctly—"Boris is not here. I take messages for Boris"—he would have known by the strain in her
voice. Poor Paulette. Her life would not end well. But she
had lived it according to her choice.

It was then that his eye caught that of a man standing at
a bar near the entrance to the tracks. The man looked away
quickly and in that second Gondrachov turned and broke
for the nearest staircase. He was incredibly quick for his age
and agile as well, taking the stairs three at a time. He didn't
look back to see if the man had followed, but from the way
people were looking at him and then behind him he deduced
that he had. At the street level he took yet another stairway
leading to the Galerie de la Gare, a clutter of stores below
ground. He passed a food shop and then a clothing shop
and then went through a series of unmarked doors that took
him to another hallway. Ahead were three other doors. He
took the one on the right and found himself in an underground garage. There was a door at the far end. He ran for

it and went through it to the basement floor of an office building adjoining the station. On the left was a short flight of stairs leading to the street. His breath was labored, but his adrenaline kept him going and he took the steps two at a time. On the street, he turned right into another parking lot. At the rear was an elevator and an escalator and a sign that said Accés à la Gare. He took the escalator to the second level, stopped at the entrance to the main hall and studied the crowd for a minute. If his pursuer was there, he couldn't spot him. Nothing ventured, nothing gained, he told himself. He stepped into the main hall and then turned left to the tracks. The train to Dreux was on Track 15. He walked through the automatic turnstile, validating his ticket in the process. Twenty seconds after he boarded, the train began to move. He sat in the nonsmoking section of the second car, trying to catch his breath, wiping his brow with a handkerchief. Only then did he realize that he was still clutching the bag from the bakery.

No one followed him from the station at Montfort L'Amaury and no cars were parked anywhere near the safe house. He dismissed his taxi at the driveway to another house, waited until the taxi was out of sight, and then walked back to the safe house. Still no cars and no sign of life. He advanced cautiously nonetheless, stopping at the French windows to peer into the living room. The couches and chairs were covered with sheets. He let himself in, walked into the living room, and pulled the sheet from the couch nearest the fireplace, where he had begun so many pleasurable bouts of love and sank gratefully onto it.

"Colonel Gondrachov," a voice behind him said. "What a pleasure. I am Gauthier of the DGSE."

Gondrachov turned. With Gauthier were three other men.

At some point during the next hours, before he passed out, Gondrachov managed to say to Gauthier through battered lips, "Is this how you got the woman to tell you where I was?"

"You misjudge us," Gauthier said. "First, that we would disfigure such a beautiful woman and, second, that we would have needed her to determine where you were. We have known about this house for a very long time, but until this moment it has been in our interest to let your people enjoy it. I'm sure you know what I mean. As to you, once you were sighted at the Gare Montparnasse we were certain that this was where you were coming." Gauthier paused. "Now, before these gentlemen begin again, let me repeat my offer: tell me where the dossier is and you can be in Moscow tomorrow."

"I don't know what you're talking about," Gondrachov said. "I've told you. What you're doing doesn't change that."

Gauthier shook his head and motioned his men forward. From the looks on their faces, Gondrachov could see that they were reluctant to resume. He had earned their respect. To his great surprise, he had even earned his own.

27

From the moment he finished talking to Charles Houghton, André had turned to his task with a degree of ferocity never before applied to a reporting assignment. He was absolutely certain that Meredith's life—and, for all he knew, his own—depended on the diligence and accuracy with which he collected information on the life and habits of Kurt Hoepner.

"Don't you want to rest before we start?" Eshel, the Israeli ambassador, asked, frowning at André. "The altitude . . ."

"I couldn't rest," André said quickly. "I'm too upset." Yet it was obvious from the concern with which Eshel regarded him that he looked as bad as he felt. He knew that his pulse was racing, as though he had drunk a dozen cups of coffee. He could feel the tremors coursing through his body and, although he'd had nothing to drink, his head throbbed with the equivalent of a massive hangover. "I'd really like to get started as quickly as we can."

"Very well," Eshel said. He picked up the telephone, dialed a number, and spoke rapidly and briefly in Hebrew.

Then he led André back to his office, a modest room in the rear of the building looking onto a garden. "I'll only be a moment," he said. Before André had had time to do more than look at what he imagined were pictures of Eshel's grandchildren, the ambassador had returned. With him was a man of thirty, a cut-down, younger version of Shlomo, with the same big shoulders and muscular arms, the same paradoxically gentle expression on his face. André was certain the man was the Israeli equivalent of the station chief.

"This is Aryea," Eshel said. "He'll tell you what we know."

They knew a great deal, it developed.

The year before, they had recruited Hoepner's maid and paid her a retainer in exchange for information on what happened inside the house. The maid was uneducated but bright. She needed the extra money for her husband, who had a dependency on cocaine. Not only had she given them details on the house, but they had a schedule of all regular deliveries and Hoepner's unlisted telephone number. There were two bodyguards and a third man who spelled one or the other on their days off. One bodyguard always accompanied Hoepner wherever he went, doubling as a chauffeur; the other remained in the house. Both slept there, but not simultaneously. One man was awake and on sentry duty at all times.

Hoepner traveled a great deal, as much as six months of every year, but when he was in La Paz his schedule was absolutely rigid. Whatever his business was, he conducted it from his home every workday from nine until one-thirty. Then he went to the Club La Paz for lunch. He almost always had a guest. After lunch, which could end as late as 4 P.M., he might play cards at the club or call on business associates. Twice a week he visited a young woman he kept in an apartment near the center of town. Every night at eight-thirty he returned to his home, a small villa in

Calacoto surrounded by a fence, drank sherry for an hour with his wife, and then sat down to dinner. After dinner he watched television until midnight, long after his wife had gone to bed. They slept in separate rooms. On the weekends, Hoepner took walks, read, watched more television, and attended sporting events. He was a maniac about soccer, taking both his bodyguards to every Sunday game.

Hoepner had one other passion: he was a collector of antiques. A new piece arrived at the house at least once a month, the maid reported. Sometimes she wondered where her employer would fit it.

The information seemed ample, but André listened to Aryea with a mounting sense of panic. Either he wasn't processing the information well or else something was missing. Was the oxygen deficit compromising his brainpower? Was he simply overwrought and fatigued? Whatever the reason, his reportorial instincts told him that he didn't have everything he needed. "Is that all?" he asked.

"Yes," Aryea said.

His answer was half a second late, but that pause was all André needed to know that they were holding back. He looked quickly at Eshel, a challenge in his eyes.

"It's all we can tell you," Eshel said quietly.

It was then André knew what it was he didn't know. What did Hoepner *do?* How did he make his living? What was the nature of the business he conducted from his home each day? What kinds of discussions did he have with his business associates in La Paz? To what end was he away from La Paz six months of every year? It seemed inconceivable that the Israelis wouldn't know the answers. "You haven't said a word about how Hoepner supports himself," he said to Eshel.

"That information has no bearing on the rescue of Miss Houghton," Eshel said.

Anger stirred in André. He knew there had to be a reason

why the Israelis were holding back. He knew they were trying to help him to the extent they could. It didn't matter. Nothing mattered but knowing everything he possibly could about Kurt Hoepner. "I would rather you not be the judge of what has bearing and doesn't have bearing," he said, controlling himself with an effort.

"I am sorry," Eshel said. "I won't lie to you—and I can't tell you the truth."

"Why not?"

"Because I'm under orders not to."

"Then I'd like to call Shlomo again."

Eshel smiled forlornly, obviously full of sympathy for André. "I don't believe that will help you," he said.

"Why not?"

"Because it was Shlomo who gave the orders."

André closed his eyes and willed himself to stay calm. He knew that if he exploded his cause would be lost. When he opened his eyes, he looked pleadingly at Eshel. "I'd like to try," he said.

"Of course," Eshel said. He rose, beckoned to André and led him back to the communications room in the basement.

They did not connect with Shlomo right away. It was now early morning in Israel, and he had already left for his office, but hadn't yet arrived. Eshel left a message for him to call as soon as he came in. "Please rest," the ambassador counseled André. "There's nothing you can do for the moment."

He could think. Even as he stretched out on a sofa and shut his eyes, André had visions of Meredith being forced from the hotel, pushed into a car, tied or handcuffed or perhaps even drugged and then, finally, thrown into a room somewhere. Or had they killed her already? The thought sent a shock through him so great his body twitched. He sat up abruptly and rubbed his face.

Each minute that he waited seemed like an hour. He

knew that he had never experienced anxiety like this before, not simply its intensity, but its quality, as well. It was a participant's anxiety, not a spectator's, and it was unbearable.

At last, Shlomo called. André wasted no time. "They're holding back on me, Shlomo. They say it's because of you. Is that true?"

There was a long silence. "What can I say, André? As you can imagine, the Israeli government is very interested in Mr. Hoepner."

"In what way?" Even as he asked the question André knew it wouldn't be answered.

"Please, André. I would tell you if I could."

Suddenly, André's mind was racing. As overcome by events as he was, he was at least grateful that his mental processes seemed to be restored. They flashed a word: Eichmann! Were the Israelis planning to grab Hoepner?

"Look, Shlomo, I don't know what you guys are up to or what kind of problem I'm causing. All I know is that I wouldn't be here if it weren't for you. More than that, goddamnit, a woman's life is in danger and while I'm directly responsible for that, you're responsible, too. She's not just any woman. She's the woman I love. I'm not even going to try to persuade you on the basis of sentiment or friendship. I swear to you, Shlomo, that if anything happens to that woman, I'm not only going to tell the world it was because you guys held out on me, I'm going to reveal that the Mossad was penetrated by a Russian agent."

"André! André! Please!" Shlomo said. "I can understand how you feel. I beg you not to threaten. You know it won't do any good . . . André?"

He couldn't respond. He was overcome, ashamed of how he'd just acted, aware that for the one and only moment in his life, he had been completely out of control. It had been a moment as frightening as a nightmare in which he was falling into a bottomless chasm. He could end the nightmare by awakening. This one would go on.

"André?"

"I'm here. I'm sorry."

"Don't apologize. I understand."

"What do I have to say to you to make you help me?"

"You've already said it. I *know* I'm responsible, and I *will* try to help you, but it will take some time. If I can get clearance, I'm going to 'fax you a report that should answer your questions. I've got to go all the way to the top on this one. I'll do it provided you give me your word you'll never disclose where you got the information."

"You've got it."

"All right. It may take several hours, maybe a day."

"We may not have a day."

"I'll do my best. And, André—I have a feeling I know what you're thinking. That's not what it is."

Charles Houghton, Dick Sexton, and Barry Schloss took off in a Learjet from a private airfield in Virginia shortly before midnight, five hours after Houghton's telephone call to Sexton. Schloss, the former station chief in La Paz, was in his early fifties, but he moved with the power and agility of a man fifteen years younger. Small and wiry, weighing no more than 140 pounds, he was the one who heaved the baggage into the hold of the airplane. Houghton had remembered Schloss as soon as Sexton mentioned his name. He'd been an able field officer. The son of a corporate executive who had managed an American subsidiary in Buenos Aires, he was not only bilingual but knew the continent well. The deputy director had been sorry to see him go. But what had made Schloss valuable to the CIA had also made him valuable to the corporate world; in the last decade, he'd developed a thriving business, based in Washington, advising corporations on political conditions in areas where they hoped to invest.

Schloss had jumped at the chance for a little action. In the hours between Sexton's call and their takeoff, he'd made all the arrangements in Bolivia while Sexton arranged for the transport.

They flew to Lima, stopping twice en route to refuel, and landed in the Peruvian capital just after 10 A.M., local time. They transferred at once to a waiting Piper Cheyenne, an eight-passenger turboprop with good takeoff and landing capabilities at high altitudes. Two and a half hours later they set down on the runway near a hacienda fifty miles from La Paz, where Schloss and his family had often been guests during his tour in Bolivia. Two Bolivian men in their late thirties, wearing nondescript suits, were waiting for them alongside the runway, next to a twenty-year-old Dodge station wagon that had been repaired so many times it was barely recognizable. But the engine was hearty, they discovered as soon as they were on the highway, and they raced to La Paz. At one point they were stopped briefly at a roadblock set up to look for drug smugglers, but the officer in charge took one look at the occupants and, apparently deciding that they were tourists, waved them through. By four o'clock they were at the Israeli Embassy.

André awaited them in the ambassador's office, along with Eshel and Aryea. He'd had no further word from Shlomo, but he put that matter from his mind in order to brief the newcomers as fully as he could. It was the first time in his life he'd ever *given* the briefing, another reminder that he wasn't an observer this time.

"The scenario seems self-evident," Schloss said after André had mentioned Hoepner's penchant for antiques. "We make a delivery while he's at his club, take out the guard, and wait for him to come home. Anybody see any problem with that?"

"What about all-clear signals from the on-site guard?"
Sexton asked. "Anyone know anything about that?"

No one did.

"That could be a problem," Sexton said.

"I doubt it," Schloss said. "Not with my two friends
here." He turned to the Bolivians and spoke to them rapidly
in Spanish. Their expressions indicated that they could handle the problem.

"So the only question is, when?" Sexton said.

They all turned to Houghton. "Where is Hoepner now?
Does anybody know?" Houghton asked.

"Yes," Ambassador Eshel said. "He is at lunch at his
club. We will get a call as soon as he leaves."

"Does he ever return straight home from the club?"

"Never," the ambassador said.

"Do you have enough time to do it today?" Houghton
asked Schloss.

Schloss looked at his wristwatch. It was now four-thirty.
"Give me thirty minutes on the phone," he said.

"This way," Aryea said, leading Schloss off.

André turned to Houghton. "There are no words to tell
you how sorry I am," he said.

Houghton nodded. "I know you are."

There was nothing more to be said. They stared at one
another awkwardly for a moment. Then Aryea returned. He
whispered something in Hebrew to Eshel and then left. The
ambassador rose. "Excuse me," he said and moved toward
the door. As he passed behind Houghton and Sexton, he
caught André's eye and moved his head almost impercepti-
bly, a signal for André to follow him.

André's heartbeat quickened. He waited fifteen seconds,
then excused himself to go to the bathroom. Eshel was waiting for him in the corridor. Without a word, he led André
back to the basement communications room, where Aryea
handed the ambassador a sheaf of papers. Eshel turned to

André, a look of the gravest concern on his face. "When you have read this, you will understand why the information it contains could never have come from us. You have given your word to Shlomo that you will never divulge your source. I pray that you will keep it."

André reached for the papers, but Eshel held onto them for just a moment longer. "There is a further condition," he said. "When you have finished reading the report, we will destroy it. And you are not to make notes."

At last, Eshel held the papers out to André, but with such obvious reluctance it seemed even then that he might withdraw them. André took them and glanced at the top page. It bore the title, *Kurt Hoepner: From Clermont-Ferrand to La Paz, Including "Operation Detox."* A minute into the report, André gasped audibly. Eshel and Aryea exchanged grim smiles.

At seven that evening, a small van pulled up in front of Hoepner's Calacoto villa. Two Bolivians, dressed in coveralls, hauled a fine chest of drawers from the van and carried it to the gate. Then they rang the bell.

Half a minute later, one of the bodyguards came to the gate. "What's this?" he said. For an answer, he was shown a waybill, made out to Wilhelm Kurtz. "No one said anything to me about a delivery," he said.

"You don't accept it?" one of Schloss's men said. "We take it back." He turned to his colleague. "Come on." Together, they began to move the chest of drawers back to the van.

"Wait a minute!" the bodyguard said. "I didn't tell you I wouldn't accept it."

"Make up your mind, man!"

The guard opened the gate. One of the men handed him the bill of lading and a pen. As he was signing, the other man moved behind him, shoved a knife into his back and said, "Don't make me stick you."

At that, Schloss emerged from the van and covered the guard with a pistol. Quickly, his men moved the chest back into the van and closed the door. In a moment, the van was gone.

"Into the house," Schloss whispered to the bodyguard. They followed him inside. One of the Bolivians went immediately for Hoepner's wife, the other for the maid and the cook. They took the women to a garden room at the rear of the house and bound and gagged them. Mrs. Hoepner, a stout woman with gray hair that scarcely covered her scalp, seemed about to expire of fear. The cook and the maid were too bewildered to register their fear. "You won't be hurt," Schloss said to them in Spanish. With a nod, he sent the two Bolivians off to make a room-to-room search for Meredith. Then he spoke into a small walkie-talkie. "House secure," he said.

"Roger," Sexton said into his walkie-talkie. He was seated in the station wagon half a block away with Houghton and André. They left the car at once and hurried to the house. Schloss and the two Bolivians met them at the door. "Meredith's not here," Schloss said.

Houghton nodded without expression. "I didn't expect she would be. What about the 'all clear'?"

Schloss turned to the two Bolivians and said a few words in Spanish. They grinned simultaneously, said something to Schloss that made the guard recoil, and then led him away. "They said they would show him a little of his blood," Schloss reported. Seconds passed. There was a cry from another room. Schloss smiled. "He's not very brave." In a minute all three men were back, the guard holding a blood-soaked handkerchief to the back of his right hand. One of the Bolivians reported to Schloss.

"It's very simple. Just a lamp next to the window in the

center of the living room. If it's not turned on, they don't come in."

"Are they sure?" Houghton asked.

Once more Schloss spoke to the Bolivians, and once more both of them grinned and spoke at once to Schloss. Schloss turned to Houghton. "They say he has no balls."

Houghton nodded. "Is the light on?"

Schloss shook his head. "No. The chauffeur honks. *Then* this guy turns it on. That way they can see him."

"They're sure?" Houghton repeated.

"They told him he's a dead man if his *patrón* and his *compadre* don't both come in the house."

"Let's hope," Houghton said.

Ever since Houghton had arrived, nearly four hours before, André had watched the deputy director for some sign of emotion. Nothing. Not an inflection, not a twitch, not a sudden flash of anger nor a baleful glance. Anything the man might have said to him would have been excusable under the circumstances, but he'd said virtually nothing. For all anyone else could tell, the hostage might have been a total stranger. "Let's hope," Houghton had said. He should have said, "Let's pray."

André, the lapsed Catholic, the half Jew, hadn't prayed in years, but he had made up for it in the twenty-eight hours since Meredith had been kidnapped. The prayer was unfocused; no one deity was invoked; he simply prayed: for her safety, her deliverance, her forgiveness and love. He couldn't begin to imagine where she was or how she was being treated; when he was finished praying for everything else in her behalf, he prayed for her comfort and ability to bear up. He thought of the strength she would bring to any ordeal, her poise and independence and clarity of thought. He prayed that because of her singularity of character her captors might respect her, but given what he now knew about them, he doubted that they would. The stakes were too great; to them, Houghton's daughter was a windfall. He wondered how much, if any, of the information in that Israeli report was known to Houghton. There *had* to be a way to use that information as a lever to free Meredith; he would pass the information to the deputy director as soon as he could and pray that he would know how.

"Do you want to come along?" Houghton had asked him as he was preparing to leave the Israeli Embassy.

"Of course," André had said.

"I can't guarantee your safety."

"I couldn't care less about my safety," he'd said. It was true. He'd never thought of himself as an especially courageous man. Now he knew that fear was a component of courage, and that purpose tipped the balance. Whatever was about to occur, he wanted to be part of it. He wanted to take Hoepner by the throat and choke Meredith's whereabouts from him.

The entry of Hoepner's house was a large tiled space with a cathedral ceiling. A circular staircase at the rear of the entry led to the upstairs. To the right of the entry was a living room, to the left a study with floor-to-ceiling bookshelves, filled not with books but with primitive Indian figures.

The maid had said that Hoepner would enter alone by the front door. The chauffeur-bodyguard would then put the car in the garage and enter the house through the kitchen in the back of the house. They had positioned themselves accordingly. Schloss and one of the Bolivians were in the living room with the other bodyguard to make certain he gave the signal. The other Bolivian was hidden at the side of the house to take out the chauffeur as he parked the car. Sexton was in the garden room with the women. Houghton was in a corner of the study, from which he could see into the entry but would not be seen unless someone peered inside.

André was in the corner across from Houghton, with the same advantage.

At eight-thirty exactly a horn sounded in the street outside the house. A moment later the bodyguard walked to the lamp and nervously pulled at the cord. Twice he tugged and nothing happened. "Pull it!" Schloss hissed at him in Spanish. On the third try the lamp went on. Schloss covered the bodyguard with his pistol as he moved to the front door to open it for his employer. The car crept up the driveway, its beams playing on the side of the house and filtering through the curtains into the study. They heard doors opening and closing and footsteps, first on gravel, then on the stoop. At last a man came through the door and into the entry. André stiffened. It wasn't Hoepner. His eyes darted to Houghton, just as he saw the man. To André's bewilderment, Houghton smiled.

Then Hoepner came into the entry. As he cleared the doorway, the bodyguard uttered an unintelligible cry and bolted for the gate. Instantly, Schloss was into the entry, a gun on Hoepner and the stranger. The Bolivian who had been in the living room raced through the door and after the bodyguard but he was too late; the man had already reached the street. He turned to see the second bodyguard leveling a gun at him, but in the next instant that threat was removed by a chop to the neck from the Bolivian who had hidden himself at the side of the house.

In the entry, Hoepner and the stranger stared in stupefaction as first Houghton and then André appeared.

"Houghton!" the stranger said. "What the hell?"

"Craig," Houghton said, still smiling. "I had a feeling you'd be here."

Suddenly, everything clicked for André.

Schloss moved Hoepner and Craig into the living room.
Then Sexton appeared, then the two Bolivians. Houghton
and André followed.

"What's the meaning of this?" Hoepner said.

"We want the girl," Schloss said.

"I don't know what you're talking about," Hoepner said.

Schloss nodded to the two Bolivians. They grabbed
Hoepner. One of them held his head back, exposing his
jugular vein, and laid the edge of his knife on it.

"Where is she?" Schloss demanded.

Incredibly, Hoepner laughed. "Kill me and you'll never
find her."

For a moment there was no sound or movement. Then
Houghton gestured toward Craig. "Kill this man if he
doesn't tell us."

"What! You're crazy!" Craig cried.

Schloss put his gun in Craig's back. The other Bolivian
advanced with a knife, bent Craig's head, and put the knife
to his jugular. Craig said nothing. Nor did Hoepner. The
Bolivian looked at Houghton for a sign. Houghton nodded.

The Bolivian cut into Craig's throat. He screamed. "Tell
them!" he cried to Hoepner. There was hysteria in his voice,
but authority as well. It was a command, not a plea.

Hoepner reacted at once, as though control had passed
from his hands. "I'll have to take you to her," he said.

"Let's go," Schloss said.

"Just a minute," Houghton said. His voice was steady, its
volume low, but the tone reminded them who was in command. "I have other business with Mr. Hoepner."

André caught Schloss and Sexton exchanging incredulous
glances. Then he looked at Houghton. The man appeared to
be transfixed by the sight of Hoepner, as though, for the
moment, he was the only man in the room.

Sexton moved close to Houghton. "Charlie," he whispered, "we've got to get out of here."

If Houghton heard him, he gave no sign. He advanced on Hoepner, and for the first time André could see emotion in his eyes. What poured out was the passion of a man who believed he was within moments of solving a great mystery. "Mr. Hoepner," he began, "you have probably figured out who I am. I am going to ask you some questions. How you answer will determine what we do with you after we liberate my daughter."

"What do you wish to know?" Hoepner asked, his voice barely audible.

"Charlie," Sexton whispered. "The police . . ."

Again, Houghton ignored him. Balancing on his canes, towering over Hoepner, who was seated in a chair, the ex-deputy director was acting for all the world as though he were in a comfortable CIA safe house on a back road in Virginia. "What has been your principal occupation since your arrival in Bolivia?"

"Odds and ends for the first years. Then I became a consultant."

"In what kind of matters?"

"Mostly political."

"Any others?"

"Labor relations."

"And who are your clients?"

"Mostly corporations."

"What kinds of corporations?"

"All kinds. Mostly multinational."

"Any other clients?"

"Some governments."

"And what kinds of services do you perform for these clients?"

"All kinds." Hoepner looked uneasily at Craig. "Why are you asking me these questions? You know all about this. You are the ones who put me here."

"When you say, 'you,' whom do you mean?"

"You. The CIA."

"I see," Houghton said calmly.

André looked quickly at Sexton and Schloss, who once more exchanged incredulous glances. Then Schloss turned to Houghton. "Charlie," he said, "I used to live in this area. I know exactly where the nearest police station is. If that guy who got away went directly there, I figure he'll be arriving in another five minutes, assuming he ran all the way. That gives us no more than five minutes to get out of here."

"No problem," Houghton said. He turned again to Hoepner. "Now what, precisely, are those services you perform?"

"I say no more," Hoepner said.

For a moment, Houghton glared at Hoepner. His eyes hardened. André could see little ripples in his cheeks.

"I remind you, Mr. Hoepner . . ."

Hoepner cut him off. "I say no more."

The threat wasn't working. André had known it wouldn't, just as surely as though he had written the script and was watching the actors rehearse. Hoepner knew that Houghton wasn't going to kill him, not even after he took them to Meredith. What Houghton wanted was information about his agency's complicity with ex-Nazis, and a dead Hoepner couldn't supply it.

André could see the spirit leeching from Houghton's eyes, the strength leaving his body. In a moment, he was immobilized, like a ship dead in the water. What had Meredith said? That he would put country over self—and he had done so just now, even though self involved his daughter.

"Four minutes," Schloss said.

"For chrissake, Charlie," Sexton said. There was panic in his face.

André felt it, too. No matter how lofty or understandable their motives, they had committed half a dozen crimes against a citizen of Bolivia. There was also the matter of illegal entry into the country. If they were taken by the police—who seemed to be in Hoepner's pocket—God only knew what would happen to them. And what would happen to Meredith, in that event? "I can tell you what those services were," he said suddenly, shocked by his own voice.

Houghton, Sexton, and Schloss looked sharply at him. "Quick, man," Sexton said.

"Hoepner runs a paramilitary organization. The headquarters are in La Paz, but the operation covers all Latin America. The troops are nationals, but the leadership is all ex-Nazis. For a fee, the organization will make sure that the wrong people don't become important, people like radicals and Communists in governments and trade unions. If a politician wants to get rid of a powerful rival who happens to be a leftist, he hires the organization. If a corporation feels a radical labor leader has gotten too powerful, it hires the organization. A lot of the work is accomplished by threats, but when the threats don't work they kill them."

"Who set them up?" Houghton asked.

"You really don't know?"

"No."

"The CIA. This man," André said, nodding at Craig.

"What?" Craig exploded, the blood rushing to his face, turning it a deeper red. "That's the biggest piece of rubbish I've ever heard. I know your line, Kohl. I've listened to your crap." He turned to Houghton. "You know me. You know my record. Are you going to let this media creep defame me?"

"Three minutes," Schloss said.

"Have you proof?" Houghton said to André.

"Enough for my purposes. If you need more, I suggest you make a deal with Mr. Hoepner. He tells you the truth, you let him go. I'll ask him the questions—and I'll know if he's lying."

"That's a deal, Mr. Hoepner, as far as I'm concerned. I

don't care about you, I care about my agency. Cooperate and you're free. If you don't, you're going to be flown to Lima tonight and put aboard a private jet. That jet will fly us to France—where we'll turn you over to the French."

Hoepner blanched. "Go on," he said.

"Two minutes," Schloss said. Houghton nodded to André.

"What was 'Operation Detox'?" André said.

For a moment, Hoepner seemed dumbstruck. Then, in a small voice, he said, "It was an American intelligence operation in Vichy France during World War II."

"Were you employed by American intelligence?"

"Yes."

"Who employed you?"

"This man," Hoepner said, looking at Craig.

"How did he pay you?"

"He put money in a Swiss bank for me."

"In payment for what?"

"For making certain that Communists did not take over the French Resistance."

There was the briefest silence. Houghton's eyes darted at André, who nodded affirmatively. "Dear God," Houghton said.

André stole a quick look at Sexton. He was looking at Craig in horror.

"One minute," Schloss said.

"Let's go," Houghton said.

For a moment, Sexton and Schloss turned to look at Houghton with relief. And in that moment, only André saw Craig lean down, as though to scratch his leg, remove a pistol from an ankle holster and aim it at Hoepner. It flashed into André's mind that the only man who knew where Meredith was was about to be killed. He lunged—not simply at Craig, but from one life to another. He hit the pistol, knocking it away just as it fired. The bullet caught

Houghton in the chest and knocked him to the ground. Craig's next shot crashed through Hoepner's temple, killing him at once. A second later he, too, was dead, as both Sexton and Schloss fired into his head.

André was the first to reach Houghton. Then Schloss and Sexton knelt down and gently turned him over. Schloss pulled his coat back and ripped away his shirt. There was a small hole in the right side of his chest, from which blood was slowly oozing. "The bullet didn't go through," Schloss said. "It must be in his lung."

Then Houghton opened his eyes. He looked first at André and then at each of the bodies. "Both dead?" he asked, looking at Sexton. Sexton nodded.

For a moment, he seemed dazed. Then his eyes brimmed with tears. "Oh, God," he said, "what have I done to Meredith?"

For a moment there was silence. Then André said, "I think I may know where she is."

28

Schloss and one of the Bolivians carried Houghton outside. The other Bolivian raced for the station wagon and swung it into the driveway.

"What about the other bodyguard?" Sexton said.

"Let's bring him," Schloss said. "We may need him." He spoke in Spanish to the first Bolivian, who immediately disappeared.

Sexton opened the tailgate. Inside were blankets, already spread out. He and Schloss lifted Houghton onto the blankets. By then the Bolivian was back with the bodyguard. His hands were tied behind his back, a rag covered his mouth. His eyes bulged with fear. The Bolivian pushed him into the front seat. Sexton, Schloss, and André got into the backseat. The two Bolivians got in front, sandwiching the bodyguard. Seconds later, they were out of the driveway, speeding down the residential street, away from Hoepner's house. Schloss watched through the rear window to see if they had been followed. "Okay, we made it," he said. Then he said something to the driver in Spanish. At once, the car slowed to normal speed.

"Now, where to?" Schloss asked André.

"There's a warehouse near the railway station where Hoepner stores small arms and ammunition. It's on Cordova Street. Number 16."

"Where'd you get *that* information?" Schloss said.

"Never mind," André said. It had been one of the half-dozen facts he had memorized while reading the Israeli report. He thanked God he had chosen it and prayed that Meredith would be there.

Schloss gave the instructions to the driver, who immediately changed course. Then he turned around to look at Houghton. "How you doing?" he said.

"I'm okay," Houghton said.

"I've got a kit with some painkiller. I can give you a shot."

"It's not that bad," Houghton said.

Then Schloss leaned forward, cut the bodyguard's gag, and spoke softly and rapidly to him in Spanish. The bodyguard nodded several times, then spoke rapidly himself. When Schloss leaned back, he said, "He'll help us. He says there's only one man at the warehouse. He's sure the guy will be sleeping. He'll get him up by calling through a window. The guy should let him in without any problem. He's used to odd-hour visits."

"But doesn't somebody usually call first?"

"Negative. They just go."

"Does the bodyguard know if Meredith's there?" André asked.

"Negative. Or at least he says he doesn't. He doesn't know who she is."

"Turn him around," André said.

Schloss looked quizzically at André. "What for?"

"I want to see his face. One of those guys was in on the kidnap. I saw him the day I had lunch with Hoepner. If this was the guy, I'll recognize him—and I'll know if he's lying."

Schloss turned the bodyguard's head. Then he reached in his pocket and brought out a tiny but powerful flashlight and shone it in his face. It was an Inca face, the skin a deep, drawn brown, with reddish spots on the cheekbones. The mouth was thin, and the lips were stained an even deeper brown.

"Okay," André said. "This wasn't the guy."

"Which means that the other guy has probably figured out where we're going, and he'll tell the police," Sexton said.

"I doubt it," André said. "He'd have to tell them about the kidnapping."

There was a silence of several seconds. "You know what?" Schloss said at last. "I'll bet that mother never went to the police. I'll bet he got lost—in which case we're home free."

"*If* Meredith's at the warehouse."

They parked on a side street, just off Cordova. Schloss and the two Bolivians took the bodyguard with them and flattened themselves against the warehouse wall while the bodyguard tapped at the window. He exchanged a few words with the man inside, then walked to the door. In a moment, it opened. The two Bolivians were inside in an instant. Then Schloss pushed the bodyguard inside and closed the door.

An eternity passed for André, watching from the car, his eyes fixed unwaveringly on the warehouse door, lighted by a streetlamp.

"Anything?" Houghton said.

"They're inside," Sexton said.

A minute passed, then another. At last, the door opened. One of the Bolivians appeared in the doorway. He peered cautiously into the street, then suddenly made a dash for the car.

"Lookin' good," Sexton said softly.

Just as the Bolivian reached the car, Schloss appeared in the doorway. But he was alone. Only when the Bolivian had driven the car in front of the warehouse door did they see Meredith, a few feet inside, slumped against the other Bolivian. He and Schloss brought her outside.

Sexton sprang from the car. "What about the guards?"

"They're not going anywhere," Schloss said.

They put Meredith in the backseat. Schloss got in beside her. Sexton got in front. Without a word, the driver sped off.

"She's drugged," Schloss said, "but I think she's okay."

André put his arm around Meredith and rested her head on his shoulder. Tears welled in his eyes. "Thank God," he whispered, "thank God."

They drove through the city in silence, wary that if the first bodyguard had gone to the police, after all, the police would surely put out a call and they could be stopped by a patrol car. It didn't matter that the police didn't know what kind of car they were driving. At this hour—it was nearly eleven —there weren't that many cars on the streets.

"I think we're okay," Schloss said at last.

"What about that roadblock we passed coming in?"

"You noticed we didn't get stopped," Schloss said. "My local friends distributed a few gifts this morning on their way out to get us. They left something for the officers in charge of the other shifts." He turned around to look at Houghton. "How you doing?"

"Okay," Houghton said.

"How about that painkiller?"

"No. I've got to be alert." He paused. "I've got to talk to André."

André turned around. "We'll have plenty of time to talk," he said.

There was another silence. "I want to be sure of that," Houghton said.

At the outskirts to the city, they saw the roadblock. Schloss reached behind the seat and retrieved a bottle. "I'm going to pour some whiskey on you, Charlie. If we get stopped, pretend you're sleeping."

This time the officer in charge chose to make a show of his inspection. When he saw Houghton in the back, his eyebrows shot up.

"Drunk," the driver said. He held his nose.

The officer caught the odors, laughed, and waved them on.

There was almost no traffic on the highway, so the driver began to speed, gearing down instead of braking at the curves, taking most of them at better than fifty miles an hour. But the old car swayed, causing the passengers to shift. At one turn they heard a moan from Houghton. "Better slow down," Schloss said.

No one said anything, but André was sure they were all thinking the same thing. There was no safety for any of them until they were out of Bolivia. Given what the Bolivians would find at Hoepner's house, why should they believe the Americans' version of events? But could Houghton make it? And what would happen if they had to summon a doctor or, even worse, put him into a hospital?

A few minutes before they reached the hacienda, Meredith opened her eyes. For a moment, she stared, uncomprehending.

"It's okay," André said. "You're safe."

She sighed, attempted a smile, and drifted off again.

At the hacienda, the car went directly to the airstrip. The

pilot came out and helped André put Meredith into the plane.

"What do you think, Charlie?" Sexton said to Houghton.

"I don't see any alternative," Houghton said.

"It's no good if you can't make it."

"Let's go."

They made a bed for him in the aisle. As the plane bumped down the dirt runway he had to grit his teeth to keep from shouting out. The moment they were airborne, Schloss leaned down to him. *"Please* let me give you some painkiller," he said.

"After I talk to André," he said. "Ask him to come here." In a moment, André was at his side. "Between the two of us, do you think we can put this together?"

André knew exactly what Houghton was asking: to trade information. It was an acknowledgment of the obvious, that André had something he didn't have and desperately needed. André had no such assurances; he didn't know whether he would be paid in kind for the information he would give. Knowing Houghton, however, and remembering his obsessive questioning of Hoepner, he had to believe that the deputy director had made other efforts to ferret out the awful truth he now knew. "Let's try," André said.

For the next half hour, the two men, alone, engaged in the kind of transaction that has existed since the beginning of journalism. For Houghton, it was probably a first, André suspected, but for him it had happened hundreds of times. The rules were simple: you kept your sources to yourself, but you told a version of the events that you believed to be true. Nothing Houghton might have offered in exchange could have persuaded André to identify the Israelis as the source of his information on "Operation Detox" and Hoepner's subsequent activities. He understood why the Israelis had never informed the Americans. The information would inevitably leak; the news that the OSS had connived

with a Gestapo butcher during World War II and that subsequently the CIA had—even unwittingly—abetted ex-Nazis and sponsored them in new acts of terror would be an
appalling embarrassment for the United States. The Israelis
could never afford to embarrass the United States, the guar-
antor of their existence.

In any case, Houghton didn't ask for sources. He accepted André's story and then told his own, beginning with
his discovery of the interrogation file on Hoepner, and his
visit to Craig in Virginia. He held nothing back, not even his
summons by the President or his convictions about the existence of an interagency network of like-minded men.

When they had finished, Houghton motioned Sexton and
Schloss to approach. "I want you to hear this," he said,
"because if it's ever necessary I want you to be able to say
that André and I agreed on the facts." He turned to André.
"Do you want to tell it or shall I?"

"Do you feel up to it?"

"I'm okay."

"Then why don't you go ahead? You're the one who's
involved."

"The whole agency's involved," Houghton said sadly. He
looked at his two former colleagues. "You're not going to
believe this," he said.

Hoepner worked for Craig, Houghton said. They all
worked for Craig, every Nazi who had been moved from
Europe to Latin America in exchange for the help they had
given the Americans after the war in setting up against the
Communists. That was what had given the Americans the
idea to use them again in Latin America. It wasn't official
policy, he said. He, for example, had never known about it.
It was the work of a subgroup within the CIA and the State
Department, men who believed that the ends justified the
means, the ends being the eradication of the Marxist threat
wherever it arose; the means, in this case, being the use of

methods official policy wouldn't countenance and people who were officially condemned.

The subgroup had arranged for Craig's transfer to Latin America in 1959. That was the year of the overthrow of Batista in Cuba and the ascendancy of Fidel Castro. The subgroup—men like Craig—looked ahead and saw many Cubas in Latin America. Official policy was correctly oriented but too moral, in their view, to confront the challenge. So they would meet the challenge themselves. Craig, the expert on Germany, the man who had supervised the movement of Hoepner and others from Europe to Latin America, was the ideal man to recruit the Nazis and help them set up an organization, paramilitary, terrorist. So the subgroup persuaded the CIA to form a front company with Craig as its chief operating officer. The company represented itself as the subsidiary of an American firm specializing in the development of high-density real estate. With his cover, Craig remained a CIA employee throughout, which led Hoepner and the others to believe that they were working for the United States. But Craig never reported on these efforts; they were special, unofficial activities, which he and his subgroup engineered. Money was never a problem because the company never lacked for clients. Corporations paid to have their labor problems "solved." Governments paid for lessons in how to deal with extremists and contracted the work out if and when political conditions inhibited their own involvement.

Craig never took any money for himself. He didn't want to profit, which, to him, would have been immoral. His only interest was in serving his country, his way. But Hoepner and the other Nazis had gotten rich. Hoepner, especially; when Craig retired and returned to the United States to live, it was he who took over the operation.

Craig had probably gone to La Paz out of fear that

Houghton, after all these years, had somehow stumbled upon his trail.

For a long time after Houghton finished, no one spoke. "Jesus Christ," Sexton said at last, "I fought those bastards in World War II."

"That's the part I find hard to swallow—that Craig was actually paying Hoepner to hunt down Communists in the Resistance," Schloss said.

"Craig shot him, didn't he?" Houghton said. "That was obviously the dirtiest secret of all, one he didn't want out."

"He couldn't have done something like that on his own, could he?"

"No. It would have had to have been policy—or, more specifically, the policy of a subgroup within the government that was looking ahead to the postwar Communist threat."

"Then tell me if I'm correct," André said. "The OSS sent you into France to capture a man who was actually working for the Americans."

Houghton looked at André as though he had just said something he hadn't wanted to hear. After a moment, he said, "That would be correct." Then, seeing the bewilderment on the faces of his two colleagues, he told them briefly about his World War II mission.

"The people who sent you wouldn't have known about Craig?" André said.

"No. No way," Houghton said. "My people were in overt work. This other stuff was covert. The people in covert work don't tell overt operators what they're up to. Most of the time, the covert people don't even tell one another. We've just seen the perfect example of how dangerous that can be." Suddenly, he winced with pain. André took that as a signal to move away, but Houghton grabbed his arm. "There's something I'd like you to include in your broadcast—that what scares me most isn't what we don't know about the Russians, it's what we don't know about groups within governments—beginning with our own. A month ago I would never have said that."

Sexton looked at Houghton and then at Schloss and finally at André. "You're going to *tell* this story?" he asked.

"Of course," André said.

"The story has to be told, Dick," Houghton said. "This thing stinks so badly the only way to get rid of it is to ventilate it. We can't arrest these people. Hell, we don't even know who they are. They could be anywhere—station chiefs in the embassies, desk officers or higher at Langley. Our best shot is to neutralize them by exposure."

They landed at Lima's Jorge Chávez International Airport in the northwest corner of the city. The pilot had radioed ahead for an ambulance, which took Houghton at once to the Arzobispo Loayza Hospital in the central district. Meredith, still groggy but otherwise recovered, went with him. Schloss and Sexton remained at the airport to talk to the police, who wanted to know how Houghton had been shot. They'd agreed with Houghton to portray it as an accident— technically, it had been—and to make a full statement through the American Embassy later that day.

Schloss had recommended the Gran Hotel Bolívar on the Plaza San Martín, so André went directly there in a taxi, all but numb to the realization that he was passing through a city as destitute as any he had ever seen, down wide *avenidas* built in expectation of good times that had never matured. It was almost 2 A.M. when he arrived; with no luggage and no reservation he had to spread out his credit cards alongside his passport before he could get a room.

If he had ever been more tired he could not remember when. But he couldn't sleep until he had called the foreign desk at USBC in New York. He left word for Mike Paul to call him at 8 A.M. Lima time and he asked the desk to set up a satellite transmission from Peruvian television to New

York for one that afternoon. The man on the desk wanted to know what the story was. "It's big," André said. "That's all I can tell you."

As tired as he was, there was still one more call to make. With the help of the hotel operator, André located Meredith at the hospital. "How is he?" he asked.

Her voice was slow and slightly fuzzy, as though she had just awakened from a deep sleep, but her thoughts were fully organized. "He's in intensive care, but he's fine. They say he's as strong as a horse. The bullet was in his lung, but there wasn't much damage."

"How long before he can leave?"

"Ten days, they say."

"Will you stay here?"

"Oh, absolutely."

He hesitated. "Try to get some rest," he said.

"I will. They've fixed me up with a bed. They're very nice."

He said goodnight, hoping she could sense the feeling that went with it.

When he finally slept, it was only for a few hours. At six-thirty he was explaining his plight to an English-speaking hall porter, and by seven o'clock the hotel's housekeeper had rounded up fresh clothing and toilet articles left behind by other guests. By the time Mike called, André had showered, shaved, and dressed, and eaten breakfast, his first food in almost twenty hours.

As he had on André's call from London, Mike listened in silence broken only by his exclamations. "There's no way I can write a story from here," André said when he had finished. "What I'd like to do is feed you as much as I can on the satellite, and let you put it together."

"Are you going to put the Laurent story in this broadcast?"

"I don't think that's the way to do it. I think I should get back to Paris, get hold of the dossier, and do it from there."

"The election's Sunday, you know."

"I'm not out to influence the French election."

"It's a better story before the election, André."

For a moment, André couldn't answer. "Let me clean this up first, Mike. If it's humanly possible I'll get back to Paris tomorrow."

"Would you like some help?"

"I'd love some, but I don't know what anyone could do."

"Okay. Give it your best shot."

By nine o'clock, André had arranged for a Peruvian television crew. Together, they went to the airport to do a shot of the plane, to the American Embassy for interviews with Sexton and Schloss, both men guarded but informative, and then to the hospital for shots of the doctors and an interview with Meredith about the kidnapping. There was still his narrative to be done, for which the crew had arranged studio facilities, but André had to have a few minutes first to say goodbye to Meredith.

She looked tired and drawn, and her manner was subdued. It was obvious that she hadn't quite gotten used to everything that had happened. "Whatever you do, don't apologize," she said. "I'm the one who said she didn't like to be left out."

"I wish you were coming back to Paris."

"I do, too."

"I mean for good."

She moved a hand to his face and ran her fingers along his features, as though that might help her remember them. "I've got a better idea," she said. "Why don't you come back to the States? Think of it as a foreign assignment."

He did his feed from the studio, working from a series of notes. It wasn't the oil-smooth delivery of the anchorman, but its very roughness and impromptu quality gave the story the sense of urgency and immediacy it deserved. He told as much as he could without giving away the Camille Laurent story, the one he would break in Paris.

New York was on the phone almost the moment he had finished. Saul Geffin spoke for the producers. "It's a great story, André, we all agree about that. But it's not complete. It's like having to read some marvelous novel without benefit of the first hundred pages."

"Well, what am I supposed to do?" he said, suddenly out of patience. "I can't say any more without saying the whole thing, and I'm not going to do that. I busted my ass for that dossier, and I'm not about to tell that story until I've got it in my hand and can wave it in front of the camera."

He did not even try to disguise his anger. He had interrupted his leave of absence, traveled more than twenty thousand miles in less than four weeks, risked his life and the life of a woman he loved, witnessed two violent deaths, and come through, finally, with a sensational exclusive: the exposure of a sub rosa, secret effort by a few American civil servants to enlist ex-Nazis in an illicit, clandestine effort to combat communism throughout Latin America. What the hell more did they want?

"Just a minute, André," Geffin said. He put André on hold. When he came back, his tone was solicitous. "Look, we know you've been under a strain. Why don't you get back to Paris, get that piece done, and then rest for a day or two. We'll go with the top of the Latin America story, the shooting of Houghton and the killing of Hoepner and Craig. We'll do it as a mystery. And then we'll do an hour special on Wednesday or Thursday next week. That sound okay?"

He said it did, but he knew it didn't. They still weren't satisfied.

It was not possible to get back to Paris the next day, André discovered when he had finished talking to New York. The best he could manage was a Varig flight from Lima to Rio de Janeiro at forty minutes past midnight the following morning, Friday. It would arrive in Rio at 7:30 A.M., but his flight to Paris, again with Varig, wouldn't leave until nine-thirty that evening, which would put him into Paris after 1 P.M. on Saturday.

In Rio, he went to the Copacabana Palace Hotel on Avenida Atlantica, across the street from the beach, because that was where he had stayed on his only other trip to Brazil, in the early sixties. Then it had been *the* hotel and social center, but it obviously wasn't any longer, judging from its appearance and clientele. The sofas and chairs in the lobby looked as though they had borne the weight of a hundred thousand people. The colors were faded, the wood scuffed. As to the people, there were no great beauties or handsome playboys among them, as there once had been. To the contrary, they seemed staid and businesslike. The overall change gave him a bad feeling, although he didn't know why, which set in alongside a general feeling of unease. He was punchy from fatigue, he knew the moment he stretched out on his bed, but it was more than that. He was upset with New York for what he felt was a challenge to his judgment. He was upset about being in yet another empty hotel room. He was upset about having been abruptly separated from the woman who had reawakened him, who made him feel that ten years of his life had been given back to him. He was upset about being upset, when he should have been soaring, no matter how tired he was. He was going back to Paris to put the cap on what had to be not just the biggest coup of his career but one of the great reportorial feats of all time.

Something was wrong that had nothing to do with finding himself alone in a has-been hotel or having poorly handled a well-meant and undoubtedly pertinent critique from New York. What was wrong was that this particular reporting job had been different from every other he had ever experienced and had put all that experience into question. On every other occasion, without exception, he'd been reporting the experiences of others. This time, and only this time, he had lived the experience himself. For a few weeks he had lived, despite all the motion of the past, with a kind of intensity he had never felt before. What did that say about the manner in which he'd been living for as long as he could remember? It was almost too painful to contemplate. And what would he do with this knowledge now that he had it?

Sleep spared him from further contemplation. And when he awakened he was once again all business. How had Gondrachov fared during his absence? Had the Russian given up on him and gone to another outlet? It had been more than thoughtless not to call. Careless, as well. Irresponsible even. Deep down, André understood why he'd acted as he had. He couldn't shake the feeling that in breaking this story he was accomplishing a Soviet objective. He didn't want to accomplish any objectives for a government whose conscience was so warped it could countenance the repression of other nations, the silencing of writers, the shooting down of unarmed civilian aircraft. You can be upset when a man walks across your lawn, but you don't get a gun and shoot him.

Well, he would know soon and it would be over soon. By the time he arrived in Paris, the adrenaline would be flowing. Motion would see to that.

The moment he dialed Paulette's number he knew that something was wrong. There was one ring and then a click, like a changing of gears, and then another, different sounding ring. And then a woman's voice, not Paulette's. For a moment, André didn't respond. "Allo, yes?" the woman said.

"I'd like to speak to Boris," André said.

"Boris isn't here. I take messages for Boris."

He hung up, aghast, and stared in horror at the telephone. It gave him no answer. There was no other number to call. The DGSE had Paulette, that was certain. Did that mean they had Gennady? Surely his friend was too resourceful to have let himself be caught in her apartment. Or was that wishful thinking? Did the DGSE also have the dossier? Had he, André, in the midst of this great story, made a beginner's mistake?

As his taxi drove him down the Quai d'Orléans, André noticed two men sitting in a car fifty feet from his building. So, he was still under surveillance by the DGSE. Did that mean that the KGB was still on him, as well? If so, they would get word to Gennady. His spirits soared. He persuaded himself that the Russian was still free and would soon know of his return. For good measure, André decided, he would go to his office on the Champs Élysées. That way there was the double possibility of being spotted. Somehow, some way, he'd get a signal from the Russian.

It was nearly six P.M. by the time he got to the office. The only sound was the chatter of the wire service machines; everyone had already gone. He was grateful for that; no explanations to make. Habit directed him to the office telex machine in the wire room. There were five telegrams—the network called them "herograms"—from New York extolling the story from Lima. It was a new record; the most he'd ever gotten on any previous story was three. He crumpled the messages and threw them in the wastebasket. A pile of newspapers lay on the table near the entry. He picked them up and took them to his office. He would spend an hour reading, bringing himself up to date.

All the newspapers had led with election stories. Almost

all predicted victory for Camille Laurent. All of the newspapers also prominently featured stories about the extraordinary circumstances surrounding the death of the Executioner of Clermont-Ferrand. They were follow-up stories, filled with speculations and unanswered questions, as the newspapers attempted to develop their own angles.

He wondered then how the papers had played the story when it first broke. That would have been in Friday's editions. He went back to the wire room, where old newspapers accumulated, waiting to be clipped, and found the Friday editions. Sure enough, it had been the lead. Hoepner's death must have relieved Camille Laurent. Won't he be surprised, he thought with satisfaction, as he turned to the inside pages.

It was then that he saw Gondrachov's picture. Only it identified him as Milos Novotny. The story said that the Czech's body had been found in the Bois de Boulogne, near the Auteuil race track, in a region frequented by transvestites. Police said that in addition to multiple bruises, there was evidence of sexual assault.

André vomited on the newspaper.

All day Sunday, André remained at home. There were frantic calls from New York: where are you? Are you all right? Please call. He listened to the messages on his answering machine, but made no attempt to respond. There were calls, too, from Tom Shaw, the youngest correspondent on his staff, who had been raised by New York and told to find him. These calls, too, went unanswered. At one point, his doorbell rang; then there was a knock at his door. He didn't move. He had nothing to say to anyone, no answers for anyone, no answers, worst of all, for himself.

He had lost a friend. Whatever else Gondrachov had been —a Soviet agent, an adversary, an unreachable cynic—he had been a friend. A conviction haunted André: that if he had remained in contact with Gondrachov, the Russian might still be alive. He shuddered at the thought of how Gondrachov must have died. Over and over he examined his motives; they had nothing to do with Gondrachov, everything to do with what he represented. And then the most sickening thought of all: had he, to even the smallest degree, been poisoned by the same sort of venom that had poisoned Virgil Craig? There was no answer; the question was bad enough.

At eight o'clock Sunday evening, he watched the election returns. Camille Laurent had been elected President of France. Of those voting 58 percent had cast their ballots in his behalf. It was, the commentators said, a mandate for a return to the spirit of Charles de Gaulle.

On Monday morning, he could barely extract himself from bed—his side of the bed, he recognized, an acknowledgment that further deepened his depression. But he knew that he couldn't hide any longer. He would have to deal with New York, with this story, with himself.

He was at the office before anyone else, just as he normally was. His office was in a line with the entry, so that his presence was the first thing they noted on arriving. And each arrival was followed by a sudden cessation of movement, a few seconds of silence, and then a resumption of movement, away from his office, as though he was putting out warning vibrations. At last, each of the three correspondents came in, one by one, to offer their congratulations on André's exclusive, but none of them stayed to chat.

At lunchtime, he walked from his building, intent on going to Fouquet's, up the block and across the Champs Élysées from his office, as he did at least twice a week when he was working in Paris. He had walked thirty feet when his eye was turned by the approach of a young woman, probably not older than twenty-seven, wearing a beige gabardine suit, carrying several packages. Two things had turned his

eye: first, she was a spectacular beauty and, second, she
looked familiar. Ten feet from André she dropped one of
her packages, but apparently unaware kept on walking.
"Mademoiselle!" he called at the same time he stooped to
retrieve the package. By the time he had turned to her, she
had stopped and turned to him.

She smiled, revealing perfect teeth framed by senuous
lips. Her nostrils were slightly flared. Her high cheekbones
were highlighted with a touch of brown makeup and her
brown eyes were lightly shadowed in black. There was a
vagueness to her beauty, as though she hadn't yet decided
what to do with it. He handed her the package, but she
didn't say thank you. She said, in perfect American English,
"Call me in an hour at 606-24-84. I have something for you
from a friend. That's 606-24-84." Then she turned and
walked on.

He turned himself and continued to Fouquet's, wanting
to make the encounter seem as natural as she had made it.
All the way to his table he kept repeating the number to
himself, but he didn't write it down until he had made a
pretense of studying the menu. *Where* had he seen that girl?
For the life of him, he couldn't remember. Did he know
her? Was she an actress? Had he seen her in a film or on the
stage? When the realization finally hit him, he didn't know
whether to laugh or cry. She was "Tricia Boogaloo" from
the Crazy Horse Saloon.

Tricia Boogaloo refused to be specific when he called her
an hour later from a public telephone. All she said was that
this fascinating and generous man from Prague with whom
she'd become friendly must have had a premonition that
something might happen to him, because he'd given her
instructions about how to contact André in case he, himself,
didn't contact her for several days. In addition, he'd given
her an envelope to hide behind one of the mirrors with
which the Crazy Horse was paneled. She'd done it to humor

him and because he'd been nice to her, but she hadn't taken it seriously until reading about him in the newspaper. What a horrible death, and what a surprise, because he'd seemed completely normal, if somewhat lecherous.

It had to be the dossier. And it was no more than five hundred yards away, at 12 Avenue George V, the same street where he'd just had lunch. It might as well be on the moon for all the good it would do him. Gondrachov had kept the hiding place a secret, but it had cost him his life. André hadn't the slightest doubt that Laurent's men would kill him, too, the moment he had the dossier. And they would know when he had it; of that he was certain. He'd always intended to do his broadcast from Paris with the real dossier in his hand. That was out of the question now. What had to be done, at once, was to get the dossier out of France. But how? "Let me think for a second," he said to Tricia Boogaloo. "Look, could you fly to London and back today for a thousand dollars?"

"That's all I have to do?"

For the first time in a week, André laughed. "That's all. Just bring that envelope to Heathrow Airport in London, hand it to me, and you can fly right back. I'll also pay for your tickets. The question is: can you get that envelope today?"

"Oh, sure. There's a whole crew there cleaning."

He was tempted to arrange her ticket and have her meet him at the airport, but he was afraid to take the chance. He told her to get a reservation on the 6:30 P.M. Air France flight. He would call her back in five minutes to be sure she'd gotten on it.

Five minutes later, he called from another booth. She was confirmed on the flight. He told her he would be there when she arrived.

He returned to the office, picked up his passport and some money, and took a taxi to the airport in time for the

four-thirty flight. New York would worry again but they
would survive. The question was, would he? Everything
now depended on Ms. Tricia Boogaloo of the Crazy Horse
Saloon. Oh, Gennady, what a *beau geste!*

She was the third one off the plane. He had waited for her in
the arrival area, without going through immigration. She
was carrying a large manila envelope. As she handed it to
him, she said, "There's a flight back in twenty minutes. I've
got to run." He handed her the money. She didn't bother to
count it. "Nice meeting you," she said. And then she was
gone, dodging through the crowd.

He opened the envelope. Inside was the dossier. He
turned to the critical page, the memorandum from Hoepner
to his superiors in Paris, the one dated October 10, 1943.
There it was, a piece torn off from the bottom. There was
absolutely no question. This was the authenticated dossier.
And he was holding in in his hands in London.

There was a covering letter, which André read in the taxi
en route to the USBC bureau.

Dear André:
  Well, old man, if you're reading this, it hasn't gone
well for me. Don't blame yourself, whatever you do; it
was I who got careless. In any case, here, as you would
say, is the one I owe you. My great regret is that I
might not be around to find out what you'll do with it.
Since part of my job was to know your mind as well as
you, yourself, knew it, I'm pretty certain I know what
you're going through. Given the circumstances in
which I'll have probably found myself by the time you
have this letter, I think I can safely say that your
thoughts are not without merit. We Soviets *are* a difficult people, intransigent, stubborn, xenophobic. I
would ask you only to consider what you Americans

would be like if everything that had happened to us at the hands of foreigners had also happened to you. As I said that night at the Crazy Horse, somewhere, somehow, at some time we have to agree on something. The alternative isn't very nice. So let us agree that a man who collaborated with Nazi mass murderers shouldn't become president of France.

Gennady

P.S. The mirror behind which I hid the dossier was the very one that reflected Miss Boogaloo's indescribably marvelous bottom. I hope you'll be amused.

The laughter caught in his throat. A film covered his eyes. Tell you what, Gennady, he said silently. I'll meet you halfway.

As soon as he reached the bureau, he called Mike Paul and talked to him for nearly an hour. It was touch and go for a long while, but he finally won his point. Then he sat at a typewriter and wrote the script for his piece on Camille Laurent, the entire story, beginning with the telephone call from Shlomo Glaser. When he finished he made one copy. He put the original in a large envelope, along with a photostatic copy of the dossier, addressed the envelope to Mike Paul in New York, marked it PERSONAL and CONFIDENTIAL, and put the envelope in the pouch that would leave London by air that night. Then he put a copy of the script and still another copy of the dossier into a second envelope and put the envelope into his bag, along with an envelope containing the original dossier. That done, he took a taxi to the Connaught Hotel. On arriving, he talked briefly to the manager, who led him to the safety deposit room, where he was assigned a box. He stuffed the envelope containing the real dossier into the box, locked it, pocketed the key, and went upstairs to his room.

He spent the night at the Connaught and flew back to Paris in the morning. As soon as he arrived at his office, he telephoned the headquarters of Camille Laurent and asked for an appointment. No, it could not wait until next week, he said. It had to be today. He was certain that if the press secretary put his request to the President-elect, he would receive a favorable response.

For the next twenty minutes, he busied himself with a letter. When it was finished, he put it in an envelope, which he then sealed with Scotch tape. That done, he summoned Tom Shaw, his young correspondent, to his office.

"Close the door, Tom," he said, and then indicated a chair. Shaw, barely thirty, attempted to make his bony frame comfortable on the stiff-backed chair and then, giving up, fixed his blue eyes on André. André held out the key to the safety deposit box at the Connaught Hotel in London. "I want you to put this key on your key chain." Then he held out the letter. "I want you to leave the office right now and take this letter to your home and put it where no one will find it. If anything happens to me before I ask you to return the key, I want you to open the letter and do exactly what it tells you to do and do it without delay. Basically, you'll be going to London and then on to New York. No matter who tells you to do otherwise, even if it's Mike Paul, that's what you do—and without saying a word to anyone. Okay?"

"If you say so."

"Good."

The President-elect received André at five that afternoon at his apartment on the Quai Anatole France in the Seventh Arrondissement. It was a classically haute bourgeois apartment, with high ceilings and spacious rooms and was furnished classically, as well, in Louis XVI style. Laurent was standing near a wall, his back to some Daumier prints, when André arrived. His thinness accented his height; he towered over André. Rays of hostility and suspicion seemed to emanate from his unwavering blue eyes. With Laurent was a man André had never met, whom he introduced as Monsieur Gauthier. André could not be certain, but he suspected that Monsieur Gauthier was probably an important functionary of the DGSE, the inside man who had been watching out for Laurent's interests, taking particular pains —and, at times, inflicting them—during the last four weeks.

"I'll be brief, General," André said. He handed Laurent the envelope he had brought with him from London. "Inside that envelope is a copy of a script I wrote in London yesterday. Just before coming here I verified that the original of that script had arrived at the office of the president of network news of USBC in New York. With that script is a copy of a dossier kept by the Gestapo on the memoranda filed by Kurt Hoepner from Clermont-Ferrand. The original of that dossier is now in a safe in London. In one of the memos in that dossier, dated October 10, 1943, Hoepner named you as the man who had helped him infiltrate the French Resistance."

Out of the corner of his eye André saw Gauthier blink, but Laurent's eyes remained steady.

"There are two circumstances in which my script and that dossier will be made public. The first is if I am killed or injured or I disappear, either today or at any other time. The second is if, within the next twenty-four hours, you do not announce your irrevocable decision not to take office as the President of France."

"Blackmail," Laurent said.

"Charity," André said evenly. "If I wanted to blackmail you I'd let you become President. Just think of the things I could make you do, the riches I could acquire, by having you in office with the dossier hanging over your head."

In the silence that followed, he could hear Laurent breathing through his fine, elongated nose.

"Your compatriot Arnaud de Borchgrave was right," he said at last. "The whole western press corps is infiltrated by Communists. You're a perfect example, Kohl. You've just accomplished a top priority job for the Soviets."

He had been certain Laurent would say that, just as he had known that the President-elect would accuse him of blackmail. "To the contrary, General," he answered serenely, "if I was carrying out a Soviet assignment, I would do a story on the dossier. That would ruin not only you but the whole conservative political establishment in France and bring another left-wing candidate to power. *That's* what the Soviets wanted. I'm not doing that. I'm giving you a chance to retire with honor, your good name secure. Your political allies will remain intact and the people who elected you to office will be able to vote for another conservative candidate, if they choose, without this scandal to distract them. I think you're getting a hell of a good deal."

For the next fifteen seconds, Laurent stared in silence at André. André stared back, boring into the general's blue eyes so intently he felt he could almost see the alternatives being weighed and a decision being reached. He knew the decision before the general spoke.

"Tell me something, Mr. Kohl," Laurent said at last, "I've never heard of a journalist giving up a great coup before. How are you going to justify that to such an important television network?"

"I won't have to, General. I submitted my resignation yesterday. It becomes effective the moment you announce your resignation." André paused. "You have twenty-four hours," he said. Then he turned and left.

He heard the news on television ninety-six hours later, at the end of a long day of practice in Varengeville. Laurent

himself had telephoned on Wednesday morning to ask for
an extension. He had worked out a scenario that would let
him resign with grace; surely Mr. Kohl would have the
grace, in turn, to let him do that. André had agreed to the
extension.

That afternoon Laurent's press secretary announced that
the President-elect had departed on a sudden vacation, his
destination a secret so that he could get a good rest. The
press was furious, but there was nothing it could do. On
Thursday, Laurent's whereabouts had been revealed in the
most distressing possible manner: he and his wife had gone
to an army base in the south of France, where the commanding officer had given him the use of his quarters. Unable to sleep, the President-elect had gotten up in the middle
of the night and attempted in the dark to grope his way
downstairs, where he intended to read. He had fallen down
a flight of stairs. Taken to an army hospital, he was found to
have a serious head injury. Surgery had followed on Friday.
On Saturday, the President-elect had managed to convey to
his intimates his conviction that France deserved a President whose health and acuity were certain. His no longer
was. For the good of the country, he was renouncing all
claim to the presidency, both now and in the future.

André turned off the television set. As the picture shrank
briefly and disappeared from view he knew that not just a
program had ended, or even an assignment, but an era in his
life. He was as sad as he was happy. Nothing would ever
replace it, yet no one and nothing new could enter his life
fully until he put the old life aside. He'd tried to explain that
to Mike Paul when he'd told him he was resigning, but he
knew he'd been no more successful in doing so than he had
been in explaining why they would have to bury for all time
the story of Camille Laurent's treason. Sometimes there are
considerations greater than even the greatest stories.

A month ago he wouldn't have understood that. There

were all sorts of things he wouldn't have understood a
month ago. He'd come to Varengeville four weeks before,
he'd thought, to get in touch with his past. He knew now it
wasn't a desire for the past that had drawn him here; it was
dissatisfaction with the present. How American that was, to
be restless with a dream life like his. No Frenchman would
ever be restless with it. And that was just the point. He
wasn't French, after all. He was American, born to be restless, to want to move on to new challenges and frontiers.
What had made him restless in France was that he had
sought to deny his birthright, assigning himself to a lovely
backwater, turning his back on the greatest story of his lifetime: his own country's attempt to redefine itself, to shake
off its sorrows, and confront its problems and move ahead
again.

It was Meredith who'd compelled him to acknowledge
that. He knew she was right—because she was the living
proof.

She'd been right about something else, as well; after almost more than fifteen years in Europe, he would view
America with the wonder of a foreign correspondent.

He moved to his bookcase, selected a recording, and put
it on the stereo. It was Dvořák's *New World Symphony*. He
closed his eyes, listening intently, giving both mind and
body to the music. Five minutes into the symphony, he
knew that he was hearing it from a totally different perspective—that of a man who had passed, for at least one brief
moment, from a passive to an active life. The performance
was by Leonard Bernstein and the New York Philharmonic.
It was a fine performance. But that was all it was. It was not
a creative act. Performance was at best a *re-creative* act, a
kind of reporting on someone else's act of creation. The
Isaac Sterns, for all the joy they brought people, were not
creators. They were performers. What had been dissatisfy-
ing about his old life, André knew now, was that it hadn't

been creative, either; it had been passive and vicarious; lived, for the most part, through the experiences of others, people doing things he couldn't or wouldn't do himself.

So "the road not taken" had not been the road to take, after all. And the road he had taken was one he now had to get off. What *was* the right road, then—the road that led to an authentic life? What *was* the authentic, the creative, life? It was a life in which you made things happen that would not have happened except for your intervention; in which you produced something that would never have existed but for you. You don't have to be a composer to qualify; truly loving another person, in a way that made her love you, would qualify. The love—which otherwise would not have existed—would be the product of your creative act.

The symphony was ending, and André was suddenly alert. As familiar as he was with the score, with its stirring mixture of European and American themes and architecture, the last moment of the final movement caught him completely unaware. After all the flourishes and crescendos, a single note emerged, sustained for several seconds. What had Dvořák meant?

There could be only one meaning. That in a new world nothing ever ends. That out of endings come new beginnings.